NOVELS BY WILLIAM MICHAEL RIED

Five Ferries (2018) "Full-hearted. This debut "A character-rich legal thriller of uncommon ambition—smart, absorbing, and surprisingly heartfelt. A taut, well-written thriller with a riveting conspiracy that stretches from flea markets to fighter jets."

~ Kirkus Review

2019 American Fiction Award for Best New Fiction Finalist

Backstory (2021) "A masterpiece, an intriguing read with a perfect blend of anger, resentment, love, hatred, excitement, and displeasure."

~ OnlineBookClub Review

Winning Mystery in 2021 New York City Big Book Awards; Silver Medal Winner in Wishing Shelf Book Awards for Adult Fiction; Semifinalist in Kindle Book Award for Literary Fiction; 2022 Eric Hoffer Award Category Finalist

Pandion (2022) "Unreservedly recommended as a genre-bending mystery of puzzlement, betrayal and love. The result is an addictively compulsive page-turner from cover to cover."

~ Midwest Book Review

2022 New York City Big Book Awards Distinguished Favorite Mystery; Red Ribbon Winner in 2022 Wishing Shelf Awards; 2023 Eric Hoffer Award Grand Prize Short List Honoree and Honorable Mention for Mystery/Crime

WRONG HAND RIGHT

WILLIAM MICHAEL RIED

Publisher's Cataloging-in-Publication Data
Names: Ried, William Michael, 1956- .
Title: Wrong hand right : a novel / William Michael Ried.
Description: New York, NY : William Michael Ried, 2025. | Summary: A lawyer chases trademark counterfeiters and romance until Navy pilots are dying and he stumbles upon the cause. His firm presses him to look away, which forces him to confront the childhood tragedy of his family deaths and his grudge against the right-handed world, putting himself and his friends in danger.
Identifiers: LCCN 2025903878 | ISBN 9781966219163 (pbk.) | ISBN 9781966219170 (ebook)
Subjects: LCSH: Murder – Fiction. | Lawyers – Fiction. | Man-woman relationships – Fiction. | Left- and right-handedness – Fiction. | Nineteen eighties – Fiction. | New York (N.Y.) – Fiction. | BISAC: FICTION / Thrillers / Crime. | FICTION / Thrillers / Legal. | FICTION / Thrillers / Suspense.
Classification: LCC PS3618.E53 W76 2025 | DDC 813 R--dc23
LC record available at https://lccn.loc.gov/2025903878

Cover design by LemonLime Designs
Left Hand Justice design by Lorenzo Contessa

Published by William Micheal Ried, New York, NY

Chapter One

It was a fine morning for a raid. Finnegan Alger liked getting out of the office to hunt trademark infringers, a break from his usual day writing briefs and yelling at people over the phone. He got out in the fresh air—and sometimes came home with a great cocktail party story.

He crowded in with the Bolger & Plotkin lawyers and their investigators at the flea market's edge. Everyone was poised to start. Ainsley Hatcher stretched a slender arm from within her tailored suit, out of place in the warm Tennessee morning. Finn checked his right wrist for his old Timex—which kept time despite the cracked crystal—as Ainsley called out, "Ten-fifteen... in four, three, two, one."

Trademark enforcement wasn't dangerous, not really, though there were sometimes angry words or threats to unleash guard dogs. The year before, a crazed shopkeeper tried to set fire to his own warehouse full of knockoff T-shirts, which would simply have saved their client the cost of destroying them. For today's flea market raid, Finn was armed only with a court order, and the defendants would be docile. The authorities—who might be US marshals or customs agents, depending on who the firm could arrange—came along to serve the order and keep the peace. Today they were using local cops, who of course had guns but would never draw them. The typical defendants were Korean or Taiwanese shopkeepers, with a healthy fear of law enforcement— at least until they were sure they wouldn't go to jail or be deported. Then they might become belligerent or, in another case last year, humorously fake a fainting spell.

Depending on the case, Finn's firm might seize boxes of T-shirts or intercept containers of athletic shoes. Today they were after counterfeit Sanchi watches. The target was three booths at an upscale flea market outside Nashville.

This was a step up for a boutique law firm like Bolger & Plotkin. Sanchi made high-end watches at the level of Swiss brands like Rolex or Patek Philippe, and this upped the stakes for trademark enforcement and meant bigger fees. This was why it was surprising that Victor Bolger wasn't at the helm himself. But Ainsley Hatcher was an eighth-year associate with experience running raids, and this was her show.

The local investigator, Terry Jones, had done the advance work of making buys and photographing the targets. "We should be able to get 'em all," he said, "long as we hit all the targets at once. These old boys down here are slicker th'n owl shit, and the minute we hit one booth, the rest will scatter like a bunch of scalded haints."

They looked at him with curious smiles.

He laughed. "I keep forgetting you folks are Yankees. They'll split like evil spirits, which is pretty damned fast."

Ainsley shook her head in what passed for amusement but to Finn looked more like impatience.

"Are we ready to roll?" she said. Ainsley rarely waited for answers to her questions, so they all just crowded around the map. They also didn't need Terry's warning about serving all the defendants at once. The way counterfeit product disappeared during a raid was one rationale for the law passed a few years before, in 1984, empowering judges to issue seizure orders *ex parte*, without notice to the defendants. The plaintiff's lawyers just had to show their clients would otherwise suffer irreparable harm because the defendants would hide the knockoffs and business records if given advance warning.

Jimmy Henderson had flown down to Nashville the day before the team to secure a seizure order. He was two years ahead of Finn at the firm, and they often worked together. Finn liked having another young guy at the firm to go out with and laugh about their bosses. Finn called him "JT" because he liked giving people nicknames, sometimes to make fun but just as often to show friendship. Back in school he made up nicknames as a countermeasure to how kids made fun of him. "Finicky" and "Huckleberry" were names he had a hard time shaking, because even grownups thought they were cute. "Scarface" was also a big favorite when he got to Missouri with the mark across his cheek, but the bullies were at least smart enough not to utter *that* name around parents or teachers.

Even with preparation and reliable local counsel to steer the Bolger lawyers through the courthouse, judges were sometimes reluctant to sign off on *ex parte* orders. "It's something they learn in judge school," JT had joked after it took him two days to get an order in Wichita, "to be squeamish about issuing orders without all the parties in court." But in Nashville the judge quickly granted the order, luckily for JT. Victor Bolger had little patience for associates screwing up raids, and clients were easily annoyed by delay. But JT had called in to report he had the order in hand, and Terry had lined up local cops, so Finn and Ainsley caught the first flight down from New York the next morning.

They met at LaGuardia before the sun came up. The late November morning was clear and crisp, unlike Finn's head. He was on his third cup of coffee, trying to pry his eyes open. Ainsley looked wide awake and completely put together, as always, and ready to devour anyone who got in her way. It was amazing how she showed up for a raid looking like she was going to a board meeting. Today it was a deep orange suit and stiletto heels.

He tried to remember the movie where the sailor says his girl is "built like a battleship." He wasn't sure exactly what that meant in the 1940s, but the description seemed to fit Ainsley. Her flawless skin and thick blond hair reminded him of the French actress Catherine Deneuve, but Ainsley was bigger, maybe five nine, with broad shoulders and legs that went on forever. In his loneliness from failing to find a stable relationship, she was often fantasy fodder.

Finn had initially tried to ask her out, but she made clear she had zero interest; she was out of his league, not to mention senior to him at the firm. He tried to chalk this up to arrogance and no sense of humor—she hardly ever laughed, no matter how uproariously funny he was—but that was just to make himself feel better. It was understandable she was wrapped up in work; as an eighth year, she had to make partner or be shown the door.

Pointing to Xs on the map, Terry confirmed all three target stalls were open for business. Ainsley told him, "You stand by and watch for moving merchandise."

Then she turned to the rest of them. "Everyone just wait by the van when you're done. Terry thinks Silk Road is the main connection, so I will not leave that booth until I get some answers."

The team split into three groups, each with a lawyer and a police officer. At precisely ten-forty-five Finn stepped up to the booth under the "Luxe Watches" sign. He handed the complaint and seizure order to the thin Asian man behind the counter.

"What this means?" the man pleaded, looking bewildered.

"This is a complaint filed in federal court for trademark counterfeiting," Finn said. "Judge Sweeney issued a temporary restraining order, which provides for the seizure of counterfeit Sanchi watches in your possession or control and all related records, pending a preliminary injunction hearing. Are you Mr. Sun Kim?"

Eyes bulging, the man turned to the smaller man beside him,

then looked back at Finn. "Ah, I am Yu-jun Lee, and this man Minjun Cho. Misser Kim not here."

"Okay. Please call Mr. Kim and tell him to come down because we are going to enforce this seizure order now."

"You wait for Misser Kim," the man beseeched.

"Sir, we will not wait. I will secure the counterfeit watches and related business records, pursuant to the judge's order. This officer will ensure you stand aside and do not interfere. Mr. Kim may appear before Judge Sweeney in one week to contest the injunction, so please make sure he gets these papers."

Lee stood frozen to the ground while Cho stepped back, wild-eyed, looking as if he might bolt into the market's maze of booths. Finn loaded an empty cardboard box with the Sanchi-branded knockoffs in the counter display and four smaller boxes of watches he found in the packing case behind the booth. He also secured two large binders and some loose papers.

Most of the writing on the documents was in Asian characters, presumably Korean. It was also par for the course for these records to be in code, so deciphering it all would have to wait until they returned to the office. For the present, he seized *all* sales records he could find. But, following the law, he ignored all the other knockoffs and took only watches bearing *his* client's marks, then gave Lee a receipt for what he took.

While Finn was pressuring Lee to identify his supplier, Cho muttered something. But a stern look from Lee shut him up. Finn wished he could separate the two so he could squeeze Cho for information, but he couldn't do this by himself, and he had no way to contact the team.

When Finn returned to the parking lot, JT was already there, sitting on the van's running board and watching the crowd as if he were spending a leisurely day at the market.

"Looks like the two of us got a lot of knockoffs," Finn said.

"You know the Ice Queen, though," JT replied, adopting Finn's nickname for Ainsley. "She'll get the Silk Road guy to give up the supplier and the importer, if not also the damned factory in Korea and his grandmother's secret kimchi recipe."

Finn chuckled. "That Silk Road guy never dealt with a tsunami like Ainsley."

JT grew thoughtful. "You know about the Star Jeans case, right?"

Finn shook his head.

"It was right before I joined the firm, so I don't know for sure it's true. Ainsley was the junior associate on this big case against our client for selling jeans with a trademarked pattern on the back pocket. Some junior lawyer at the opposing firm accidentally sent her a privileged document, stamped "Confidential – Attorney's Eyes Only," that laid out how his client had no internal protocols for applying its trademark, which obviously undermined its ability to enforce the mark."

"Damn. So what did she do?"

"Well, the document was so obviously privileged, she was supposed to return it and not even read it...."

"But she didn't."

JT raised an eyebrow. "Well, the story is Ainsley had to act ethically and return the document, or hand Victor an easy win and launch herself onto the partnership track. And we all know she is speeding up the partnership highway."

Finn pictured Ainsley's imposing image and realized that, like Victor, she seemed to find little joy in her impressive success. Was that from some buried sense of guilt?

"But *we* did pretty damn well," JT went on, looking through the boxes. "Street value's got to be in the thousands." He reached into one box and held up a fancy silver watch. "Looks real, right?"

"Except it's light and the bezel's too thin," Finn said, taking the watch in hand and peering at the back. "And the fine print says 'water r-e-s-i-s-t-e-n-t.' "

"And that's wrong?"

"Yes, James. That's not how you spell 'resistant.' "

"Well, how about this one?" JT said, taking a watch from one of the Luxe boxes.

Finn sighed dismissively and took hold of the watch, a copy of the high-end Peakstone model. He noticed none of the common defects on the face and, flipping it over and looking closely, also saw no misspellings. "Have to admit," he concluded, "this one is good. It's even got the heft of a real watch."

"Well, it looks good enough to me," JT said, slipping it into his pocket.

"What the hell are you doing?"

"What does it matter, one bogus watch more or less?"

Finn grimaced. Destroying knockoffs was part of the job, permitted by the law and sometimes ordered by the judge. The aim was to take fake merchandise out of the marketplace and recover profits made by the infringers. But what mattered most to Finn was satisfying the client and Victor, and they'd all go into a tailspin if they found out JT kept a watch.

But like JT said, no one *would* find out, and it occurred to Finn this could be a small way to get back at the wrong-handed world.

It wasn't Finn's fault he was born left-handed, always fumbling with a world designed for the right-handed. He had so many childhood memories of clumsiness with scissors and door handles. It was a lot to deal with as a kid, parents and teachers telling him he was doing things wrong so often he started to believe them. But writing with his right hand made his work sloppy and slow and left him feeling stupid, and he believed this was what caused him to stutter and further stand out when what he wanted desperately was to fit in.

One day in first grade, he came home with a big black "X" on the back of his left hand. He tried to hide it, but his father found him trying to scrub the ink off his hand and made him tell how the teacher marked the hand to remind him he should *not* use it to write. Finn pleaded with his father to let the matter drop, to no avail. His dad met the principal the next day, and Finn's teacher apologized to Finn before the whole class. After that Finn was not only the backwards kid who stuttered and could hardly write, but he was also a baby who ran to his father to protect him.

But from then on at least *his father* was on his side, encouraging him to do things his own way. He tried to buoy Finn's spirits with stories about famous people. "Lots of left-handed people have done great things," he said. "Look at Jimi Hendrix."

"Who's Jimi Hendrix?"

"Well, never mind him. There's also Albert Einstein, one of the smartest guys ever, and Henry Ford, who practically invented the automobile."

Those names were vaguely familiar to the seven-year-old Finn, but he was not reassured.

"You know," his father went on, "some of the greatest pitchers in baseball have been southpaws."

"But I play soccer," Finn whined.

"Even better. You make the defender think you favor your right foot, and when it really counts, you score with your left."

He knew his father was just trying to make him feel better.

"Okay," his father went on. "Maybe a better example is boxing. Here, get in a stance."

His father stood him up, turning him partially to the right and positioning his arms.

Stepping behind and moving Finn's arms, his father said, "Right-handed fighters jab with the left, like this." He moved Finn's arm. "The opponent thinks the hand that will do damage is the right, and so gets ready to block it." He pushed Finn's right fist out, followed by his shoulder and a turn of his hips.

"But if the other guy focuses on your right, and then you turn the other way...the wrong way." He turned Finn and repositioned his fists. "While he's looking at your right fist, you bring up a haymaker from your left...and then it's all over. Let's call it the 'wrong-hand whammy.' "

Finn liked that name, wrong-hand whammy, and took up shadow boxing to practice it. He repeated this move countless times, driven by the fantasy of delivering a crushing blow against a big bully if he ever got the chance.

But it was only weeks later when Finn was knocked down for the count. His sister, Whitney, two years older than Finn, was constantly going to ballet classes and giving recitals. One snowy winter night when Finn was seven, the family was driving home from her recital when they were hit by a drunk driver.

He came to in the hospital, his leg in a cast and his face bandaged, covering a long gash on his left cheek where a scar would never completely fade. And, as if fate had not been satisfied simply making him left-handed, nerve damage left the middle fingers of his right hand permanently numb and weak.

But then a nurse told him no one in his family had survived, and Finn's world shattered. There would be no more catches with his dad, no hugs from his mom. In the lonely months and years ahead, he would even miss squabbling with his sister. They would all be consigned to cameo appearances in his recurring nightmare of flashing lights and screeching tires.

He was pulled from school in Chicago and sent to live with his grandfather in a little town in Missouri. He had to leave his home and his friends and his school. Gone was any foothold on the climb toward a normal, or at least a left-handed, normal life. He was embittered and felt entitled to do whatever he could to get back at the unfair world.

By this time Finn's sinistrality was no more than an occasional nuisance, but he still felt he had a right to even the scales against an unjust world. And so here was a chance, in a small way, to balance things out. These watches were headed for a landfill, anyway, and JT was right that no one would miss just one... or even two. He looked through the Luxe box for another Peakstone. Holding it up to the light and admiring the craftsmanship, he tried to ignore his grandfather quoting Plato: "Theft of money is illiberal, and rapacity shameless."

This wasn't money; it was a watch, and a counterfeit at that. Besides, he had so often seen even the cops help themselves to "samples" during raids. He brushed his sermonizing grandfather off his shoulder and decided to put the watch in his pocket.

He had no idea how much he'd regret that choice.

Chapter Two

Finn and JT leaned against the van, people-watching. JT nodded to a young woman in a sundress who threw him a look.

"Man, I'd climb that tree," he said lasciviously.

"You are a rutting dog," Finn said.

"Hey, a girl like that? I've got just what she needs."

Finn wondered if JT would dare refer to Ainsley that way. He felt prompted to say, "What do you think about women who object to being called 'girls'?"

"That's such crap," JT chuckled. "Does any guy squawk when you talk about 'going out with the boys' or 'hanging with my boys'? No. What, are women insulted by being thought of as young? They're supposed to like that."

"Well, calling someone 'boy' can be insulting."

JT scoffed. "It's all bullshit. Now," he said, mimicking Terry's southern drawl, "if I said, 'I'd put my raccoon in *that* cage...' " He got up, laughing at his own wit, and headed for a food truck.

Returning with a corn dog and a box of fried pickle chips, JT sat in the doorway of the van to eat. Just seeing all that fried food made Finn feel greasy, so he took a walk into the market. He admired his friend's audacity with women, and wished he could be that confident. But he wondered if JT could really be satisfied with relationships that timed out when the sun came up. The whole "woman versus girl" debate also stuck in his head, but it wasn't his problem on this beautiful day.

Everything had returned to normal after the commotion of the raid. People again ambled in the sunshine, haggled and drank lemonade. Record albums spread on a table drew Finn's attention, and recalling how his father used to bring home gifts from business trips, he thought he should pick up something for Dani. He looked through the albums, which seemed in decent shape, though you never knew with used LPs. He found a copy of U2's *Under a Blood Red Sky*. Dani loved Bono, and throughout his on-again, off-again pursuit of her, a line from one U2 song had looped in his head: "No matter what you do, I'm still hungry for you." He had played that song so many times he could even sing the French refrain.

Dani was other-worldly. Her bleached blond hair was always tied in some fantastic mess, the only feminine touch being maybe a floppy bow or a side braid. He called her "Madonna," although not to her face, because she was straight out of the movie *Desperately Seeking Susan*, all vintage boutique beads, leather and lace, and always in high heels. It might have been her short stature that incentivized her to master walking in heels, nothing like lady lawyers he knew who stumbled over cracks in the sidewalk or just kept their high heels in the office. Dani had no trouble moving quickly on heels, like when it came time to pay the bill.

When he was with her, he floated on air. But then he'd go days unable to reach her. She had no answering machine and, while she spent two spectacular nights with him at the loft, she never invited him to her apartment in Hoboken or even gave him the address—though she sometimes talked about getting his help to throw a party there. Even when they were together, it drove him crazy how he could not predict her moods. She tacked from thoughtful to oblivious, playful to remote, sometimes openly affectionate and at others maddeningly detached. And despite her stunning looks and shocking outfits, she seemed unfazed by the attention she attracted. Irrepressible and irresistible, she was also totally unaffected by him; he could come by or not, take her out or not; she really didn't seem to care. But it all occupied too many of his thoughts.

Past relationships had taught him that, after the third night together, the girl got serious, what he thought of as his own twist on the "rule of three." He just needed to sleep with her one more time to win her over.

For now, though, the album would get her attention. It was almost impossible to find this recording in vinyl—and Dani hadn't yet moved on to CDs. As he turned back to the van, he plotted how and when he'd give her the present. But the thought nagged at him that a record album was too impersonal a gift for what he wanted to express.

Then he spotted a pair of silver, cross-shaped earrings, glittery and ostentatious, just her style. He hesitated only a moment before laying out the rest of the cash in his wallet. But he was no fool; he'd hold onto the earrings until he saw how she reacted to the album.

When Finn returned to the van, JT asked, "What's with the record?"

"It's a present...for a *girl*."

"Still chasing Madonna?"

"Well, 'chasing' may not be the right word."

JT kidded Finn for putting serious effort into pursuing *any* woman, insisting there was always another one just around the corner or waiting in the corner bar. Finn regretted ever having shared his dating woes—and Dani's nickname—and was not surprised when his friend said, "You should give Madonna a watch."

Finn turned away, looking for solace in one of G-pa's quotations, annoying when he first heard them but so often on point. Nietzsche, of all people, apparently had said, "Unrequited love forces us to develop a sense of humor about ourselves." This put

Finn in good company, but laughing at himself hardly lessened his loathing of looking foolish.

Ainsley finally returned, visibly dissatisfied.

"The Silk Road owner says Luxe Watches is the connection for all the booths," she said impatiently to Finn. "What did you get from them?"

Finn panicked. "A load of watches," he said, suddenly unsteady, gesturing at the boxes beside the van, "and business records. Nothing else, except..."

"Except what?"

"Well, I had the feeling this second guy, named Cho, would have talked, but the head guy, Lee, shut him up."

Ainsley's frustration turned to anger. "And you were keeping this to yourself?"

Finn fumbled to explain, but Ainsley didn't wait for an answer. "Jimmy," she barked out, "you stay with the van. Terry, get one of your cops to come with us, and you," gesturing impatiently at Finn, "come along; you're the good cop."

They returned to the Luxe booth as the two Koreans were packing up, looking beaten by the day. When they saw Finn, Lee seethed with suppressed anger. Cho started inching toward to the parking lot, but Terry blocked his way.

"Mr. Lee," Ainsley said, "I am the chief lawyer representing Sanchi. You and I need to talk."

Ainsley edged Lee toward the end of his booth, her voice low but threatening, while Finn pulled Cho aside.

"Mr. Cho," Finn said quietly, "My boss will not let this rest. I think there's something you'd like to tell us about the source of the Sanchi watches, something that will make this go much easier for you."

Cho shook, darting bird-like looks around the market and toward his partner. "You take watches, but no trouble," he said.

"Whether you are in trouble depends on several things," Finn replied. "Are you legally in this country? Have you got papers?"

"I..." Cho muttered. "papers not here; at home." He stopped, sweating profusely, and then burst out, "I say place; but no jail, no send Korea."

"We just want the source, Mr. Cho. That's all we care about."

"Okay," Cho said, looking like he was about to wet his pants. "Okay...old factory building...by railroad."

"Cho!" Lee shouted, trying to push by Ainsley, which was never going to happen. His way blocked, Lee unleashed a torrent in Korean.

Cho looked more scared of Lee than of the trademark team or the cop standing at the edge of the drama. And with everyone's attention on Cho, Lee reached beneath the counter and pulled out a handgun.

Cho dove for cover. Ainsley jumped back. Finn tripped over a box and hit the ground. The cop fumbled for the pistol in his holster.

Lee waved the gun wildly and shouted. The cop was just drawing his firearm when Terry leaped over a table and grabbed at Lee. A shot went off.

Chapter Three

Finn stepped away from the conference room table covered with watches and documents. He poured a cup of coffee from the pot on the credenza and surveyed the room.

The purplish bruise on his chin from the Nashville raid, together with the old scar on his cheek, made Finn look like a tough guy...or maybe someone who still got beaten up by bullies. It was lucky for them all that Terry had the reflexes—and the courage—to tackle that crazy vendor before he shot someone. But they were all safe. Yu-jun Lee was in jail, and Minjun Cho was in the wind, the police showing little interest in finding him. The trademark case was moving forward.

The question remained why Lee went after his partner like that. Even if Cho *was* giving up the watch supplier, could this be a reason to shoot him?

The gun incident made this case stand out. Cho's tip might lead to more than just a few bogus watches; it could be the key to taking down a nationwide counterfeiting operation. The factory Cho described was easy to find, and Terry set up surveillance. With some luck and patience, they could follow the trail up the supply chain.

Late in the morning, Victor's secretary told Finn the boss wanted to see him. With a satisfied grin, Finn entered Victor's corner office, spacious and opulent enough to make clear his status as chairman. Victor was rotund and ruddy in a tan linen suit and Hermès tie. He gestured at a guest chair facing his huge, mahogany desk, upon which sat a marble bust of Niccolò Machiavelli. "Sit down," he said with unctuous charm that could without warning snap into rage. "We need to talk."

"About the raid?"

"Yes, well, luckily the results were good, despite your bungling."

That was a blow to the head. What was Victor's problem? They seized product and got an invaluable lead. What more did he want?

"I don't understand," Finn said. "You mean about the gu-gu-gun?" He couldn't believe his old stutter was back, and at the worst time. Victor had no patience for weakness, just like he deplored showing adversaries any kind of sympathy. One of his favorite lines was, "You're not in litigation to make friends."

"Yes, Finnegan," Victor said, pausing as if he wondered about what he just heard, then resuming in anger. "Something about almost losing two of my attorneys sets me on edge."

Finn braced for a tongue lashing.

"What is the first thing we do after we serve an order?" Victor said.

"Ask if there are firearms on the premises?" Finn asked rhetorically.

"Ask if there are firearms!" Victor shouted, blood rushing to his face. "What the hell is wrong with you, returning twice to that booth without ever asking?"

"I..." Finn said, stumbling. But seeing no alternative to taking a beating, he went on. "I screwed up, Victor. I'm sorry. But we..."

"There's no 'but we' about it. You could have gotten killed, and what's worse, gotten Ainsley killed. Have you lost your mind?"

"I know. I don't know why I didn't check—even if that guy would definitely have lied."

"Oh, don't even go there. Defendants lie; that's what they do. But it was an absolute fuck-up not to ask the question."

Finn waited while Victor breathed heavily and then pounced again. "This kind of shit cannot happen at Bolger & Plotkin. I won't allow it."

"I understand," Finn said.

"If you understood, it wouldn't happen."

"At least we got the information," Finn said in a voice that sounded weak, even to himself.

"We got information," Victor said condescendingly. "Good thing for you. And the client seems ready to forgive the fact that you almost got shot. But *I* can't overlook this."

Deep silence settled over the office. Finn scrambled for something to say. He had messed up, but Victor couldn't be upset about the end result. Still, Finn was used to the world singling him out for torment; the important thing was to keep cool and hang on to his job.

Finally, Finn couldn't stand the silence and said, "I'm really sorry, Victor. I know I can do better. You have to let me show you."

Victor scowled. "I don't *have to* do anything." He paused for an excruciating moment. "But I will. I'm going to gamble you'll straighten out your act. You will *show me* I can trust you and that our clients can rely on you. And for now, I'm taking you off Sanchi—after you help Jimmy with the post-raid declaration. Then I want you to focus on the copyright case for Videoblock. You'll draft the opposition to the summary judgment motion and handle the argument in Chicago; Alice will give you the date."

Finn was relieved he wasn't fired and that Victor trusted him to handle the hearing in Illinois. But he couldn't believe he'd landed on Victor's shit list just when he'd be setting year-end bonuses. Still, he had been part of the raid and wanted to see the results, and so before getting to work on the Videoblock brief, he returned to the conference room.

Two legal assistants were poring through seized looseleaf binders, trying to match stockkeeping units, or SKUs, with brands and tallying sales figures. In addition to Sanchi-branded watches, the defendants dealt in bogus Rolex and Tag Heuer, and who knew what else. To calculate damages they had to decode the documents and segregate out those copying Sanchi marks. The firm had no interest in other brands—not unless another company also retained them.

"I think I've got the symbol," Imani called out. She was the brightest of the legal assistants, not to mention quite attractive in an athletic sort of way. Finn loved the crazy things she did with her thick, black hair, currently set in short dreadlocks spouting in all directions, which made her look as tall as Finn. Were she not a subordinate at the firm with a husband who could easily break Finn in half, he'd have asked her out. But she never showed that kind of interest in him, and more important was how helpful she was in comprehending assignments and anticipating issues. He encouraged her to think about applying to law school.

Ainsley looked up from a pile of documents at the other end of the table. JT leaned over Imani's shoulder and said, "Imani found a listing for delivery of the four boxes to Luxe. The symbol looks Korean; no telling what it means literally."

"Who cares?" Finn volunteered, coming to see. "With a match we can figure damages for Luxe and get a clue about the other defendants. Toss me a pen and I'll draw those symbols."

Ainsley squinted at Finn. She was obviously aware Victor had reassigned him, and she hadn't forgiven him for almost getting her shot, but she didn't say anything.

One of the legal assistants pushed a pen across the table to Finn.

"I can't use this," he said. Writing left-handed with an ordinary pen left ink smudges on his hand. "Has somebody got a Pilot or anything with fast-drying ink?"

Imani handed him another pen just as Victor Bolger made his appearance. "So what have we got?" he asked the room, casting a disparaging glance at Finn.

Ainsley jumped up before anyone else could respond. "We may have found the code to identify the Sanchi brand," she said. "Anyway, we seized two hundred and forty-four watches altogether, in four models. Most have typical cosmetic flaws, and we'll have to get the client to identify substandard parts in the workings. The cheap ones are also flimsy; I wouldn't give them the time of day."

Victor paused, apparently assessing whether she was making a joke.

"But then there are these," she said, handing Victor one of the Peakstone models. "Not only do they feel genuine, but so far we can't find any defects."

Victor held up the watch and tested the weight in his hand. "The client will be very concerned about this," he said. "Send off one of these to Sam Eddings right away, and ask him to rush an analysis of the workings. Make sure we have a way to identify it as counterfeit." He looked again at the watch, handed it back to Ainsley and returned to his benevolent despot tone. "Two forty-four: that's a good number. The client will like the sound of that. And what about up stream?"

Ainsley responded, "We got a lead to identify the local supplier. I may be able to trace that back to the US distributor, or even the factory."

She might be able to trace it, Finn thought derisively, as if the rest of them were only there for the free coffee.

"Korea?" Bolger asked.

"Well," Ainsley replied, "given the defendants, that looks to be the ultimate source."

"Well, let's try to close up this case quickly while we look into the supplier. Have any of the defendants lawyered up?"

"That's the really strange thing," Ainsley said, obviously baffled. "The guy who pulled the gun is already out on bail, and I got a call from his lawyer...from *Hune & Buchanan*...."

Victor looked at her in surprise.

"I know," she said. "Hune swooping in to represent a flea market vendor in a criminal case? It makes no sense."

"And a vendor so scared of giving up his supplier he was ready to shoot up the market," Victor said, ominously. "What did the Hune lawyer say?"

"Well, first he wanted to make sure I was suitably impressed by his firm. Then he advised they were not only appearing for Yu-jun Lee in the criminal matter but also representing Luxe Watches *and the other two vendors* in the trademark case."

Victor's surprise turned to astonishment.

She went on. "And we are not to speak directly with his clients."

"Does he know that guy at Luxe gave up the supplier?"

"He didn't say, but he did suggest they would complain to the judge about our threatening his clients with deportation."

"Will they oppose the preliminary injunction?"

"He wants to work out a settlement. He clearly does *not* want things going any further."

A national law firm like Hune, known for corporate deals and white-collar criminal defense, had no place taking on this representation. How could these vendors afford that firm? And it was unheard of for the same lawyers to represent three separate defendants when there were bound to be conflicts of interest. The Hune appearance—on top of the Luxe guy pulling a gun—made this case extraordinary and portentous.

"Joint representation only works," Victor mused, "if all three defendants consent to judgment."

"That seems like their plan," Ainsley said. "Hune doesn't want us taking discovery or having any contact with the clients."

"Well, so, talk to this guy. We won't be scared off. Clearly Hune has stepped in to stop us from digging into these operations, so we look for a quick settlement of the flea market case and don't let on we're watching the supplier to pursue the next level up."

Victor turned to the room. "Good work, Ainsley...and everyone. We've never seen a case like this before, so we better be on our A game. Keep your eyes open, and report anything out of the ordinary."

Victor left the room. Looking pleased with herself, Ainsley returned to her seat. Finn rolled his eyes at JT, who stifled a laugh. They were used to her taking credit for any success.

Finn looked at her profile as she peered through big reading glasses. Despite her grandstanding and her condescending air, she aroused him by how she abstractedly ran a fingernail across blood-red lips. Why was he drawn to a woman who treated him like a grunt?

When he left the room, JT followed and pulled him aside. "Just wanted you to know," he said conspiratorially, "that the number of watches came out two short of the receipts."

He didn't have to tell Finn the missing watches were the two they had pocketed.

"But no worries," JT went on quietly. "In a raid, who can help when the numbers don't match up exactly?"

"Normally. But Victor will tell the client we got two-forty-four, and that number will go into our filing with the court...."

"No one's going to count the pieces they pour into an incinerator."

Finn peered at him. JT grinned and returned to the conference room, apparently unconcerned. And JT was right that the bogus watches would be destroyed in the end, so there was nothing wrong with saving one from the steamroller. As to any sense of morality, right versus wrong was a nuanced question, a matter of degree, different for Finn than other people.

Finn returned to his office. The room was small but serviceable, with a couple of filing cabinets, two extra chairs for guests and a view down the avenue—if you pressed your face against the window. Moving to a better office would only come with rising in the ranks of the firm.

He took the fake Sanchi from his desk—he had been careful not to let anyone at the firm besides JT see it. They should reduce the count in the declaration, but the total number seized needed to comport with what Bolger already told the client.

Recalling his problem with the pen in the conference room brought him back to the annoyance of his sinistrality. He had almost entirely grown out of the stutter that came from struggling to fit into a right-handed world; he had become accustomed to finding the one left-handed desk in a lecture hall; he was deft at maneuvering not to sit to the right of a dinner companion. But he continued to obsess over the distinction between left and right. In a body with two sets of limbs and everything else symmetrical, at least from the outside, why were only one percent of people ambidextrous, or "even-handed" as he called it? The much larger number of left-handed people simply had to deal with doing things from the "wrong side." This could sometimes be an advantage, like when he saw the flaw in a design no one else could see. But the rare benefits hardly made up for the difficulties, like Finn's inclination to offer the wrong hand to shake.

At the end of the day, he and JT were going to head out to a bar reputed to be teeming with available women. Finn took out the fake Sanchi again. The genuine version sold for thousands of dollars, so would wearing it really impress anyone? Then again, why have it if he was never going to wear it, and this evening— away from the office—was an opportunity to try it out.

He paused for only a moment, then put his old Timex in his desk drawer and strapped the knockoff on his right wrist.

Chapter Four

Bolger & Plotkin did not pay at the big-firm scale. This, together with Finn's substantial student loans and the prospect of helping pay for an assisted living home for his grandfather, required him to save all the money he could. When his last sublet ran out, he turned to "Apartments to Share" in *The Village Voice* and found a room in a commercial loft on Duane Street, downtown near the courthouses.

It was the only apartment in the building and not a legal residence in a block zoned commercial. The space was enormous, the entire second floor of an abandoned nightclub with twenty-foot ceilings, a stage and a dance floor. Three bedrooms divided by drywall lined the side of an industrial kitchen, and the ladies' room at the back had been converted into a fourth bedroom. A shower was rigged up in one stall of the old men's room. The large windows at the front and back of the loft would soon be inviting in winter drafts.

Finn sublet his room from the main tenant, Larry, a lanky thirty-five-year-old. Finn needed no nickname for his landlord, who had made up his own in the form of the stage name "Lance." Lance had built a studio in the front of the loft, where he composed the music for his debut album, eponymously titled "Lance." He had done a decent job insulating his studio, which at least muffled the noise from his rehearsals. The studio also served another purpose when Lance sublet his bedroom from the converted ladies' room and moved his stuff *on top* of his studio. This meant lifting his crane-like body up a long ladder to reach his mattress, but it provided more steady income than was likely from record sales.

Three others occupied the loft, leaving aside Bogart, Lance's ten-year-old collie-shepherd, who probably should have counted as a resident since he was virtually self-sufficient and displayed more personality than his owner.

The next resident was Satchel, a marketing copywriter and sometime actor who quickly became Finn's closest friend. He showed his genial nature by putting up with Finn nicknaming him "Satchmo." Satch complained his job made him a mere "cog in the machine," and he longed for a creative career in theater or television.

Mandy occupied the end room. Finn called her "Party Girl" because she lived too hard, out every night. She and Finn occupied alternate time zones; as he prepared for bed, she'd be applying makeup and choosing her outfit for the night; as he left for work in the morning, he'd pass her on the stairs coming home.

One very hot early morning in August, the sound of his door squeaking woke Finn. He looked down from the platform that held his bed to see Mandy wander in, drop all her clothes and lie back on the sofa. She could have just been hot or sleepwalking, but Finn didn't think so. Mandy was reasonably attractive—except maybe in the bright light of day—but Finn intuited that sex with her would lead to nothing good. He pulled a pillow over his head until she was gone.

The newest tenant, Petra, had taken Lance's place in the old ladies' room. She was a short, round-faced woman who worked at a restaurant but spent her free time painting at easels set up at the street end of the dance floor. Finn saw no way to improve on her name and so left it alone. She was cute, and he was impressed by her dedication to her art, but she appeared to reserve her winning smile mostly for women, so he left her to herself.

In addition to the human and canine residents, large centipedes, water bugs and in the summer a swarm of mosquitoes also shared the loft. The wildlife at least stayed mostly hidden when the lights were on, and mosquitos were easy to squash at night with the ceiling less than three feet over Finn's mattress.

When Finn got home that evening, Satch was sitting in the kitchen.

"I got the part!" Satch said with a self-satisfied grin.

"Oh, right," said Finn. "You auditioned at your club."

Satch belonged to the Amateur Comedy Club, a private "gentlemen's club" started in the 1880s that seemed to focus mostly on drinking and camaraderie but also put on plays at their old carriage house in Murray Hill. Satch had become a member—through some sort of arcane ritual—and in the fall had helped build the set for the previous show. Finn attended that play and found it surprisingly well done for an amateur production and the clubhouse a fascinating relic of old New York. That evening brought Finn back to *Oliver!*, the show he had helped put on in junior high. That had been a rare happy moment of fitting in, although even that memory was colored by how "stage right" and "stage left" being the opposite of "house right" and "house left" screwed with his always befuddled sense of direction.

"What's the play?" Finn asked.

"*What's Funny About Crime & Punishment?*"

"Good question," Finn chuckled. "Not quite Dostoevsky, I guess."

Satch smiled. "Well, a little livelier we hope. In this version, Raskolnikov is a student barred from graduation because of a long-overdue library book, and when the bursar squeezes him for a bribe, Raskolnikov pushes him out a window."

"Sounds ridiculous."

"Well, yeah, and the real challenge will be running a slew of actors on and off."

Finn laughed. "And how will you do the window thing on that tiny stage?"

"Oh, we'll build a window frame and lay a mattress behind it. I hope so, anyway, since I'm the bursar who gets thrown out the window. But my main role is as Raskolnikov's friend, Dimitri Prokofich Razumikhin."

"Is that one character or three?"

"Only one, but altogether I have three parts."

"Sounds like chaos."

"To be honest, it will be, but it should also be fun. And hey, we're amateurs."

"It *is* called the *Amateur* Comedy Club."

"Exactly."

"But—just wondering—have you read the novel?"

"Dostoyevsky? Are you kidding?" Satch paused. "Wait, you read it?"

"Yeah," Finn said, "in college. You know, Raskolnikov spends a lot of time sweating in bed, torturing himself about murdering the pawnbroker?"

"I think we skip over that bit with a light-hearted song."

Satch had been inviting Finn to join him for a "worknight" at the clubhouse, where Satch assured him actual work was always preceded by a home-cooked meal and followed by cocktails. Finn was intrigued about the club, but it was dinner that lured him to stop at the clubhouse before going to intercept Dani.

They caught the uptown local to Murray Hill and crossed 36th Street. It was not until Satch took out his keys halfway down the block toward Third Avenue that Finn remembered this was where he had come to the play in the fall. There was nothing to indicate there was a theater in this two-story brick building.

Inside the doorway they stepped through a curtain into a

theater. Power saws, worktables, piles of wood and paint cans took up much of the space where chairs would be set up for the audience. A man and a woman seated behind a folding table conversed with actors on stage. Another man standing off to the side shouted a greeting to Satch.

The others all looked up. The woman at the table checked her clipboard and said to Satch, "We'll run through the first Dimitri scene when this is done, in half an hour."

"Tonight is unusual," Satch told Finn, "because rehearsals are going on while we're building."

"Sounds crazy but okay, put me to work."

"First let me buy you a drink upstairs, and then we'll have dinner. By then the stage should be clear."

Finn was thinking he could easily get used to this club.

Satch led the way back toward the front door and up a narrow staircase. It felt like stepping back in time. A posterboard on the wall showed illustrations of the actors in a 1921 performance of *What the Public Got*, and the hallway leading from the stairs was lined with more posterboards, some recent but others ancient. Past a kitchen they reached the "Green Room," where the green of the walls was mostly covered with more posterboards hung between bookshelves crammed with plays. The floor beneath the worn carpet listed toward the hallway, making Finn wonder about the building's structural integrity. But this didn't seem to concern the elderly woman with dyed red hair and cat eyeglasses who was on her knees pinning up a long, billowing dress. The young woman wearing the dress looked over with a welcoming smile.

"Glad you made it, comrade," she said to Satch. "We should run our lines."

"Gen," Satch said in greeting and, following her gaze to his friend, turned to Finn and added, "Genevieve Bejart, meet Finnegan Alger."

"And I'm just chopped liver?" growled the woman on her knees.

"Yes, no, of course," Satch said. "And this dear lady is Sylvia, our consummate professional costume designer. Sylvia, this is my roommate Finn."

Sylvia nodded and returned to her work, as if this introduction was all the conversation required. Genevieve returned her smile to the two men. A shaft of sunlight through the window caught both her dangling crystal earrings and grey-green eyes.

"Nice to meet you, Finnegan," she said and held out her hand to shake. "Are you an actor?"

"Me?" Finn said, caught off guard. "No, I'm more a backstage guy."

"That's perfect," she chirped. "I think we're still looking for grips."

Finn laughed this off. He had "gripped" once in junior high school because he liked one of the actresses, but why would he do that now?

He followed Satch through a doorway to an even more eclectic room, glancing back to see Genevieve hold up a mask that hid her mouth but not the smile in her eyes. Many of the club members he had seen so far seemed past their use-by date, but if young women like Genevieve also acted or helped out, maybe there was a reason to volunteer besides the food.

"This is the workroom," Satch said. "You wouldn't have seen this at the show because we close it off for the cast, at least until the crowds clear and we break out the hard liquor and cigars."

"I thought there was no smoking in this old wooden building," Finn said.

"There really are no rules for the members. This is *our* house."

Finn laughed. "And I assume Puffy Dress Girl is *the* Genevieve."

"Puffy...what?" Satch said and smirked. "Yeah, man, of course. She's so awesome. And that tent of a costume she's wearing does *not* do her justice."

The workroom looked like a theater museum. Over a bar hung ancient steel buckets whose faded labels suggested they held paint pigments. Hanging from the low ceiling were a dozen chandeliers from plays probably no one could even remember. Stuffed in odd places hung a dart board, a wooden sword and an old tennis racket. A vaudeville-era sign read: "We Do Not Lease Rooms To Theatricals." Two walls were lined with lockers, some painted with designs looking as old as the clubhouse itself.

Seeing Finn inspect the lockers, Satch said, "Those were installed during Prohibition for members to keep their liquor."

Finn looked at him in confusion. "Wasn't that illegal?"

"Prohibition didn't make *drinking* alcohol illegal, just making and selling it. And this has always been a private club."

"So no trouble with the law?"

"To the extent our members stocked up enough to last from 1920 to 1933, anyway."

A bell rang, and Finn lined up at the kitchen. They waived the five-dollar charge because it was his first worknight. He took his plate of beef stew and roasted vegetables to the workroom, where he and Satch joined a tall man in his forties and another perhaps seventy.

"Satchel, great to see you," said the young man dressed in cargo shorts—despite the season—and a paint-stained Talking Heads concert T-shirt.

The older man peered at Finn. "New blood?" he said to Satch.

"Right," Satch responded with a laugh. "Gentlemen, this is my roomie, Finnegan Alger. Finn, meet Derk." The young man half rose and extended his hand. "And Hudson." Hudson remained seated but also held out his hand. "Hudson is the esteemed chair of our Play Committee, which selects and produces our shows; you must be nice to him if you want a part. But Derk is the guy who actually runs the place; he builds sets and fixes the refrigerator and gets the late-night call when the heat goes out."

"Are you rehearsing?" Hudson asked Satch.

"Yeah," Satch said, rising with his still-full plate. "In fact, I've got to finish this and get downstairs. I'll leave you two to deliver the hard sell. Finn really wants to get involved in theater."

Finn grinned at Satch, who laughed, cupped him on the shoulder and disappeared.

"So," Hudson said to Finn, "what do you do?"

"Me? Well, I'm no actor. I'm just a lawyer."

"Oh, really? I was a proud member of the bar for thirty-five years. What law do you practice?"

"I mostly enforce trademarks and copyrights."

Hudson and Derk looked at each other. "That's an odd coincidence," Derk said.

"Yes," Hudson added. "We just heard we can't secure the rights for our spring play."

"The playwright won't give you a license?" Finn asked.

"Not the playwright; the company that handles the rights."

"Well, that's too bad. So you have to find another show?"

They both nodded ruefully.

"It's such a bother," Hudson said. "What ever happened to artistic license?"

"Of course," Finn said quietly, "copyrights exist to protect artists."

"Right," Hudson said, "but we don't sell tickets, so there's no public performance. Couldn't we just say it's like putting on a show at home for friends and family?"

Finn couldn't help looking skeptical, and Hudson turned away, called out to someone and left with barely a nod.

Derk turned back to Finn. "I think you spooked him."

Finn laughed. "He may be right that you could get away with it. I was just pointing out the risk; that's what lawyers do. But you can't separate the written law from human behavior and the discretion of judges."

Derk looked doubtful.

"It comes down to whether the copyright owners will even

notice you're putting on a show. And if they do notice, will they care? And if they care, will they care enough to complain? And even if they complain, is it worth spending the time and money to sue you? Where's the upside for them?"

Even as Finn repeated, by rote, this advice for which he normally over-billed, his thoughts returned to how the law was riddled with ambiguities and conflicting interpretations. Here a small, local club quietly ignored regulations about liquor and put on shows for its members and guests. How could buying liquor be illegal but not drinking it? What was "fair use" of a play? Should the analysis come down to Plato—channeled by G-pa—and focus on the accused's disposition and character in benefiting or injuring someone else?

"Well," Derk said, rising to bring his plate back to the kitchen. "The law is above my pay grade. I've got to pull some furniture from the basement." He paused. "And I could use a hand."

Finn followed Derk down a back stairway to the stage, where men—and a few women—were putting up molding and painting a set taking form as a Russian library.

Derk said, "The director is asking for a small round table, and I think there's one buried in the cellar." Then, pulling open a trapdoor in the stage, he shouted, "Trap open!"

From somewhere in the house, two over-loud shouts rejoined, "Trap open!"

This outburst got no rise from anyone except one woman on stage holding a script, who was visibly annoyed.

"Actors," Derk spit out. "They think the sun rises and sets on them, but there's no show if we don't build their set and turn on the lights."

Finn followed Derk down a wooden ladder bolted to the wall to what looked like a timeworn antique shop and a chaotic lumber supply store stuffed together into a cave. Derk moved a box of two-by-fours and shoved a wooden platform across the gravelly floor, scattering a nest of black mice.

"Watch your head," Derk said, gesturing at a low-hanging pipe.

Everything about this building was fascinating. The cellar felt like Paris, rough-hewn from bedrock atop old sewers and caves. Finn noticed an opening in the back wall barely large enough to climb through. "What's through there?" he said.

"It connects to the front cellar."

"There's another room like this?" Finn asked, incredulous.

"Something like this, but it's where we keep costumes and props. And there's a stairway from the cloakroom by the front door."

The young boy in Finn wanted go spelunking through the opening. But he was supposed to work for his dinner, so he returned his attention to the table search and trying not to get too messed up before he met Dani.

Back on stage Derk asked, "How about helping me move this light?" He pointed at a large black device bolted to the ceiling. "But you might want to remove that watch. No sense putting it at risk."

"Oh, no worries," Finn said, looking at his wrist. "It's a fake."

"Really?" Derk said with interest. "Where can I get one of those?"

It was illuminating how people didn't care if watches were genuine as long as they looked real. He wondered if anyone even cared how well they kept time. This posed a huge challenge to marketing products whose price was boosted by branding—basically *all* luxury items. Of course, Finn had no reason to complain since that challenge paid his salary.

They used a battery-powered drill to bolt the light to the ceiling. As Finn put his back into holding the light in place, he mused about how his concern about the watch was not that he might damage it but rather that he wore it at all. It was JT's idea to steal watches, but that hardly excused Finn's theft. It brought him back to one particularly bleak episode of his never-blissful teenage years.

At sixteen Finn worked part-time at the one supermarket in town, assisting the cashiers by packing groceries into paper bags. The monotony of this job and resentment at making minimum wage fed his resentment of his narrow world.

Then right before Thanksgiving, Matt Handy, the cashier he was working with one afternoon, turned to say under his breath, "Watch this."

Matt fiddled with the paper tape running through the cash register. Then, after the next customer, a middle-aged man stepped up with just a turkey. Matt keyed in the price, and the tape jammed.

"Oh, I'm so sorry," Matt said. "I'll fix this."

As Matt worked on the cash register, the woman in line behind turkey-man moved with a huff to the next line. And after two minutes, turkey-man looked like his head might explode. He growled, "How long is this gonna take?"

"Oh, only a few minutes. I just need to pull the ripped spool out and load another."

Matt ripped the tape out of the machine as the man's face reddened further. Then Matt looked up and said, "Listen, you've got only one item. If you want you can pay, and I'll ring it up after I fix the tape."

Turkey man didn't need a receipt. He handed over cash, Matt made change, and Finn bagged the bird and wished the man a happy Thanksgiving. Matt then fixed the tape in an instant and rang up the next customer. In the next lull, he covertly handed Finn a five-dollar bill. "Your cut," he said.

In a way it was the perfect crime, although not really a crime since nobody got hurt. The customer took home his turkey at the listed price, Matt and Finn made a living wage—for one hour at least—and the company, well, the company would hardly notice ten bucks off the day's receipts. Justice, or at least fairness, was served all around.

After Thanksgiving there were no more one-off turkey purchases. But Matt was always on the lookout for customers with single, big-ticket items and pulled the torn tape scam several times over the following month. One Saturday afternoon he pulled the scam twice. The first was with a man buying a ribeye steak for exactly twelve dollars. Finn's payoff for that scam equaled his salary for almost three hours. The second guy bought a case of imported beer, but Matt's lousy arithmetic in adding the bottle deposit did them in. The customer recalculated the deposit at his car and returned to complain to the manager. No, he hadn't been given a receipt, but he had the change from his twenty and a story about a torn register slip. That was enough to land Matt and Finn in the police station. And the worst part was having to call G-pa to come get him.

As always, his grandfather didn't scold or impose punishment, but his look of disappointment hurt so much more. On the way home he said, "It reminds me of a quote."

"No, G-pa, please," was all Finn could reply. These quotes were maddening because they imbued his grandfather's homilies with thousands of years of gravitas that allowed no comeback. And the quotes were annoyingly on point.

This time G-pa's look told Finn he was getting off easy. He only said, laconically, "The Laws of Plato: the unrestrained and insolent things done by the young."

Finn lost his job and had to pay back the store for each ripped-tape incident the manager could identify. That depleted his bank account, and the arrest killed his chance at a soccer scholarship. The only escape route after that was a job digging irrigation ditches and later enrollment at the community college in Neosho. But he saved enough money living at home and did well enough in his classes to transfer to the University of Missouri for his degree. From there he just had to borrow his way through law school.

The racket of Derk's drill brought Finn back to holding the heavy light in place—and not falling off the ladder. No, there was no need to worry about his watch. Any cause for alarm came from how cavalierly he was wearing it, like some kind of big shot, even though he also had to make sure no one from work, other than JT, ever saw it. He had outgrown the belief that the rules of the right-handed world didn't apply to him, and yet morality and justice remained nebulous concepts. He wondered if he was overdue for a re-set conversation with his grandfather.

When they wrapped up working on the set, Finn joined Satch for a drink in the workroom, along with a couple of men from the crew and two who apparently had remained upstairs over cocktails and never made it downstairs to work. This seemed to be the tenor of the club, that people helped out as much or as little as they wanted, without disapprobation, while never passing up a chance to share a drink and chat about the next show or their vacation plans.

One older gentleman launched into a tirade about the Iran-Contra scandal, which met with stony silence. He walked away, muttering.

Another man, watching the old guy storm off, leaned into Finn. "The unwritten rule is no talk about politics or religion. It keeps the atmosphere congenial."

It was hard not to be alarmed by Reagan's right-wing policies, but Finn was happy to try. These were new friends eager to enjoy each other's company. The rule about politics made sense, regardless of the world outside. Even the recent Black Monday stock market crash, which Satch told him had hit some rich old members hard, was absent from the workroom chatter.

Finn tuned back into the conversation about how the work crew could help the women building life-sized police puppets for a climactic scene.

"I'm a little confused," Finn said to one of the crew. "There's no crowd of police in *Crime and Punishment*."

"Much less *singing* police," the man laughed. "And these cops even do a little dancing."

"I see you two are working hard," Genevieve interrupted with a gentle, teasing smile as she took a seat between Finn and Satch.

"We can't overtax our recruits if we hope to sign them up," Satch said, gesturing at Finn.

There was no mystery why Satch liked Genevieve. Her disposition seemed to brighten the whole room. Now in a baggy sweatshirt, painter's pants and backwards Yankees cap, she looked almost like a young boy, although there was something undeniably feminine about her laughing eyes and the faint freckles on her nose and cheeks.

She joined in talk about the puppet costumes, but when the conversation turned to the British Premier League, she turned to Finn. "So, Satch says you spend your days harassing Asian shopkeepers?"

"That's the job, I'm afraid. We go after counterfeiters."

"Are you a detective or something?"

"No, nothing like that. Just a trademark lawyer."

She looked pensive.

"They deserve it," he went on. "It's big business churning out cheap merchandise with infringing trademarks."

"I guess when you're talking about large corporations," she said with a sad smile.

"Big brands usually hire us, but last year we brought a claim for 'reverse confusion' for a string of small bakeries when a nationwide corporation copied their trademark, making people believe it was the bakeries that were infringing."

"Did you win?"

"Sure did. And we finally had to ask our client to stop sending over pastries in gratitude."

Genevieve laughed.

"Oh, it wasn't funny," Finn said. "I put on five pounds."

Satch broke in to say to Genevieve, "Can you make it a half-hour early for rehearsal tomorrow, so we can go over the hotel scene?"

She perked up at this. "I think I can. Just have to check I don't have to work late. Let me give you a call during the day."

"Good enough." Satch said, and to Finn he added, "Genevieve works at Scribner's."

"The store on Fifth Avenue?"

"That's the one," she replied proudly. "I thought they were hiring me to replace Maxwell Perkins, you know, to edit the next Hemingway or Thomas Wolfe, but I've started off reshelving books."

Satch had to go uptown when they left the clubhouse, so he accompanied Finn on the subway.

The train pulled out, and Finn was lost in thinking how to approach Dani, when Satch grabbed his elbow. "I can't tell if she likes me," he said, sounding desperate. "She's nice to everyone."

"Who, Puffy Dress Girl?"

"Of course, you idiot! Who do you think I'm talking about?"

"Well, I agree she's nice...and serious about her acting and her publishing career. And she seems to like working with you."

The train pulled in, the outsides of most of the cars plastered with graffiti. The splashy images reflected the city's kaleidoscope of characters and strangely made Finn feel at home. Still, there was something dystopian about all the paint. What was colorful on the outside of the trains—from the obscure "TRAP DEZ DAZE" to the AIDS-inspired "SILENCE=DEATH"—was often just a mess of black tags inside the cars. And whether this was art or desecration, Mayor Koch was on a mission to wash it away. Year by year, the message of street artists was supplanted by Madison Avenue ads. It was debatable whether this was progress, but it lessened the sense of anarchy in the gritty backbone of the city.

"But that's just it," Satch said, loud enough for Finn to hear over the kid's ghetto blaster at the other end of the car, and pulling Finn's attention from "ART IS THE WORD" on the passing uptown local. "She's so serious about her acting and making the play come off that, well, I can't tell if that's all I mean to her."

When they pulled out, Finn surfed the curves of the track without holding on, proud this hard-earned proficiency marked him as a New Yorker.

"Well," Satch took up again plaintively, "What would *you* do? What are you doing about Dani?"

Finn grabbed a pole to keep from stumbling. He saw he had to forget about Dani for a minute and focus on Satch. It seemed his loftmate was pretty far gone on this woman. "All I can tell you, Satchmo," he said with a sigh, "is what *doesn't* work."

But Satch looked desperate, so Finn went on. "Remember when I dog-sat for that partner at my firm?"

"Like three weeks ago?"

"Yeah. I had this classic seven on Riverside Drive all to myself—except the little Westies I had to walk and feed. An ideal setup to invite Dani, right? And on top of the gorgeous apartment, I bought tickets to *Burn This* on Broadway."

"I think I see where this is going."

"Right, well, I wish *I* had seen it coming."

"And so...?"

"Well, she loved the apartment and liked the dogs...and the play was good, too."

"But other than that, Mrs. Lincoln, you enjoyed the play?"

"Exactly. Once again I ended up putting her on a PATH train after just a kiss on the cheek."

Finn paused for a long sigh and went on. "I'm the *last* person you should ask for dating advice. I guess just ask her out. No sense wasting time."

"Like you?" Satch said with a sad grin.

"Right. Like me."

Chapter Five

St. Mark's Place stretched the few blocks between Astor Place and Tompkins Square Park, where Eighth Street became a bohemian center of open-front markets, mohawks and tattoo parlors. One writer called the aura of this street "superglue for fragmented identities." By 1987 Thelonious Monk no longer played at the Five Spot, and Andy Warhol and the Velvet Underground had moved on from the Dom, but there was still no shortage of late-night parties, drag queens and shadowy drug dealers hissing, "Smoke, smoke." And mid-block sat the Café Kabul, serving Afghani food at small tables, including one in the front window, where diners sat on woven cushions.

It was not surprising this was where Dani worked as a waitress. Her bedazzled ankle boots and fluorescent rubber bracelets hardly even stood out in this shabby wonder of a neighborhood. But her ethereal beauty made it hard for Finn to see anything else when she was nearby. And now he would ambush her after her shift and try once again to get her to take him seriously.

He could just call and ask her out, to a movie or dinner maybe. Their date to see *Babette's Feast* at the Paris had gone so well, she spent the night with him at the loft. But that was weeks ago, and she was still so hard to pin down or even reach on the telephone. Still, that last night together left him hopeful. He had known two women in college who been only mildly interested in him until the *third* time they slept together; he was confident it could be the same with Dani—if only he could get her to come back to the loft once more.

This evening he would surprise her, make it spontaneous and flattering so she had to give him a chance. And the U2 album would break the ice; she wouldn't turn that down.

He steeled himself to limit his expectations. Success would be getting her to walk with him and making her smile with the album. He could be patient about the rest. It was worth the wait if he could start to wear her down.

He arrived early and had a beer on a pub stool with a view of the café. Looking at his knockoff Sanchi reminded him of coordinating the raid in Nashville, but this time he had no backup team; he smiled thinking it might help to have a police escort. He tried not to think about where he got the watch; this was no time for moral appraisal. And Dani liked jewelry so much, maybe it would impress her.

At ten twenty-five he stood in front of the restaurant and caught her eye. She was removing the apron from over her flowered, calf-length dress. Her face showed recognition but hardly surprise. He held up the album wrapped in newspaper, and she tilted her head in curiosity.

This would work; he was confident as he waited for her to emerge to the sidewalk in her gold jacquard jacket. She looked at him with big hazel eyes, seeming to ask both what was in the package and why he was there, while not particularly caring about the answers.

"Horatio," she said, using her literary nickname for Finn, "what are you doing here?"

"I was in the neighborhood," he said with a grin. Clearly, that wasn't true. "And I wanted to give you something I picked up in Tennessee."

He had thought the reference to Tennessee might pique her interest, but she simply reached for the album and unwrapped it.

"That was nice of you," she said, a smile revealing she was happy with the gift.

"I thought you'd like it."

After a moment of awkward silence, he went on. "So, can I buy you a drink or something?"

"I need to get home," she said absently, "but I could eat a slice of pizza."

"You mean a 'slab.' "

"What's that?"

"It's just what my friend at work calls it."

He regretted bringing JT into the conversation, as it belittled his serious intentions. But she stopped walking and pondered. "We can grab a slab just across Astor Place, on the way to the PATH."

"Great, then I'll walk you to your train."

Her response was an enigmatic smile. She was pleased, he guessed, but still irksomely aloof. But she did let him walk with her and carry the album. Maybe he was finally breaking through.

They ate standing at a counter facing the street. People streamed in and out, but Finn saw only Dani. He told his story about an LA raid, where they raced to the bank before it closed to freeze half a million dollars in illicit profits, but she seemed distracted.

When they reached Sixth Avenue, he walked down into the station with her, planning to join her on the train if she'd let him.

At the bottom of the stairs, she searched her red-tasseled bag. "I can never find change when I need it," she said.

"Oh, here," Finn volunteered and pulled a handful of coins from his pocket.

Without hesitation, she selected the exact change from his hand, giving him an involuntary thrill at her touch.

"Should I come with you?" he blurted out, his confidence wavering.

"I don't think so."

He was deflated. Did she really not see he had gone way out of his way to meet her, and to buy her a gift, that he wanted to spend time with her and would do almost anything to go to her apartment?

"I thought," he stammered, "maybe we could get a drink or something. I don't know...."

She smiled patronizingly. "I have an early morning and work in the afternoon. I really need to sleep."

Before he knew it, she had passed through the turnstile.

But she stopped and reached back a hand. He stepped in close. She leaned in and kissed him on the cheek. "Thanks for the record, Horatio," she said with disconcerting good cheer and then laughed when she added, "and the slab."

He tried to think of something to say to delay her leaving but came up with nothing. She turned and walked off without looking back.

He felt sucker-punched. But even in ignominious defeat, he couldn't help seeing the encounter as a grand romantic scene, imagining her disappearing into the mist at the end of *Casablanca*.

Finn dragged himself into work the next day, feeling hung-over despite having had only one beer the night before. An early meeting with Victor was torture, but then he hoped to spend the day alone in his office, sorting through the results of the Nashville raid and his plans for wooing Dani.

Peace and quiet were short-lived, though, as Ainsley soon appeared at his office door.

"The new associate is here," she said, peering at him suspiciously as if he had shown up for work drunk, "and Victor wants you to settle him in."

"What about Jimmy? Can't he do it?"

"Victor said *you* should do it. What, are you above mentoring a baby lawyer?"

"No," Finn said resignedly. "What's his name?"

"Theodore Cummings, Jr. He was recommended by some country club friend of Victor's. Texas A&M."

Finn distrusted anyone hired through a family connection. They were always entitled brats with inflated views of themselves. And then a thought occurred to him. "Isn't A&M a military school?"

"I think the cadet corps is an undergrad thing. But Victor said he's from a military family, back to the Civil War or something."

Ainsley brought the new kid to his office minutes later. He was tall and thin and neatly dressed in an inexpensive suit with pants pressed to a knifelike crease. Most friends of Victor were Ivy League types, but this new lawyer looked like he just got off the bus from Missouri. This normally would be a reason to go easy on him, but Theodore was too damned bright-eyed and eager for Finn's dour mood.

"Welcome aboard," Finn said listlessly.

"Thank you, sir," the young man responded with too much enthusiasm. "It's a pleasure to be here."

Ainsley chuckled at Finn from behind the young lawyer. "Well," she said, "I'll leave you in Finn's hands, Theodore, and will see you in the trenches."

Theodore turned to her and said, "I appreciate it, ma'am."

Finn tried not to laugh at Ainsley's attempt at battlefield humor and his impression that Theodore Cummings Jr. almost saluted her. Then he resigned himself to twenty minutes of answering questions about the firm, after which it was time to get back to work.

He handed Theodore the index of watches seized in Nashville and a copy of the client declaration JT had filed to get the seizure order. "We have to report at the hearing Thursday," Finn said, "on what we seized at a raid last week. Sam Eddings, at the client, will testify about how to identify a counterfeit. Use Eddings' earlier declaration to state his title at Sanchi, etcetera, and Jack Wilson's declaration from the Nike case as a model to lay out each seized watch model, with details of how we know it isn't genuine. June, one of our legal assistants, can get you that template and help with photographing the watches. And the other assistant, Imani, will give you a memo about common cosmetic errors, like misspelled words or mis-sized parts. You should examine each watch model for discrepancies. Leave blanks for the client to fill in mechanical differences. Put that all together right away, and let me see it. You'll finish up this declaration with me, but JT is running the case."

"Will do, Mr. Alger, sir," Ted said eagerly.

Finn let out an exasperated breath. "Victor is the only one to call 'sir,' if you must," he said, "although we call him 'Big Niccolò,' but not to his face. "

Ted scrunched up his face.

Finn laughed. "Victor keeps this bust of Machiavelli on his desk. He'd say it venerates a respected advisor of the Medicis during the Italian Renaissance, but we're pretty sure he's more about seeing to business and taking no prisoners. It tells you a lot about Victor."

Ted smiled uneasily as if he was unsure if Finn was serious.

Finn went on. "But everyone other than Big Niccolò goes by first names. Got it, Junior?"

"Yes, sir, but..."

Finn cut him off with a stern look. The kid was obviously about to say he preferred not to be called "Junior," but he needed a nickname, like everyone else, and Finn would see that the name stuck.

Back at the loft that night, Finn sat on the threadbare couch that took up the entire wall beneath the big windows in his room, looking at the earrings he bought for Dani. Petra popped her head in the doorway and said he had a call.

He jumped up, sure it was Dani. He was glad Petra didn't see his disappointment when it turned out to be his grandfather.

"My boy," the gravelly voice said, "haven't heard from you in a week. Still rolling that big boulder up the hill?"

Finn's grandfather had taught philosophy and could inject a quote from a philosopher or reference to mythology into just about any conversation. And if Finn ever forgot to call, it was like some national emergency. "We spoke three days ago, G-pa," Finn said. "I was travelling for a case."

"Oh, don't mind a bearish old man," his grandfather said. "It's the privilege of age to grouse." He paused long enough to make Finn feel guilty for making excuses and then turned serious. "Listen, my boy, I hate to do this, but I must ask a favor."

"Of course, G-pa. Whatever you need."

"Well, it's actually for Charley." Finn had known G-pa's next-door neighbor most of his life.

"What's the trouble?" Finn asked.

"You know his grandson, Julian...."

Indeed, Finn did know Julian, who was ten years younger than Finn and so constantly raising Cain that Finn felt some affinity for him. The difference was Julian rebelled as a way of establishing himself as a local bad boy too cool for his home town, while Finn had always focused on getting out.

"As you know, he's been trouble his whole life," G-pa went on, "but this time it's serious. He was picked up in New York for robbing eighty-seven dollars from a convenience store. I don't know what he was thinking or even what he's doing in New York. But he's in a holding cell and will be arraigned in the morning."

Finn was more surprised Julian was in New York than that he was in trouble. In any event, the thought of this kid held in a jail cell over eighty-seven dollars struck home; the watch Finn stole had to be worth at least that much.

"That must be devastating for Charley," he said. "Can I do something to help?"

"Well, he knows you're a lawyer in New York, and..."

"G-pa. I've never even been in the criminal courthouse."

"Yes, I know, and I told him he'd need a criminal lawyer. But he'd also like your help hiring someone...after the hearing tomorrow."

Finn ran down the pile of work he had to do in the office, and cringed at what Victor would do if he found out Finn was moonlighting during business hours.

"He really doesn't know what to do," his grandfather went on. "Is there any way...?"

"Wait," Finn said, cutting him off and trying to complete this thought. "Okay," he said reluctantly. "Tell Charley to call me with all the details. I'll get him a name and take care of the arraignment."

Finn would take no money for handling the arraignment. He knew Charley would go into shock if he learned Finn's billable rate. But more importantly, Charley was a good friend to G-pa; Finn would do all he could for him.

Finn wondered if Julian could get through this mess and return to Lebanon. At seven years old, Finn had been unhappy to be moved there to live with his grandfather, but with his parents gone, there was no other option. Certainly, no one gave *him* a choice. At first he hated leaving his friends and his school, but as he grew his resentment focused on being stuck in a tiny, moribund town, which paled against his embellished memories of the big city. He came to see this as an extension of the alienation of living in a backwards world.

But looking at that time now, he saw how much he owed his grandfather and felt bad about neglecting him, even though he sometimes felt burdened by having constantly to check on him. All through his seventies G-pa had been active, playing golf and cards with his cronies and walking every day, but one after another his friends were dying or sinking into dementia. He had now given up golf, though he still mowed his lawn—and apparently sometimes the neighbor's. Besides tearing through mystery novels, Finn couldn't imagine what else filled his days. And so Finn normally called every couple of days to check in, even though their conversation was often the same old talk about taking meds or playing bridge.

Although he had been tempted to go to the Bahamas with two law school friends over Christmas break, he would go home instead. This was not entirely for the old man. G-pa had rescued him from a sea of despair and raised him through the really tough years. From the death of his parents and sister, Finn became all too familiar with tears; from his grandfather, he learned how to suffer them. And now his grandfather was all the family he had; he needed to keep him close.

Despite his declining memory about recent events, Finn's grandfather remained the voice of morality. G-pa's lectures and inexhaustible cache of maxims helped Finn get over his socio-pathic resentment of the right-handed world, and deal with the challenges of grown-up life. He had to admit he still needed G-Pa sitting on one shoulder to counteract the devil on the other.

Chapter Six

Speaking with his grandfather was sometimes painful for Finn. G-pa inevitably called him out for his foolishness. If he had seen Finn lunge for the phone, thinking it was Dani, he'd have proffered something from Aristotle or Thomas Aquinas about puerile youth. Finn would not only be embarrassed for jumping up like a puppy dog but once again would be browbeaten by some venerable authority. He didn't need the old man to tell him his fruitless longing for Dani was not a good look for him.

Nonetheless, after G-pa's call Finn was back on the couch in his room thinking again about Dani. Maybe he could get her to go see *Guernica* at the Modern. But thinking of Picasso's enormous depiction of Franco's fascist regime reminded him of the recurring *Saturday Night Live* announcement in the '70s that the Generalissimo was "still dead." Debbie Harry was scheduled to appear on that show, and Finn had a friend who worked as a lawyer at NBC. What if he could get tickets? Dani would definitely join him for that.

Bogart pushed Finn's door open and rested his big snout on Finn's lap. It brought a smile to his lips to remember his grandfather wasn't the *only* one who loved him.

"What do you say, fella?" Finn said. "Groceries?"

Because the loft was in a commercial district, it was a bit of a walk to the supermarket. But Bogart was always up for going out, and as they prepared to leave, Petra said she wanted to join them. He grabbed his wallet from the top of his dresser, where he had left the earrings. He still had no idea how Dani would react to them.

"Are those for Dani?" Petra asked.

Petra had met Dani the second time she came to the loft. She volunteered no opinion at the time, but it was obvious she thought Dani was bad news for Finn, and he felt that was completely out of line. How could she understand what he felt? Surely the women who attracted her were nothing like Dani—and after all, who was?

"Yeah," he said, embarrassed. "I picked them up in Nashville."

As they headed for the grocery store, Finn said, "I need to stop at the Raccoon Lodge."

"Isn't it a bit early?" Petra said with a squint.

"Not for a drink. My friend and I were there Friday, and think I left my glasses. I want to see if someone found them."

When they turned on Warren Street and neared the bar's red neon sign, lighted even against the day, Petra said, "I'll stay outside with Bogart."

"Oh, he can come in. He's a regular."

"Really? Isn't that against the law?"

"Well, 'the law' is a malleable concept."

She looked skeptical.

"We came in during that big storm in April because we were both sopping wet. The owner is this Irish lady. She immediately barked out that dogs were not allowed."

"Barked?" she laughed.

"Yes, barked. You'll see when you meet Bridie. Anyway, I said, 'You mean *this* dog?' tilting my head toward Bogart sitting next to me like the perfect gentleman he is. She leaned over the bar, and I swear he smiled at her from beneath his dripping hair. Then she just shook her head and walked away. Bogart's had a free pass ever since."

Petra laughed as they entered the darkness of the classic

dive bar a few blocks north of the World Trade Center. He had wondered what she would think of the frat-house setting, walls covered with old signs, police and fire department patches, duck decoys and posters from *The Honeymooners*.

Petra asked where the name came from.

"Two sad-sack stars of that show," he said, gesturing toward Jackie Gleason and Art Carney in one of the posters. "They belonged to a fraternal society called the Raccoon Lodge."

Bridie was behind the bar, dyed blond hair pulled back in a bun and a no-nonsense expression on her ruddy face. She met them with a scowl that broke into a smile at seeing the dog.

"Well, here's what I call a treat," she said with a slight brogue, leaning over the bar and growling playfully at the dog. Bogart threw his front legs up on the bar, and she scratched behind his ears.

When Bogart dropped back down, Bridie turned to Finn. "What are you two at?" And then she added specifically to Finn, "Don't usually see you this early."

"I was checking if someone turned in a pair of eyeglasses. I think you poured too many free shots Friday, and I left them somewhere, back by the pool table maybe?"

"Well, isn't that a typical bit of shite?" Bridie said to Petra. "Sure, it's the first sign of dependency when you blame someone else for drinking yourself into a stupor." Then she turned back to Finn. "You and yer man—who I noticed struck out with nearly every woman in the bar—needed none of my help catching the midnight train to petrification."

Petra laughed, and Finn was surprised how she seemed to connect with Bridie. He left them to their joke and headed toward the back of the room, past the moose head on the wall above stacks of Budweiser cases. The moose was real, unlike the red hippopotamus hanging upside down from the ceiling.

"Wait," Bridie said as she rummaged under the bar and came up with a cardboard box. On top of forsaken scarves and hats was a pair of glasses, with one arm bent.

"That's them," he said with a grimace, "and I guess a broken pair is better than nothing."

At the office next day Finn was deep into the research for the opposition brief in the copyright case in Chicago. Just three years before, the Supreme Court had found that home videotaping of television broadcasts was non-infringing "time-shifting" rather than "library building." The defendants in Chicago had moved for summary judgment that electronic content could not be accessed *at all* without some kind of "copying," and so copying broadcasts on private televisions could not be the "reproduction" prohibited under the law. Finn would counter that his client's content scrambling system, which prevented taping of television broadcasts, protected copyrighted works from unlicensed "reproduction."

As he outlined the argument, he thought about how Satch's club had to license plays. This requirement was consistent with his client marketing a device to prevent unlicensed use of broadcasts. Was it arrogant to argue for strict enforcement of copyrights in his client's case but excuse unlicensed use of copyrighted work by his friends?

Still, there was no need to reconcile his feelings about the ACC's fair use of plays with the position he would argue in Chicago. He was hired to advocate his client's position in the case at hand, which was at least arguably correct. Someone else would argue the other side, and a judge would decide what was "right" under the law and the facts—legal realism in practice. He wondered if everyone was hypocritical in applying abstract laws to themselves.

Late in the day he called Ted into his office and asked, "Have you finished the Nashville declaration?"

"I have examined the watches and put together the exhibits. I'll have a draft to you this afternoon."

"That's good. I'm so wrapped up in this copyright brief that I haven't been able to focus on Sanchi."

"Can I just ask, though...?"

"What?"

"Um, I'm also working with Jimmy on the upcoming Orchard Street raid, and I wondered if you, well, if you had any advice for me, you know, so I get everything right?"

Finn paused, eyeing Ted's eager expression and cheap suit. How did he become this kid's big brother? "Well," he said reluctantly, "first thing to understand is nothing ever goes entirely right on a raid. That said, this case is about counterfeit T-shirts, which the Taiwanese have been selling since they moved in."

"Moved in?

"Yeah, Junior. It's Orchard Street."

Ted looked puzzled.

"Oh, right," Finn said, "you're from...?"

"Minnesota, sir."

Finn threw him a grim look to knock off the "sir" business and said, "Orchard Street is a mostly pedestrian stretch of a few blocks of discount retail on the Lower East Side below Delancey. It was traditionally Jewish, but Chinatown has been pushing in. Our investigator, Ray Bagatoni—or 'Ray Bag-a-Donuts' as they call him in the old neighborhood—made buys of knockoff T-shirts in several stores. JT then got a seizure order—just like in Tennessee—and we will set up a raid, seize the goods and try to squeeze the shopkeepers to give up their suppliers. It's all straightforward." He paused. "You getting all this?"

"Yeah," Ted looked up from his notebook. "Is that Bag-*a*-Donuts or Bag *of* Donuts?"

Finn held back a laugh but was thinking this kid might actually work out.

Ted's smile broadened. "They didn't teach us any of this in law school."

"Right. Well, welcome to the real world, Junior. And there's one more thing—and while this is not my case, I'm guessing your most important assignment..."

Ted's eyes lit up.

"Well, Ray and his associates at the pre-raid meeting will all be ex-cops. You, Junior, will no doubt be in charge of buying the donuts."

After Ted left him in peace, Finn absentmindedly watched a window cleaner on scaffolding high above the street. He needed a memorable way to give Dani the earrings and reminded himself to call about tickets to *Saturday Night Live*. He wondered if he was pushing too hard with her...or maybe not hard enough? He lingered on their last night in the loft, watching her climb the ladder to his mattress in nothing but his dress shirt.

"Finnegan, old boy," JT said, entering the room. "Missed you at Jack's party Saturday. How was the weekend?"

Done with court appearances for a while, JT had returned to the three-day stubble he told Finn made him irresistible to women.

Before Finn could answer, the phone buzzed and the receptionist said, "Raymond Bagatoni and another gentleman are here."

"More exhibits for Orchard Street?" JT said.

Finn shrugged.

Ray was a real piece of work, a squat, hairy Italian from Brooklyn, the kind of guy whose childhood friends, like in the old movies, all ended up as cops, priests or criminals.

"We're the same," Ray had blurted out when he once saw Finn taking notes.

Finn doubted that, and said, "What do you mean?"

"Both *keivhendt*."

Finn had no idea what that meant.

"It's Norwegian for left-handed," Ray said. "It actually means 'wrong-handed.' "

Finn sighed. He was sure Ray didn't speak Norwegian. He likely picked up that bit the same way Finn had learned the Hungarian for "right" also meant better and "left" bad, or "sinister" was Latin for "on the left." Since Finn had more or less made peace with a world designed backwards, or with being backward himself, he wasn't going to become best friends with some pai-san just because they were both left-handed. Then again, Ray was good at his job—and Victor liked him—so it made sense to play nice.

Ray came into the conference room with Ernie Vulpe, a de-tective they had met on a raid the prior year. Vulpe was a tough guy, big and barrel-chested with massive arms and shoulders, a thick mustache, no neck and a huge, mostly bald head.

"Hey, guys," Ray said, as if they were old frat brothers.

Vulpe just nodded, as if to say, "You guys are Ray's friends, so I suppose you're okay."

"You know Ernie, right?" Ray said, "from Midtown South?"

Both Finn and JT nodded.

"What's up, Ray?" JT said.

"I got passes to the Hard Rock Café tonight, and since it's just around the corner, I thought my best clients might want to come with me and Ernie."

"But that place just opened," JT said. "It's, like, impossible to get in."

"Yeah," Finn added, "I'm not waiting on a line to get into a bar."

Ray chuckled. "No problem there, not for friends of Ray Bagatoni."

Later in the day Ainsley buzzed for Finn to come see her. As soon as he entered her office—not in a corner like Victor's but with a sofa and decent views out three windows—he could see she was unhappy. She was a fine-looking woman but her scowl was chilling. He was pretty sure she was not still steaming about the gun in Nashville; what else was she steaming about?

"You sent off the Nashville declaration to Sam Eddings?"

"Yeah, Ted said it went out last night."

"Ted said?"

"Sure. What's the matter? It's just the follow-up about the seized knockoffs."

"In the format we used for Nike?"

"Sure, but about watches, of course...and Eddings needs to fill in the technical details."

She lashed out. "The signature line called Sam the chief product engineer *at Nike*!"

"Oh, shit."

"Oh, shit is right. And Eddings has already given Victor an earful. What's wrong with you?"

"Look, it's a minor error, easy to fix."

She scoffed. "Easy if this wasn't a new client...and Eddings wasn't a prima donna." She paused. "You say Ted sent this out? Did he draft it?"

"Well, yeah."

"Victor will want him gone."

Finn bristled at this. It was a pain hiring a new lawyer, and he liked this kid. Besides, the error was really Finn's for not supervising. "We can't fire him for that," he said. "Look, it was my responsibility. He just started. I should have reviewed it."

"Obviously you should have, and if we didn't need you right now, Victor would throw *you* out."

Finn saw his mistake in taking a hit for an associate he had just met. But the error really was his, and that would come out if Victor wanted to fire someone, so he might as well take the blame. He should have had Ted work with Imani; she had been with the firm for five years, two since Finn got her promoted from secretary to legal assistant. She wouldn't have let that slip through.

"Okay," she said, returning to a calm voice, "this muck-up is fixable, and Victor will handle the client. You need to give our new associate the lecture, explain that his ethical obligation—even beyond his responsibilities to the firm—is zealously to protect our clients' interests. Failing to proofread a document filed for a client fails in that duty." She stopped and looked at him, then added, "Can I leave this to, or do you need a refresher yourself?"

Finn could not contemplate lessons and lectures without hearing his grandfather spout from his bottomless reservoir of axioms.

"Do you find this funny?" Ainsely asked. Finn realized he was grinning at how even Ainsely would be no match for G-pa in a debate on ethics. "No," he said. "No, of course not. I'll talk to Ted, and I'll give myself a good talking to." Her look was patronizing but then perplexed as she said, "And there's something else. That first watch we sent to Eddings? They couldn't find any flaws except an unregistered serial number."

"You mean...?"

"It's real."

"You mean, like, worth thousands of dollars? How is that possible?"

"That's something we need to find out."

Still puzzled about how a seized watch could be genuine, Finn went to meet with Victor. He admitted up front it was his mistake to not supervise Ted more closely. "I shouldn't have relied on a new associate just because he came recommended," he said, hoping to remind Victor they hired this kid as a favor to his friend.

But like his hero Machiavelli, Victor never second-guessed himself; instead, he vented his frustration at Finn. This wasn't so bad; Finn had long since learned to weather a scolding by distracting himself with pleasant thoughts. As long as there were no lasting consequences, Victor could shout all he wanted.

"And I assured Eddings that kid won't work on his cases," Victor was saying when Finn tuned back into the harangue.

"That's ridiculous. We're going to need his help."

Victor turned severe eyes on Finn, who wiped the cynicism from his face to look contrite. Apparently appeased, Victor went on. "That's the only way I kept *you* on their work. Someone's head had to roll. From now on we bury Ted in the back office—and *don't* let him send anything directly to a client!"

Ted stood at attention in Finn's office. He was trying to look stoic but was clearly mortified.

"You fucked up, and I got the blame," Finn said. "Another mistake like that and we'll both be on the bus back to the hinterland."

"You mean...I'm not fired?"

"Not yet. But stay away from the client, especially Eddings. For now, we'll have you focus on Orchard Street."

Ted was relieved but still pale.

Finn saw a bit of himself in the kid and felt sorry for him. "Look," he said, "the hard lessons are the ones you don't forget. You have to just take the time, print everything and read it before it leaves the office."

Finn was impressed the kid took responsibility without making excuses. He attributed that to Ted's military upbringing. What would growing up with that kind of discipline have done for Finn? A rigid structure could have straightened him out, that and a family that stayed alive...or could as easily have pushed him to rebel harder.

Finn worked late to make up the time wasted on the declaration screw-up. Results mattered, but what mattered most was billable hours, and time wasted on repairing their mistake would not be billed. Strangely enough, JT also worked late. He came by Finn's office at seven-thirty.

"I'm ready to knock off here," Finn said. "You want to go join Ray and ape-man at the bar?"

"Nah," JT said, "I've got to watch the Knicks game."

"Oh, right. They're playing Detroit?"

"And I've got the Pistons with the spread."

"You rat bastard. How much did you bet?"

"You don't want to know."

Although his friend bragged about his winnings, Finn guessed he didn't come out ahead over time. Besides, having money on a game kept JT from rooting for his team, the true joy in watching sports. Instead, games became a business, one tilted to lose JT money in the end.

"You know," Finn said, "if those Peakstones are essentially genuine, they're worth like twenty thousand each?"

"Well, you couldn't sell them for that, not without the serial numbers."

Finn paused and searched JT's face. "Even half that, a quarter of that, rates a Class D felony."

Chapter Seven

In December Finn flew to Chicago for the district court hearing. A short taxi ride past Wrigley Field brought him to the rectangular glass and steel courthouse, so unlike the Romanesque structure down the street from his loft. There were no grand marble steps, only a modern elevator on his way to the assigned courtroom, where he took a seat in the back row to listen to the cases called before his. Victor had taught him this was like scouting how your ref called a basketball game. It might provide clues about what he could get away with in making his argument.

Finn was joined by Larry Gardner, his local counsel. It was just a formality to have an Illinois lawyer with him, though in theory he was there to help. But Finn knew the case and the law as well as anyone. Still, it was some comfort to have an ally in the courtroom, and he had every hope Larry would know a good place nearby for lunch. He had skipped breakfast—he could never eat before going to court—but arguing before a judge always left him ravenous.

When the case was called, Larry moved up to the plaintiff's table while Finn gathered his papers and grabbed his briefcase. He should have known the gate in the rail between the public benches and the counsel tables would swing the wrong direction, but reaching for the right-handed latch he dropped several documents. This was *not* the image of an imposing New York attorney he wanted to convey. He quickly picked up the papers, hoping no one had noticed.

The judge's questions focused on whether his client's technology prevented consumers from shifting purchased movies to other devices for personal use, as they could do legally with audio works. He countered that this was not "time-shifting," in the words of the Supremes, but rather use beyond the limited license that came with a purchase, and restricting his client's technology would unfairly damage its business and hamstring a burgeoning security industry.

The hearing went as well as could be expected, but the issue remained unresolved. It was always a crapshoot predicting how a judge would weigh realistic or moral considerations, so there was no use fretting until she handed down her decision.

Finn turned his attention to getting something to eat before heading back to the airport. Ably filling his role, Larry suggested an authentic Italian trattoria nearby.

As soon as they were seated and had ordered, Larry went to call his office. But he quickly returned with a look of concern. "There was a message for you," he said. "A hospital in Missouri. They want you to call as soon as possible."

When Finn remembered to breathe again, he rushed to the phone booth. The receptionist at Mercy Hospital in Lebanon forwarded his call to a nurse's station in intensive care. His grandfather had taken a fall and was in surgery.

"Is there family nearby we can call?" the nurse said.

"I'm the only family he has. How bad is it?"

"Quite serious. Someone should be here for him."

He rushed back to the table and told Larry, "My grandfather took a fall. I have to fly right away to St. Louis."

"I'm so sorry," Larry said. "Anything I can do?"

"Just tell me where to get a cab."

Finn picked up his briefcase just as the waitress appeared with their lunch. She looked at him in confusion and then at Larry.

"My colleague has an emergency," Larry said. "Just leave both plates."

Chapter Eight

On board the short flight to St. Louis, Finn tried to keep from worrying about G-pa by concentrating on the logistics of where the car rental office was located at Lambert Field and the fastest route to the hospital.

Once on the ground, he rented a car and headed west. The drive to Lebanon would take almost three hours, a long time with nothing on his mind but apprehension. G-pa was old—he had been well past his prime even when he first took Finn to live with him—but somehow Finn thought he would live forever. That was crazy, he knew, but he needed it to be true. G-pa had been there for him when his parents and his sister died, when he arrived in Lebanon lost and scared. Now the old man was all he had left. Finn couldn't be losing his family again. This had to be just a scare.

He arrived at the hospital late in the evening. He wasn't able to see G-pa in the intensive care unit, but the surgeon came to talk with him.

"Surgery of any kind is hard on a man your grandfather's age," the doctor said, "and that fall did serious damage. He hit his head, apparently on a staircase or banister, and also broke his arm and dislocated a shoulder. We were able to get the shoulder back in line and set the bone, but the head injury is severe. And at this point, given his age, we are uncertain how, or if, he'll come out of the anesthesia. For now, all we can do is wait."

Finn's knees gave way. He reached for a doorjamb to hold himself up. The doctor took his elbow and walked him to the waiting room.

"Can we get you something?" the doctor said. "A cup of coffee? It may be a while."

Finn shook his head. He didn't want coffee or conversation. He just wanted to see G-pa or at least hear he was okay. Beyond that, he needed to be alone with his thoughts.

How many times had G-pa pulled him from the muck, not only springing him from jail after the supermarket debacle but all the other times when there was trouble at school or Finn lost himself in his mindless retribution against the world? G-pa never got angry; he just let Finn know he would help him get through whatever it was. How could Finn have resented needing to check in with his grandfather; how did he not see this was a precious privilege rather than a burden?

Feeling he had let his grandfather down, he tried to recall times when G-pa had been disappointed in him. Finn once stood up a neighborhood girl he had asked to a dance. Her mother told G-pa the girl shut herself up in her party dress and cried all night and then refused to go to school. G-pa didn't raise his voice, but he made clear this was a failure of kindness and empathy, which embarrassed him as Finn's grandfather. It was clear this really shook G-pa—because he didn't even quote Socrates or Kierkegaard. That was Finn's equivalent of being lashed with a tongue and whipped with a belt.

Accepting responsibility for that incident in one sense conflicted with Finn's philosophy of taking all he could get from a right-handed world, where physical disabilities mark you as a target and families disappear in a flash. But reflecting on it later, he saw his grandfather was espousing the essentialism Finn would later adopt as a guiding philosophy. There was no law saying a young boy had to keep his word to an innocent girl, but in breaking his word, Finn hurt her. The real-world pain he caused was the issue, not whether he broke a law.

Thinking of accountability reminded him the boss was expecting him to return right after the hearing. He found a phone booth and made a collect call to Ainsley.

"Finn, what the hell?" she said, clearly perturbed.

"Wait," he said, "let me explain."

"You'd better. Victor was looking for you all afternoon. Local counsel's office said you flew to St. Louis?"

"Yeah, well, my grandfather took a fall and is in the hospital. I'm his only family and had to come home to Missouri straight away. I'm sorry I didn't call sooner. I've been...I don't know, kind of upset about it all, and there are things I have to take care of."

"Oh," she said, clearly taken aback. "I didn't know. I'm sorry to jump on you like that. How serious is it?"

"It's been hours since the operation, and he's still unconscious. He's eighty-eight, and they don't know if he'll come out of it."

"Oh, Finn, I wish there was something I could say. Is there anything we can do for you?"

"There's the Nashville follow-up and Terry's surveillance of the warehouse."

"Jimmy will handle Nashville. You just take care of your grandfather, and let us know how we can help."

"Thank you, Ainsley. That's really nice...." He was touched by this unexpected sympathy and at a loss at what else to say.

"Well," she resumed. "You have things to do. Please check in when you can. We'll be thinking of you."

The call to the office really did help. He felt less on his own and relieved he didn't have to think about work deadlines. He also realized he hadn't eaten all day and was really hungry. He asked the receptionist to call him when there was news and went in search of the hospital cafeteria, where he shared a near-empty dining room with a couple of tired-looking residents in scrubs.

The soup and chicken cutlets he ordered tasted like they had been warming behind the counter all day, but at least his stomach stopped growling. He took a bottle of seltzer back to the waiting room and tried to interest himself in magazines, but they were all vacuous. Celebrities, fashion, fly-fishing, what did any of that matter?

Late that night a nurse took hold of his arm to wake him.

"Mr. Alger," she said. "I'm Mary Franken, your grandfather's night nurse. You were shouting in your sleep."

Finn was disoriented but quickly realized he was in the hospital for his grandfather. However disorienting this was, it beat flashing lights and crashing cars.

"I'm sorry," he said, wiping sweat from his forehead and feeling a pain in his neck. The nurse was a big woman in crisp green scrubs. She stood before him, a caring smile on her face.

"Your grandfather is still not conscious," she said, "but we are hopeful he'll be awake in the morning. Maybe you should go home and come back tomorrow?"

"But he could wake up any time, right?"

"Well, if he does, we will be sure to let you know."

"I..." he said and stopped. "I want to be here in case he wakes up."

She bit her lower lip. "Well, you can't spend the night in that chair. You'll end up in traction. Why don't you come with me; I'll put you on a couch in the residents' lounge."

The next morning Finn's neck still ached. He rose on unsteady legs to find the restroom. He doused his face and tried to smooth wrinkles from the clothes he had worn and slept in since flying to Chicago the day before. He was unsuccessful, but it didn't really matter what he looked like. He needed an update and emerged into the bright lights of the waiting room.

A cheerful young nurse with "Alice Tilson" on her nametag came up to him. "Good morning, Mr. Alger," she said. "I'm Nurse Alice. The night nurse said you stayed over in hopes of seeing your grandfather…" she checked her clipboard, "…Nelson Alger, when he woke up."

"Yes," Finn replied, surprised at the hoarseness in his voice. "Is there news?"

"Nothing yet, but the doctor expects Mr. Alger to come around later this morning. He's been moved to a recovery room and is sleeping peacefully."

"Can I see him?"

"Not quite yet. Why don't you get yourself some breakfast and then hopefully Mr. Alger will be ready for visitors."

He was encouraged things were looking up. At least Nurse Alice acted like it was a hopeful new day, although you never knew with those eternally cheerful types. He walked to the cafeteria, where men and women in scrubs congregated at a few of the tables. It seemed odd no one paid attention to him, even though he looked like he had rolled in off the street.

In the waiting room for the recovery unit, he tried to stay positive and think of something to occupy his mind. A crossword puzzle in a celebrity magazine was indecipherable with its clues about actors and their love lives. That left him taking in the beige walls and chairs cushioned in neutral patterns. He understood hospitals were designed to be aseptic and communicate cleanliness, but everything he saw also spoke of detachment, as if the business carried on there was impersonal. Yet, these rooms witnessed the *most* personal human drama: life and death. Didn't they call the surgery an "operating theater," and could any theater be more real, more consequential to its audience? Shouldn't the décor reflect humanity, or was humanity inherently incompatible with hygienics?

Morning turned to afternoon, and Finn still sat. A few times he stepped outside and breathed cold, fresh air. Finally, he decided the one thing he could do for G-pa was befriend the hospital personnel and let them know G-pa had someone looking out for him. In the gift shop, he bought a large box of candy, which he left at the nurse's station. Then he wandered the building, expressing gratitude to all the staff he met, from janitors to nurses and doctors. The cleaning people and nurses responded in kind; the doctors, not so much.

Mid-afternoon he returned from another break outside to find Nurse Alice all smiles. "Your grandfather is awake," she said. "Dr. Hammond says you can visit with him now."

It was a shock seeing his grandfather with tubes running to his thin arms and monitors beeping all around. G-pa had always seemed preternaturally vigorous. Now he looked pale and ancient, a stolid fixture in a scene of time finally winning out.

"G-pa," Finn said cheerfully.

His grandfather turned toward him, a light coming into his listless eyes. "My boy," he said. "What in the name of Gaia are you doing here?"

In the doorway Nurse Alice scrunched up her face at G-pa's unusual choice of words, but then said, "Your grandson has been here all night."

Finn hardly heard what she said, he was so jolted by the image of his grandfather and determined not to show his alarm. He had to be positive, hopeful. This was payback to G-pa for all those years, Finn's time to be strong.

"I heard you took a fall," Finn said, moving to the bedside and taking his grandfather's bloodless hand. "I was already in Chicago, so it was no trouble to come home."

"No trouble," G-pa said with sarcasm that encouraged Finn to think he was feeling better than he looked.

"Well, not much, anyway. And hey, you know they've got a twenty-four-hour cafeteria here?"

"Yes, and I bet they serve the same kind of gourmet meals you're used to in New York."

About on par, Finn thought, but he said, "Well, it's good to see you haven't lost your sense of humor."

His grandfather squeezed Finn's hand. Feeling how little strength there was in the old man's grip raised a lump in his throat.

"You've got some pretty nurses here," Finn said with a grin.

"Maybe you and I can rustle up a couple of dates for later."

Finn laughed.

G-pa turned over Finn's wrist, saying, "Say, that's a fine-looking watch."

"Just an imitation. We seized it from a counterfeiter."

The old man leaned over to look more closely. "Looks real to me," he said.

"That's the point. The infringers make cheap copies and sell them as genuine. They undercut the market at a tenth of the price and destroy our client's reputation by selling timepieces under their brand that don't even keep time."

G-pa let go of Finn's hand and grew thoughtful.

"As a matter of fact, G-pa," Finn said, beginning to unstrap the watch from his wrist, "you should take it. Like I said, it's not really valuable, but it might impress your bridge buddies."

His grandfather held Finn's hand to stop him, his grip suddenly strong and his expression turning reflective. "I couldn't keep something that fancy in here—even if it isn't *real*," he said. Then he added slowly, as if carefully choosing his words, "But tell me again: you protect your client by taking cheap replicas out of the marketplace?"

"Yes...."

"But you wear these replicas yourself—and give them away?"

"Well, not usually."

"I see," G-pa said sadly, cutting off Finn's rationalization.

Finn felt again like a wayward child, about to get a lecture. But he was a grown man and needed to turn this dynamic around. He wanted to explain how his taking the watch really didn't hurt anyone, how it was going to be destroyed anyway and how the world owed him whatever he could grab. But the old man had done it again. Finn was the misbehaved teenager who needed to be taught a lesson.

He flashed back to the night his grandfather got him out of jail. G-pa had not scolded or lectured; he had simply quoted Plato. At that age, Finn lacked the education to express his belief in terms of legal philosophy, that the right-handed world had done him wrong and owed him recompense. He had nonetheless yearned to make G-pa understand. As his grandfather had brewed decaffeinated tea to calm them both down, Finn blurted out, "I always have to deal with a backwards world. I'm always the one who has to try to fit in, with no parents or sister, all on my own..."

"Except for me," G-pa said, sounding a little hurt. "Don't forget me, Son."

"Of course, G-pa, you," he said and rose to hug the old man's shoulders.

And now, even in a hospital bed, trussed up with tubes and wires, G-pa retained the high ground. "You are espousing legal realism," his grandfather said, in a weary version of his professorial voice, "that judges should consider, not only abstract rules but also social interests and public policy. You're saying your sociopathic episodes should be excused—and expunged—because you have had a rough life."

"It sounds ridiculous when you say it like that."

"Possibly, but nothing new. You simply fall into the school of philosophical naturalism, where biological, social and economic forces dictate behavior and fate."

"The devil made me do it," Finn concluded morosely.

Here was Finn again disappointing the one person he loved, disheartening the man to whom he owed everything, even as he stood at death's door. Finn was a grown man, a professional, living a responsible life and working for the good—for the most part— but he was still being schooled about right and wrong. What was worse, he *needed* to hear this and stop making excuses.

"And I think, Finnegan," G-pa said with a forced smile, as if to change the subject, "we should talk about your clothes. You are a big-city lawyer now, but it looks like you slept in your suit."

"Well, yeah, I did. I meant to go to Chicago and back the same day, so I didn't bring any clothes."

"Why didn't you go to the house and change?"

"I could...I mean I will."

"You should. Listen, my boy, I appreciate your racing here to be with the old man. Prometheus knows, it means the world to me. But you have to look after yourself. It isn't healthy to sleep in a hospital if you don't have to. Besides, it's embarrassing having my grandson looking like Rumpelstiltskin."

"I'm not sure I get the mixed analogy," Finn said and laughed.

"Oh, not the myth or the fairy tale, of course, but the name seems to fit."

"And if the sound fits...?"

"Exactly."

Finn was encouraged the old man's mind was working in its usual arcane manner. "I'll go back to the house tonight," he said, "and tomorrow try to revive the Alger family's fashion-forward reputation. But for now, tell me, what kind of trouble have you and your cronies been getting into?"

Finn sat with his grandfather through the afternoon. The old man drifted to sleep a few times but woke and resumed the conversation where it had left off. Finn tried to ignore the beeps and whirs from the monitors as he told stories about his job, his colorful loftmates and Satch's clubhouse, continuing his stories after the naps as if they had been interrupted by commercial breaks.

At one point, G-pa moved his legs and appeared to be uncomfortable.

"You need me to do something?" Finn asked.

"No, my boy, I just get these cramps in my feet sometimes. The nurse will rub them for me when she gets the time; but they are always so busy, and I hate to trouble them."

"I can do it," Finn heard himself say.

He knew nothing about giving massages but this couldn't be hard. His grandfather hesitated but then gave in, and Finn went to work gently rubbing circulation into one foot and then the other. It felt strange to touch his grandfather this way; they had never had much physical contact. The old leathery feet, with calluses that must have solidified for a dozen years, felt bloated and stiff. But G-pa's involuntary sigh said the massage felt good, which was all that mattered. When Nurse Alice stuck her head in the room and saw what was happening, she watched dreamily for a moment and then quietly closed the door.

"And what about romance?" G-pa said later in the afternoon. "Have you got a girlfriend?"

"Uh, no, not really."

"How can that be, a handsome young lawyer like you in the big city?"

"I don't know, G-pa. With the job and all, it never seems to work out."

"What happened to that free spirit you were dating, the one with the sparkly boots?"

Even G-pa was kind of in love with Dani, just from hearing Finn talk about her. "Dani...yeah," Finn said, regretting having shared those stories when things seemed more hopeful. And now the old man was looking at him, his tired old eyes suddenly piercing.

"A Sisyphean task?" G-pa said.

"Yeah, yes...a lost cause."

"Well, Nietzsche said unrequited love was something a lover would at no price relinquish for a state of indifference."

"Right, G-pa, better to have loved and lost...."

"Well, in your case it seems even worse."

"Thanks for the support."

"Buck up, Son. You just need to move on from quixotic fantasies. Stop wasting time on *ignis fatuus*."

Nurse Alice came to the door to announce dinner, just in time to save Finn from having to share details of his latest humbling in pursuing Dani. And G-pa would have pressed him.

He seemed to have taken on a new tone of concern about Finn's farcical love life.

Finn got his dinner on a tray so he could eat with his grandfather. This latest meal actually looked good next to the pablum and Jell-O served to G-pa. Then Nurse Mary, back for the evening shift, said it was time for Nelson to get some sleep, and suggested Finn come back in the morning.

"That's right, my boy," said G-pa. "You need a break."

The prospect of getting out of his suit and into a shower was tempting, but Finn didn't want to leave his grandfather alone. "I'll get a change of clothes and something to read and be back in an hour," he said.

The nurse and G-pa sighed theatrically and looked at each other, and then together at Finn. "You get along now," G-pa said. "I plan to sleep through the night, so you do the same—in a bed."

The nurse nodded emphatically, and Finn gave in. "Okay," he said, taking hold of the old man's boney hand. "I'll see you first thing."

"You are my best comrade, Finnegan Alger. Thank you again for making the trip."

"I love you, G-pa. Get a good night's sleep."

It was strange being in the house where he grew up with his grandfather not there. Finn had been back often while he finished school and a few times a year since, so it was not like his bedroom was a time capsule from the '70s, but the rest of the house remained much as he knew it as a teenager.

He was grateful for a hot shower—that went as long as the hot water held out—and a change into jeans and a sweatshirt. But his next step, to the kitchen, was disappointing. There was very little in the refrigerator, which made him regret not picking up takeout food on his way home and also left him concerned about G-pa's eating habits. The house also needed a serious cleaning, which was a curious observation from the resident of a loft that would win no Good Housekeeping seals. But G-pa deserved better than how Finn lived. Everything Finn saw advanced his belief it was time to move G-pa somewhere where people would take over day-to-day tasks like cleaning and laundry and preparing healthy meals.

There had never been much liquor in the house, except when Finn was a teenager and snuck it in. But a distant memory sparked, and he climbed a stool to look in a high cupboard. Behind some cleaning supplies he found an old bottle of Puerto Rican rum. He poured a large tumbler, to go along with fried eggs and stale bread that wasn't so bad once he toasted it. The only other food he found was a can of peaches, but he decided his day had been long enough without fighting a right-handed can opener.

While he ate and drank he made a list of things to do while G-pa was in the hospital. He had to go food shopping, of course, as well as stop at the beer store. Then he had to get serious about cleaning and airing the place out. The yard also needed work. but that was a project for the spring. And he guessed he'd have to sort through the pile of mail to pay bills and throw out the junk, tighten loose doorknobs and change out dead batteries.

More important than any of this, though, would be finding G-pa an assisted-living situation he'd be willing to try. Between his grandfather's university pension and Social Security, and what Finn could kick in, they could afford a nice place nearby, where G-pa could still stay in touch with his neighbors.

After dinner Finn called the office. Neither Ainsley nor Victor was there, but he reached JT.

"Hey, man," his friend said. "Ainsley told us about your grandfather. Is he okay?"

"No, he's really not. Looks like I'll be here for a bit."

"Sorry to hear it. Anything I can do?"

"Fill me in. What's up with Orchard Street?"

"None of the defendants will put up a fight, and damages won't amount to squat. But it's cool. They'll default or we'll get consent judgments, and we pulled a load of shirts off the street, along with a dozen screen frames."

"Guess it would be overreaching to seize the printing presses, too."

"Yeah, the judge would never allow that. But at least we've got a lot of counterfeits. Victor will spin everything to satisfy Nike."

"Planning a bonfire?"

"Funny thing: Imani suggested we donate the shirts to something called World Vision; they distribute that shit in disaster areas and war zones."

"Right, like the client wants to see refugees on the news wearing Nike shirts."

JT laughed. "Exactly. But—if you can believe it—Ainsley is looking into it."

"You know, she's also been really nice about my grandfather. Did she fall asleep next to an alien pod or something?"

"I guess even the Ice Queen melts down once in a while. But I wouldn't count on her staying that way."

"Oh, hey, I'm no idiot. But I have to go. Really tired. Tell Ainsley I'll call tomorrow to brief her on the hearing and give her some kind of timeline for my coming home. And can you also switch me over to Imani if she's still there? I need her to follow up on the space-shifting case."

"You mean you want to hear about the Knicks' win over the Pacers, which by the way cost me a bundle."

"Well, that too." Imani was not only a great legal assistant, but she knew basketball. She had played at City College and followed the Knicks even more closely than Finn did. In fact, he had told JT he could improve his NBA bets by taking tips from her.

"She's gone for the night. And oh, I forgot the best news. Part of what's distracting Ainsley is that factory building in Nashville has led us to the importer."

"That's great! So where's it all coming from?"

"The US distributor is a huge Korean company called GlobalX, with a US sub. Ainsley and Victor are at a dinner right now with Sanchi's counsel to come up with a game plan. Could be big things ahead."

"Wow, this sounds serious."

"Serious is right. Oh, and those bastards from Hune are threatening to move for sanctions because we squeezed their clients without their lawyer present."

"That's ridiculous. No one told us they had counsel."

"No shit. But Hune is throwing its weight around, like we should just kowtow to them."

"So what's going to happen?"

"Who knows? It's not like they have any defense to liability, so Victor figures this is just a distraction to force a quick settlement. But that works for us, since they don't know we've zeroed in on the importer."

"Well, I wish I was there for this, although it sounds like these guys are not playing around."

"Ainsley says it's like no case she's ever seen. But hey, she'll do the dance with Hune while we start building the next case. You just take care of your grandfather. There'll be plenty to do when you get back."

After hanging up, Finn felt exhausted. When he rose, the room swirled a bit from the rum. But that didn't matter; it was a welcome relief. It had been a long couple of days. It felt good to be out of that crumpled suit, and he headed for bed.

He first made the rounds of locking doors and turning off lights without thinking too much; nothing in the house had changed in years. It was all so familiar and yet didn't seem right without G-pa, so he pretended his grandfather was asleep in his room, and everything was right with the world.

He didn't remember his head hitting the pillow. What he did remember—and could never forget no matter how hard he tried— was the phone call waking him in the dark. It was the hospital. G-pa was dead.

Chapter Nine

The next week was a sad slog. There were hospital bills and funeral arrangements and closing up the house—which meant sorting through G-pa's things.

Finn had had little respect for much during his school years in Lebanon. But he did defer to G-pa's right to decide how much of his life to share with his grandson. This came from Finn being plucked out of Chicago when he was not yet eight. Ever afterward he clung to the few things he felt were his own, from his first soccer jersey to the action figures he kept in his closet long after he stopped playing with them. And unhappy as he was being shuffled off to Lebanon, he recognized G-pa had sacrificed his quiet, comfortable life to take him in. This didn't stop Finn from rebelling, but it did make him considerate of G-pa's privacy.

But now Finn had to go through everything, or he wouldn't know what he needed to keep. The financial papers were organized, but sixty years' worth of everything else crammed into that house presented a monumental task.

In the top drawer of G-pa's dresser he found his father's college ring, the one he never took off. It was in an envelope with a newspaper article about the accident. Looking at the article, Finn found himself crying and suddenly weak, so he sat on the bed. But again he teared up and then just gave in and let himself cry and sob and wail, not caring who heard him.

Over the next two days, a few neighbors stopped by, and Finn invited them to take whatever they wanted. It made no sense to bring much back to the loft. There were the record albums and books that sustained him as a teenager, but his room in New York was too cluttered to fit any more memories.

G-pa's books presented another complication. An entire floor-to-ceiling shelf held his philosophy library. Those volumes certainly were the source of many of the aphorisms that had peppered G-pa's moral lessons to his mutinous grandson. It would have been profane to discard these books, but Finn had nowhere to keep them. He called the department head at G-pa's old university, who sent a truck to pick up the collection.

And then there were the family photos. Sorting through G-pa's closet, Finn found a shoe box full of prints and lost himself in images of his mother and father, almost as young as he was now, and a sister who never got past age ten. His memory of his family was so hazy that each shot brought them more into focus. He stared fixedly at how their poses and expressions acknowledged each other, how they touched. The touching part got to him. That was missing from Finn's growing up, beyond an occasional squeeze of G-pa's bony shoulders. But in these pictures his family seemed always tethered together, making each of them stronger for the connection. Where would Finn ever again find that kind of closeness and strength? Marking the disaster that divided his life into two distinct periods, there were no pictures from after the accident.

Finn also needed to deal with legal matters. He hired a law school classmate to handle probate—which should be simple given the modest estate. The lawyer would also coordinate with the broker to sell the house, which would net little because G-pa had taken out an equity loan. He changed his name for his grandfather's on the local bank account that Finn would use for estate matters, and one small annuity that would continue to pay directly into the account. All told, there wouldn't be much money, but it would still be simpler to keep everything in Missouri. There was no telling how the New York tax authorities might try to get their piece if they found out about the estate.

Finn held no wake but did arrange a brief funeral service at the cemetery. The pastor at a church G-pa pointedly did *not* attend agreed to preside.

"He was not religious," the pastor told Finn, "but he was one of the most spiritual men I've had the honor of knowing, and he could quote the Bible better than I could."

Finn asked Charley Ringle, the next-door neighbor, to get the word out. Charley would do anything for Finn after his help in getting his grandson out on bail. Nonetheless, Charley's first loyalty was to his neighbor, and he apparently felt compelled to say privately to Finn, "He did right by you. At a time in life when he deserved peace and quiet, he got anything but."

"You're so right," Finn responded. "I only wish I had appreciated that while it still mattered."

"The way Nelson saw the world, it matters more now than it ever did while he was alive."

Finn realized Charley was right. He wondered how many of the axioms G-pa had called up for every occasion would stay with him. But it was the man, more than his erudition, that left the void. He wondered if he might be able to imagine G-pa, not as dead but as still living off in Missouri, just a phone call away. Could this alleviate the pain, put off Finn's overwhelming feeling of being alone?

Finn was surprised at the turnout at the cemetery. He was also overwhelmed by two opulent flower arrangements sent by his firm. Even more moving was the fervor of tributes to G-pa. Lately, Finn had worried about how his grandfather was able to fill his days. It turned out he had been busy spreading kindness throughout the town, running errands and sharing a philosophical perspective about the ills and foibles of the world.

A Christmas card from an old colleague of G-pa's arrived at the house the next day and reminded Finn the holidays were barely two weeks off. The firm would be closed then, and it hurt to think how he had been resenting giving up a trip to the Caribbean to come home. Now that he wouldn't be visiting Lebanon, he'd have the time to join his friends, but he couldn't see making a party out of his time for grieving.

Driving to the airport some days later, Finn heard John Lennon over the radio. The words of the song reverberated in his head: "And so this is Christmas...."

The night Lennon was murdered was etched in his mind. He had been studying for his copyright law exam when the news came over the radio. He was devastated but had to put his emotions aside until he completed the test the next day. In a way he had to do that now; leave off bemoaning his solitude and repenting his neglect of his grandfather to get on with life.

Time hadn't lessened the blow of Lennon's death, the first among the four Beatles. Finn had a premonition that this death ushered in his own middle age, and the passing of the last of this seminal musical group—all fifteen years older than him—would signal the onset of his old age. And now, with no John Lennon and no G-pa or family in any sense, there would be no Christmas.

He mulled over how, in their last conversation, G-pa had pressed Finn about finding someone to love, as if he knew he would soon be leaving Finn alone. Why had Finn pushed back against that conversation? Why hadn't he just been forthcoming? It would have hurt, but G-pa might have shared some insight beyond simply that he should stop chasing after fantasies, like Dani. But before he could hope to deserve someone solid and sincere, maybe he needed to make something of himself, become a man G-pa would be proud of. Maybe he could get this right. Maybe next Christmas could be a first Christmas—if stealing that watch didn't land him in jail.

Chapter Ten

 While he was occupied wrapping up G-pa's life, Finn had been able to keep busy and avoid thinking about his loss. But once on board the flight to New York, there was nothing to distract him. He kept reliving his grandfather's final night, when Finn went to the house and got drunk instead of sticking it out at the hospital. It had been his duty to see this through, but he had failed the old man...once again. It tortured him to think G-pa might have regained consciousness during his last hours and wanted Finn.

There was no way now to rerun that night; he'd just have to live with it. And he didn't even have G-pa to put his loss and his failure into philosophical terms.

As the jet started its descent, a flight attendant announced the time in New York. Finn adjusted his watch, but the stainless-steel face sneered at him. It felt safe wearing the watch away from the office and anyone connected with Sanchi, but any pleasure or pride he had felt wearing the watch was gone. It had taken G-pa only an instant to zero in on this hunk of metal dressed up as something elegant. Finn's masquerade of a man who could afford the real thing was no clever feint against his grandfather or a cruel world; it was just pitiful. He put the watch in his briefcase so he wouldn't forget to take it off before he reached his office.

Finn resolved to look ahead. His grandfather had been a good man who lived a long life, and there was nothing sad about his passing. Finn was left more alone than ever, but that was no one's fault, and he couldn't let it define him. He had a good job and was living in New York City; how many people would give anything to be able to say that?

Everyone in the office expressed condolences. JT for once made no wisecracks. Ainsley seemed sincerely sorry. Imani wrote him a sweet sympathy note. Ted handed him a mass card, which would have made G-pa smile, given his skepticism about organized religion. Even Victor offered a drink, his way of expressing human emotion. In the swirl of commiseration, it slipped Finn's mind to ask who had arranged to send the extravagant flower displays to the funeral. Finn's only thought was to let them know he was all about getting back to work and digging into the case against GlobalX.

Before Finn started working, Ainsley asked him to join her and Jimmy in her office. "There are a couple of things you should know about GlobalX," she said. "We haven't shared this with everyone because we don't want to cause a panic or distract anyone from the work."

Finn was puzzled. Nothing about this case seemed normal.

Ainsley took a deep breath. "Yu-jun Lee, the Luxe vendor who went after his partner with a gun, was freed on bail right after his hearing...."

"Arranged by Hune & Buchanan," Jimmy cut in.

"Yeah," Finn said. "JT told me over the phone."

"Right," Ainsley said, glancing over at Jimmy but returning her gaze to Finn. "The Hune lawyer sprang him, but two days later he was in the hospital with multiple fractures. It seems he fell out a second-floor window."

"What?" Finn said, amazed.

"Yes," Ainsley responded. "Not a credible story. But there's more. The other man, Minjun Cho—the one who gave up the distributor—was found face down in a drainage ditch. He either tripped and fell while he was on a nature walk, or he was murdered, the police haven't yet decided."

Finn's head was spinning. "What's going on here?" he said, exasperated.

Ainsley continued. "We're not sure if the people behind these 'coincidental' mishaps know we have identified the supplier, and it's still unclear where the GlobalX watches come from. They appear to carry on parallel distribution of cheap knockoffs and quality watches that are genuine, as far as we can tell. Victor is working with the client to look into the factories in Korea, and our legal assistants are collecting everything we can find about GlobalX. Meanwhile, I've been stringing the Hune lawyer along, agreeing to a settlement in Nashville but squabbling over details of the agreement. Hune's involvement suggests the firm has a connection with GlobalX, and it is essential not to tip off the company about what's coming."

In past cases Bolger & Plotkin had targeted overseas factories that made genuine merchandise during the week and knockoffs over the weekend, which made it almost impossible to tell real from counterfeit. That appeared to be what was happening here, at least as to the high-end watches. The investigation in Korea thus proceeded on two tracks. First, the client instituted week-end surveillance of its own factories. But investigation into the manufacture of the cheap knockoffs was more difficult because Korean law didn't permit investigators to pretext—like pretending to be a buyer—in gathering evidence. This forced the firm to focus on the US subsidiary, to shut off importation and hit the sub for damages.

This was a major case and a big deal for the firm. But because the target was a substantial company, which would *not* disappear once it was served, they had to hone the argument why their client needed to conduct a raid without advance notice to the defendant.

Victor told Finn to draft the supporting brief. This was exactly what Finn needed, a chance to dig into something challenging and prove himself to Victor while staying busy so he wouldn't dwell on his grandfather.

A seizure order without notice was appropriate, even for a big company like GlobalX, because it had the resources and the motive to move merchandise and hide records. And if this company had willfully infringed Sanchi's trademarks, it was no stretch to suspect it would also hide evidence of its guilt. Finn would paint the company as untrustworthy, by describing it as the hub of a crime syndicate extending from the factories all the way to US flea markets.

Finn had told Ted to update all their past research on seizure orders. The kid caught on quickly and worked hard. Maybe it had to do with losing his grandfather, but Finn felt as if he should ease up on Ted. "I must say, Junior," he commented upon reviewing Ted's summary of new cases, "you show a lot of discipline for a baby lawyer."

Ted winced. He had apparently inured himself to the "Junior" nickname, so probably was reacting to being called a "baby lawyer," unaware that term was widely used for new law graduates. Still, he managed to maintain a strained smile.

"Yeah," Ted said, "it's the military training."

"What do you mean?"

"The Cummings are military from way back. In World War II my grandfather commanded a destroyer that went down off the coast of Virginia, my dad drove a tank in Korea, and my cousin and my brother both used to fly fighter jets."

"What, no Marines in the family?"

Ted looked dour. "I think that was supposed to be me. I had to convince my dad I should go to law school instead; he's hoping this means I'll join the Army's JAG Corps."

"Is that *your* plan?"

"It was. But I want to stick with trademark enforcement for

now. Anyway, the military upbringing is ingrained. I still salute my grandfather and call him Commander."

"Right," Finn said, smiling, "and all the 'sir' business."

"Yes, sir," Ted said and laughed at failing to catch himself. "You see, I can't help it. When I forget to say 'sir,' I almost feel my father slapping me upside my head."

Since the main GlobalX office was in Newark, Ted worked with local counsel in hopes of finding a way to maximize their chance of getting assigned to a sympathetic judge in the District of New Jersey. Victor wanted to use US Marshals for this case, so Ted would also get to see how the firm interfaced with federal law enforcement.

"You're getting the hang of it," Finn told the young lawyer as he looked over the report of a new case Ted found out of the Eastern District of Texas. It would not be controlling in New Jersey—because it came out of a different circuit—but was still persuasive due to its similar facts.

"Thanks, boss. And hey, what about putting an investigator in one of the factories in Korea?"

"Good thinking, Junior, but the local laws there are really strict about that. What we *have done* is ask Korean counsel to check legal dockets and business filings, put together everything they can from public records about GlobalX holdings and operations."

Given the magnitude of the case and the expectation GlobalX would put up a substantial defense, Victor told Finn to take the time to make absolutely sure everything was in order before they filed. The plan was to delay filing until after the holidays and in the meanwhile have investigators redouble their efforts to fill in details about GlobalX sales.

That timing was fine with Finn; the work until they filed would be stimulating enough to occupy his thoughts without requiring long hours in the office.

Having his evenings free gave Finn a chance to relax and recover, but it also left too much time for ghosts and doubts to swallow him up. He needed to focus on something uplifting and so was more than happy when Satch asked if he was free Friday night.

"We've had a setback on the play," Satch said. "The director had an accident and will be laid up for a couple of weeks. And we also have a leak from the kitchen into the house we need to fix before bringing in an audience."

"You can't just hand out umbrellas?"

"Well, for the right kind of show we might, but for *Crime* we're talking snow, not rain."

"So what do you do?"

"We curse our luck and push the show back. Rehearsals will start up again in January with the opening on the 24th."

"That sucks. How is everyone taking it?"

"The director is fine with it. The actors, of course, present some drama. Most of the cast said they can do it, but it looks like we'll have to replace one of the actresses. They have someone in mind from the women's group that uses our theater. With the opening pushed back, there will be plenty of time for her to learn the part, and the work crew also has time to fix the ceiling *and* finish the set. For now we're all taking a breather, and we're going out for a pre-show cast party. You should come along."

"Where are you going?"

"SOBs. You know it? It's a dance club over on Hudson Square."

"Sounds...interesting." Finn thought for a moment. "Can I bring someone?"

"Madonna?" Satch said skeptically.

"It's just the kind of thing she likes, but I'll kick you into next week if you tell her I call her that."

"Whatever," Satch said with a smirk. "We're meeting outside the club at ten."

Chapter Eleven

Finn called Dani that night but could only leave a message on her machine. He knew he should wait for her to call back, but this was Dani, and that might never happen. He had to entice her to come out with him, so at the office Thursday he tried again.

"Oh hi, Horatio," she said. "You caught me on my way out."

"This will only take a second. A bunch of actors and stage-hands from this play my roommate is in are going to SOBs tomorrow night. Would you like to join us?"

"Son of a bitch is an interesting name for a nightclub."

He laughed. "It actually stands for Sounds of Brazil. It's a dance club where they play Latin music. It should be fun. The crew had to postpone their show until January, and so they're blowing off some steam."

"Is it expensive?"

"Don't worry about that. You'll be my guest."

Those were the magic words for Dani. She agreed to meet Finn in the Village, where she would be having dinner with friends. He would have preferred to join her for dinner, but she already had plans. And he was happy enough she agreed to come to the club. This would be a for-real date, dancing and all.

After he hung up, Finn couldn't concentrate on work and so went to get a cup of coffee.

JT caught up with him in the kitchen. "You look like you just pulled an inside straight," he said.

Finn just smiled.

"Oh, come on now. You can't walk around with that shit-eating grin and keep it to yourself."

"It's nothing. I just set up a date for tomorrow."

"Not the inscrutable beauty?"

"Exactly."

"She agreed to go out with you again?"

"She did. I think this is the turning point."

JT shook his head. "I can't believe how much effort you put into that girl, but I guess a long shot has to come in once in a while."

"Thanks for the moral support, James."

Anticipation carried Finn through the rest of the workday, and he left early since things were quiet for the moment. On the subway home, he planned how he would use the night at SOBs to get Dani to spend a decisive third night in the loft.

She would certainly be wearing something outrageous, since that described pretty much her whole wardrobe, so he wondered how he could dress so they would look like a couple.

Back home he asked Satch, "What are you wearing tomorrow night?"

His loftmate looked at him quizzically. "Since when do you pay attention to your clothes?"

"I just..." Finn replied but paused, embarrassed. "I just thought you might have been to this place. I don't do a lot of clubbing."

"We should ask Mandy," Satch said with a laugh. "I'm sure she's been there."

It was only seven o'clock, and Mandy wasn't up yet. Anyway, Finn would not ask her for fashion tips. He felt foolish even asking Satch. But he still pondered the question, deciding in the end to go with black jeans and a sports jacket he had picked up at a thrift shop as part of a Halloween costume.

Of more concern was how to make the evening go as planned. He tried to think of things to talk about that would interest her. She read serious books, from Thomas Mann to Thomas Pynchon, so she should be interested in Satch's play, with its dubious connection to Russian literature.

He also wondered about how to dance without looking awkward. Did Brazilians hold each other or just face each other? He hoped they would dance together so he could hold Dani. Otherwise, he wouldn't know what to do with his hands when he really needed to exude confidence.

On Friday night Finn and Satch headed uptown together, and then Finn peeled off to pick up Dani. He arrived on the agreed street corner early, as usual, and focused on picking her out of the sensory overload of Friday night in the Village. He marveled at how the squeegee guys, who cleaned windshields for tips, just turned with the weather to snow removal, true capitalists on top of the market.

When she appeared late, he pretended not to notice. She wore a low-cut, white dress with multiple strings of pearls. Her hair was piled on top of her head as if she had arranged it in a windstorm. Over the dress she wore her metallic jacquard jacket with the skinny lapels and high heels, of course, bright red this time. The pearls had to be fake and the chaos of her hair was almost beyond description but the overall effect was dazzling.

They had planned to meet the crew outside the club, but they were late and found only strangers lined up on the barren stretch of sidewalk outside the entrance. Finn recoiled at breaking his rule against standing on line to get into a bar. He was afraid this was a bad start for the evening. But Dani took his hand and led him up to a bouncer as if she owned the place, and he stepped aside and opened the door for them, a lascivious look on his big, square face.

A hypnotic beat carried them into the dark club, where most people were standing or dancing before a purple-lighted stage. Derk pushed through the crowd to greet Finn with a chest bump, and then backed off to introduce himself to Dani. She greeted him with her enigmatic smile, and when she turned to look at the dancers, he gave Finn an exaggerated expression of wonder. Finn smiled casually but his heart leapt with the pride of arriving with the most stunning woman in the club.

The music heated up, and everyone danced. The beat was so infectious and the faces all around so filled with celebration that the weight of the past week started to fall from Finn's shoulders. The largely solo nature of the dancing made it awkward to take Dani in his arms, but he was transfixed just watching her move, overtly sexy without being overwrought. The way she stretched out a hand toward him in a sequined, fingerless glove left him breathless.

When Finn was able to tear his attention away from his date, he recognized comedy club faces in the crowd. One of the actresses, whose name he couldn't recall, was gyrating wildly with a young guy he recognized from worknight. Across the room he spotted Satch with Genevieve making their way toward him.

"Salsa night!" Satch shouted to him as he took hold of Genevieve's hand and twirled her.

The music was high energy and continuous, one song bleeding into the next in the same driving beat. He found himself dancing with one woman after another, some from the comedy club and others who just came within reach. He lost track of Dani but caught flashes of her blonde hair through the crowd.

When the band finally took a break, Satch waved Finn toward one of the two bars. Finn strained his neck to find Dani, but she had disappeared. So he made his way through the crowd to his loftmate and Derk, who were downing shots with two of the actors.

Derk took a moment to absorb his shot, and then shouted over the music "*Caju Amigo!*"

Finn looked at him in confusion.

"The drink, dude," Derk said and waived for the bartender to pour five more.

Finn pulled out his wallet and insisted on buying the round, which they all accepted with theatrical bows.

"What is it?" Finn shouted to Derk as they waited for the drinks.

"Cachaça and cashew juice," Derk said, handing around the glasses. "You first chew a cashew slice without swallowing it, to get more of the juice with the liquor."

They each took a slice of the nut and held up their glasses.

"To *Crime!*" one actor toasted.

"And punishment!" Derk rejoined, and they downed their shots.

With his head spinning from the liquor and the music, Finn looked in earnest for Dani. He caught sight of her across the dance floor. She was in the arms of a dark man with slicked-back hair and the moves of a real dancer. The man—who like Dani was wearing heels—twirled her so her pearls swung through the crowd.

Finn turned back to his friends. He sensed commiseration on their faces. This confirmed what he wanted to deny. A night out with the cast be damned, he was there to be with Dani. He felt betrayed and humiliated.

The next song started, and Finn eagerly looked again for Dani. He moved to rejoin her, but she never stopped dancing with her new friend. When Finn turned back to the bar, Derk and the actors were gone, but Satch and Genevieve were watching him like parents whose kid was sitting on the bench.

"You guys should dance," Satch said, nudging Genevieve toward Finn. She looked at Finn with an inquisitive smile. He shrugged and took her hand.

They were soon swallowed up by the undulating mass. Finn didn't worry about what to do with his hands as there wasn't room for anything fancy. And this time he was really dancing with one person for the first time that night. With little room, they both bounced in time with the beat, although she was much more graceful in her bouncing. They moved with the crowd, their faces flushed with laughter.

At one point the crowd pushed them together face to face. When they were able to step back, she shouted, "I'm glad you came."

"Me too," he shouted back.

He was sure things with Dani would work out. She just liked to dance, and that guy was so much smoother on his feet than Finn. The important thing was she was enjoying herself, and that boded well for their evening. He would take her home at the end of the night, his place or hers, and this relationship would move ahead. He needed Dani to be a little more real.

He hoped Dani would see him dancing with Genevieve. She was attractive enough to get even Dani's attention, a short black dress flattering her much more than the boxy Russian costume or her oversized overalls. Besides that, it was clear she enjoyed dancing with him.

When the band broke again, Finn found Dani leaning on a bar in close conversation with her dancing partner.

"I thought I'd lost you," he said.

She looked up as if she had forgotten he was there. "Oh, Horatio," she said, turning to her new friend, "this is Ricky."

Finn eyed his antagonist, trying to be cordial. The guy's hair looked oily, and his shirt was unbuttoned too far. He was not Dani's type at all. He wore a disturbing smirk as he offered a limp, moist hand to shake.

"Ricky also lives in Hoboken," she said, casting an amused smile at her friend. "In fact, you know, I have to be up early tomorrow, and Ricky is going to see me home."

"I...but wait," Finn said, his night crashing down around him. How could he be this close and lose Dani to some guy named Ricky?

"We were actually about to leave," she said, "so I'm glad I found you."

"*You* found *me*?" he said, feeling beaten on both sides of his head and unable to restrain his feelings about who was doing what.

"Well, we found each other."

"But I should see you home."

"No," she said, a with a patronizing look that cut right through him. "You don't need to do that. But thanks for bringing me. This was fun."

She kissed him on the cheek and turned to leave. Ricky nodded with a self-satisfied grin. Finn decked him with a wrong-hand whammy...in his imagination.

In reality he just watched them go.

The neighborhood was quiet when the cast left the bar sometime after three. They hugged with drunken, sloppy affection. Finn envied the camaraderie of the troupe. But more than that, he was stung by how Dani had left him. Thankfully, Satch and Genevieve were there, and they were both sympathetic but tactful enough not to mention it.

It was hard to miss the contrast between Genevieve's enthusiasm and Dani's aloofness. He had to laugh thinking how he had called Genevieve "Puffy Dress Girl" in her costume and theatrical makeup. In real life she was dynamite in a sparkly black dress, and the freckles made her unexpectedly pretty.

But what was he thinking? He couldn't get between her and Satch, not if they were a thing. He had to focus on and appreciate how the cast gave him a feeling of belonging he desperately yearned for. That, and his inebriation, led him to volunteer to help on the show.

"Terrific," Genevieve said, excited. "You'll love it."

As people peeled off in taxis, Finn walked east with Satch and Genevieve. His friends held hands, or possibly just held each other up, while Finn concentrated on holding himself up. When they reached Sixth Avenue, he said, "I'm gonna catch a cab."

"Oh, you should come the rest of the way with us," Genevieve said. "It's just across town, and then you guys can share a cab home."

Finn was sure that was not Satch's plan, but her statement seemed to decide his friend's fate. He didn't want to give her an easy out with Satch but felt helpless to do anything about it. Join the club, he thought, feeling a beleaguered camaraderie with his loftmate.

The three walked together through Greenwich Village, Satch now gone quiet while Genevieve tried to keep the conversation going. She and Satch no longer held hands.

On East Seventh they ambled past McSorley's, long closed up for the night, and Genevieve stopped in front of a brick tenement to face them.

"This is me," she said. "Front apartment, fourth floor; the stairs are my exercise. Sorry it's so late or I'd ask you up."

There was no doubt Satch was striking out. "After all that dancing and cachaça," Finn said, "I doubt I could make it up four flights."

"I've got plenty of energy," Satch said, unsurprisingly and a bit pitifully. "You sure you don't want company?"

She didn't, and Satch took this blow with a grimace but tried to look stoic.

Finn said goodnight to Genevieve and stepped away, to give the two of them space. He waited for Satch a short way off, turning his attention to Genevieve's building. It was a typical brick apartment tenement from the late eighteen hundreds. From the darkened windows Genevieve had pointed out on the fourth floor, he lowered his gaze story-by-story down an unremarkable façade until he reached the address embossed in art deco numbers over the front door. Thirty-eight—like Illinois Route 38, where his childhood ended one snowy night in Chicago.

Chapter Twelve

Back at work, Finn concentrated on the GlobalX brief. Ted had turned up a law review article about how the international marketing of knockoffs undermined US national security. This suggested a policy argument that would add color to the brief. Finn told Ted to track down the author, who worked at a Philadelphia firm. It turned out this attorney was coming to town on business, and Finn took him to lunch and retained him to give expert testimony.

Victor was pleased with this "outside the box thinking," and Finn felt on track to impress the boss by crafting papers that anticipated any defense GlobalX might mount. That, along with the prospect of time off for the holidays and a bonus check, lifted Finn's spirits, although the break looked to be more contemplative than celebratory. Still, there was a wisp of a chance he could catch Dani in a receptive mood, or more realistically find someone else to share his time off. He had to keep a positive outlook.

Then everything fell apart. A marketing rep from Sanchi named Frank Jones visited the offices and wanted to see all the merchandise seized in Nashville. He was new to the company, transparently ambitious in his expensive suit.

"It's all set," he exclaimed upon being introduced to the Bolger team. "We bring a steamroller into Times Square to crush the knockoff watches. I've already spoken with the mayor's office about a permit." He gestured at the man beside him, a cinematographer known for music videos who dressed flamboyantly enough to tell everyone he was an artiste. "Pablo will film the event. We will send a message to counterfeiters around the world not to mess with us, and give the Peakstone a tough-guy image. The inventory shows you seized a case of those."

The lawyers were silent for moment. Finn and JT looked to Ainsley to say something.

"You know," she finally said, "you can't destroy anything until the case is over, and even then there could be an appeal?"

"Of course," Jones said in an arrogant tone few people used with Ainsley. She reacted with a stony glare and made an excuse to leave the room, instructing JT to carry on. As soon as she left, JT came up with his own excuse to hand the job to Imani. Finn slipped out with him.

Jones and his cinematographer soon left. Imani and another legal assistant spent the afternoon arranging the watches by model on a conference table for review the next day.

Late the next morning Finn was in the kitchen with Jimmy when Imani rushed into the room.

"We have a big problem," she said, looking anxious.

"What's wrong?" Jimmy asked.

"There are watches missing."

Jimmy shot a glance at Finn, who nervously fingered his wrist where he had worn the Sanchi the night before, thankful he had the sense not to wear it in the office. Jimmy said, "They must have miscounted."

"I don't think so," Imani responded. "They counted them twice. They also said there was only one of the Peakstone model they want to feature, and there were twenty-five on the inventory."

"Twenty-five!" Finn exclaimed. "How could that happen?"

Imani looked at him curiously, as if asking why it was the

number missing rather than the fact any at all were missing that got his attention.

JT looked thoughtful. "We kept them locked up, right?" he said.

Imani's eyes went wide. "Absolutely," she said. "They've all been in a sealed box in my office, and I always lock the door. We've only taken them out when everyone was here working on the case or last night to set up the display—and we were sure to lock the conference room."

"It's a mystery, all right," JT said.

Imani looked about to cry.

"Don't worry about this," Finn said, trying to reassure her. "Nobody will think this is your fault."

Finn peered at JT, wondering how far his friend had gone in "liberating" knockoff watches. He hadn't shown any restraint in stealing one in Nashville and encouraging Finn to do the same. But had he taken a whole box? That was ridiculous. What could he do with so many?"

Victor's secretary came into the room and told JT and Finn, "Victor wants to see you two right away."

"How the hell could this happen?" Victor blustered. He stood with both hands on his desk, as if restraining himself from leaping over it. "What do I tell the client? What do I tell my partners? We had a successful raid, and an opening to a huge case, and then we lost the merchandise!"

"It makes no sense," Ainsley said.

"Damn right, it makes no sense!" Victor shouted. "Not to me and not to launching a case against a multinational pirate! What kind of shit show are we running here?"

Finn had nothing to say and so kept quiet. It would be unfair to taint him with a theft like this for taking a single, throw-away watch, but that wouldn't matter if he was caught with it, especially now that the watch might be genuine. He kept his eyes on the friend who had gotten him involved in this mess, trying to see if he was wearing his Sanchi knockoff.

"I know," Victor said, his anger now seething beneath a quiet tone, "none of you would steal from the client, but you must have seen something, or sensed something."

They were all silent, and Victor picked up steam again. "Well someone did! Who was it, that paralegal in charge of the merchandise?"

"Imani," Ainsley said reluctantly.

"Yeah," JT added, unnecessarily piling on in what sounded like an attempt to divert suspicion from himself, "she kept them locked in her office."

Victor fumed. "Well, she won't have an office to keep anything in before this day is out, but first I want you," turning an icy look on Ainsley, "to find out what she did with those watches. Threaten her with deportation if you have to."

"She's American," Finn heard himself say, drawing a stare from Victor.

"Well, she can still go to jail," he said.

Ainsley broke in, thankfully drawing Victor's attention back to her. "I'll talk to her, Victor. But I can't believe she's involved. She's scrupulously honest."

"Well," Victor spat out, "sometimes those who seem that way are precisely the ones you can't trust, especially *her* type."

Victor's comment cut into Finn. It exposed a dark side of the boss more starkly than he could have intended. His bigotry was clear, if only inferred. Black people might dress up and play the part but they couldn't be trusted. This enraged Finn. Imani was a better person than Victor or anyone else in the room, and they all should know that. There was no way she stole anything.

Finn had to protect her. At the risk of drawing fire again, he said, "I am certain it wasn't Imani, Victor. I'd stake my own job on that."

Silence swallowed the room. Finn realized what he had just said, as Ainsley and JT turned to him in veiled astonishment, and Victor peered as if trying to dissect him. Then Victor looked away in disgust, told Ainsley to get to the bottom of it and dismissed them all.

They left Victor's office in silence. JT followed Finn to his office and closed the door behind him.

"We're in for it now," he said.

"What do you mean, we?"

"Hey, bucko, you took a watch, too."

"That's so fucked up. *You* took a watch and convinced me no one would miss it. But what about this box of Peakstones? Was that you?"

"Are you kidding? Of course not. What would I do with a box of watches?"

Finn tried to see through JT's innocent veneer. If there was an angle to taking a cache of watches, he would be the one to exploit it. Could he trust his friend? "Well, then," he said, "what do you think happened?"

JT shrugged. "I don't know. Could have been a cleaning person; could have been Imani."

"That's nuts! You know she'd never do that."

"Well, yeah, I guess you're right. But with that turd from Sanchi here with his pet filmmaker and Victor going all batshit, someone's going to take the blame."

JT left Finn struggling to make sense of it all. If it wasn't JT, then who? Could it really have been the nice, little Polish lady who cleaned the office?

That night Finn walked part of the way home to clear his head. Times Square—with its peep shows and break-dancers, roasted nuts and steam rising from the street through crowds of people—was no place for contemplation, now with the images in his head of a steamroller crushing a mound of watches—

but he nonetheless wandered through the commotion before descending into the subway. Heading for the downtown express, he heard the Jimmy Cliff song *Many Rivers to Cross*. He used to see The Screaming Honkers play that song at Dan Lynch and found himself wishing he was back in the early '80s, a brand-new lawyer with no troubles other than finding a career, a girl and a real apartment.

He joined the eddy of people lingering around the band amidst the rushing commuters. When the song ended, he took the knock-off watch from his briefcase, wrapped it in a dollar bill and placed it in the guitar case open in front of the band.

Tension gripped the office all through the week. But Victor was able to mollify the client by pointing to the information they had squeezed out of the Nashville defendant and the prospect of shutting down all importation of counterfeits. So Imani kept her job—though she was no longer trusted with custody of the seized property—but she could not hide her apprehension beneath her struggle to smile.

And then, thankfully, Bolger & Plotkin shut down, as usual, between Christmas and New Year's Day. This left Finn with more time on his hands than he wanted.

When Finn wasn't trying to piece together the mystery of the missing watches, he went for runs in the cold, watched old movies on television and read novels. JT had a family celebration—although he wouldn't leave off complaining about combative family dinners and having to sleep on the single bed in his old room. Anyway, he had acted so strangely about the watches that Finn had begun to feel uncomfortable around him. Satch had flown out to his parents' house in Pennsylvania. Ted predicably had a Currier & Ives holiday planned with his extended family. Even Petra was gone, visiting her parents on Long Island.

None of them knew what it was like to have no one. Finn figured that was just life, never appreciating what you had, but it made him want to shake each of them by the shoulders and make them realize their good fortune. He wished he had anyone at all to share the holidays with, although he really was in no mood to celebrate.

For Christmas dinner he nonetheless fired up the loft stove for the first time and cooked a ham. The heat and activity were sure to scatter the wildlife living under the counters, but he decided the human residents of the loft were entitled to occupy the kitchen for one day in the year.

He invited Lance and Party Girl to dinner, which went better than expected. Party Girl—who he had to remember to call Mandy—bought a bottle of wine, and Lance set up a table in the middle of the dance floor, with candles all around and dinner music piped in from his studio. The meal for the three of them—or four if you counted Bogart gnawing a ham bone on the floor—felt both intimate and palatial in their cavernous space.

By agreement they each dressed in whatever red and green they could find in their closets—in Lance's case on top of his studio. Mandy wore a flaming red bustier beneath a sheer olive-green top, not exactly a classic yuletide look but very much in the spirit of the day. Lance dug up a pair of red leather pants and matching cowboy hat, from who knew where. Finn felt outdone in a plain red sweater over a green Parks Department T-shirt, but he was the cook and so took on the role of host.

"I want to thank you both," he toasted before they dug in, "or all three of you," he added, tipping his glass to the dog, who sported a red bandanna but ignored him, "for being such enthusiastic participants in this holiday dinner. Merry Christmas."

Finn hadn't had much chance before to talk with these room-mates, and found their conversation enlightening, if slightly troubling. The three of them lived amazingly diverse lives for occupants of the same apartment.

Lance was justifiably proud of the album he had recorded at Electric Lady Studios, as this put him in the company of Jimi Hendrix. Mandy filled them in on the club scene, from the Palladium in the old Academy of Music building to Area, which changed its whole interior every six weeks to a new theme.

When Mandy showed off the new butterfly tattoo on her ankle, Lance said he had thought about getting an Andy Warhol head after he died the previous winter.

"Why Warhol?" Mandy said. "Did you know him?"

"Not really. Saw him a couple of times at The Mudd Club up on White Street with that graffiti kid, Basquiat; that was a few years ago when you'd see, like, Bowie or Lou Reed hanging out there."

Finn found these stories tough to follow. His loftmates wouldn't be interested in trademark enforcement or his bumbling attempts at finding a girlfriend. Sharing an after-dinner joint brought to mind his philosophy of law; whether written laws or some more profound sense of justice made something a crime, but he sensed that also would go nowhere. He finally described humorous aspects of Satch's theater, making Lance question if he might use the club stage to put on a concert. In all, with surprisingly good cheer, and an even more surprisingly edible meal, it was a perfect counterpoint to the family dinners his friends had all been dreading.

In the following days, when reading and watching movies got boring, Finn started kicking his soccer ball against the long wall of the dance floor and the riser of the stage. One bright spot of growing up had been finding he was good at the game, quick and decent on the ball. And the injury to the nerves in his right hand didn't impede playing soccer. He often wondered where life would have taken him if he hadn't been arrested and lost his chance at a scholarship.

Visions of his glory days on the high school pitch convinced him to take advantage of an unseasonably warm day to look for a game up in East River Park. Organized youth leagues typically filled the soccer pitch at Sixth Street and the one at Grand Street, but in warmer months he could always find a pick-up game in a small, fenced-in field abutting the path along the FDR.

Many of the players were from Central America or the Caribbean, and the chatter was mostly incomprehensible to Finn. But the bigger challenge was the quality of play. Finn had the stamina to keep up on the short field but lacked the skill he concluded must be natural to anyone with a foreign accent. One advantage he had, though, was his old fake right-go left trick. He was able to get away with this over and over because his opponents rotated with each game. The feint often led to a goal—and respect from the other players—before they woke up to his "wrong-footedness" and shut him down from going left.

The evenings were the worst time of day. Even though he had sworn off chasing after Dani, he tried calling her a couple of times. But he got no answer, and visions of her shaking her mass of blonde hair as she danced tortured him through slow, lonely hours.

One evening he was stretched out on the sofa on the stage reading a novel when he was surprised to see Petra come off the elevator. He was excited to see her. He would really have been happy to see any friendly face after staring at the walls for days.

"Thought I was the only one left in the city," he said as she carted her bag toward her room.

She stopped and looked at him, apparently wondering why he had interrupted his reading to strike up a conversation. "I had to bolt from my parents' house," she said, "to avoid a New Year's Eve party."

"You don't like parties?"

"Not at my parents' house."

She continued to the back of the loft, and a bit later took up her usual place at her easels. Finn walked over to see what she was working on. He found her staring out the front windows.

"Everything okay?" he said.

She turned, again looking a little surprised. "Yeah, thanks," she said. "Was just thinking about Arnold Lobel."

"Who's that?"

"He wrote this series of *Frog and Toad* books I loved as a kid." She handed him a small paperback book with a cover picturing the two animals on a tandem bicycle.

"And so...?" he asked.

"Well, he just died...of AIDS."

"Oh." Finn said, at a loss for words. It was impossible to live in New York and not be conscious of this disease ravaging certain communities, particularly in the arts. He knew one man who had died, but the epidemic still didn't touch him personally, not nearly as much as his grandfather's death. He guessed it was to be expected Petra would be more affected than him, given her sexual predilection. But he had to admit it was possible she was just more empathetic than he was.

"It's so sad," she said, "and I had barely processed the death of Brian Buczak in July. He was a painter who lived up on Greenwich Street; really inspiring, and he was only thirty-two; such a tragedy."

Finn began to think he was being closed-minded about Petra. What did it matter whether she liked men or women? She was a genuinely kind person and had been nothing but nice to him. And now, having lost G-pa, he was counting up the few people in the world who cared at all about him. He needed to look beyond differences to what might connect him to people around him.

"You ever done a hand?" he asked, thinking about his old gripe against the right-handed world.

"Hands are harder than you might think," she said, looking at her own hand, "but it might go well with a correlative."

"A what?"

"Well, I've moved on from body parts alone to a series called

'Somatic Complements,' where each abstract body part is juxta-posed with an associated image."

"Like...?"

"Here," she said and put up on an easel a painting of a beautiful violet eye—it must have been a woman's—beside the United States seal of the pyramid from the dollar bill. "The eye refers to the god of Freemasonry, the great architect of the universe."

"You need something to pair with each body part?"

"Yes, although I don't always have the correlative in mind to start; I just leave that space open until it comes to me. I see you're looking at your own hand. You have a thought?"

"What," Finn said, snapping back from his reverie. "No, I was just thinking how being left-handed has seemed such a burden sometimes, something unjust about the world."

"Tell you what," she said. "Tomorrow I'll sketch your hand, and we'll see where that leads."

Finn returned to his room strangely affected by his con-versation with Petra. Seeing the earrings on his dresser, he de-cided to give them to her, which might make this doleful week feel like Christmas time and cement his resolution to give up on Dani. He wrapped up the earrings in a colorful page from a magazine, brought it back out to the ballroom and handed the package to her.

"What's this?" she said, confused but obviously pleased.

"Just a holiday present."

This made her laugh as she took the package, tactfully not sneering at the wrapping job, and opened it up.

"Thank you, Finn," she said. "This is really sweet."

"I know a pair of crucifixes is kind of an odd gift for Hanukah."

"Well, yes."

"But I thought, if you wouldn't wear them, maybe you knew someone else who would?"

She smiled sincerely. "I'm sure I'll find someone," she said, but seemed to be trying not to laugh as she looked at him with a question obviously on her mind.

"Yes," he admitted, "I bought them for Dani."

"No longer in the picture?"

"Yeah, well, when I developed the film, it turned out she was never there to begin with."

"Sort of a vampire who doesn't show up in photographs?"

"Exactly like that," he said, thinking how misplaced his resentment against Petra had been when she silently but clearly disapproved of Dani as a match for Finn.

"Well, she is stunning and certainly dances to her own tune, but I think she's sort of consumed by the persona she's trying to create. You're better off without her."

"You're not saying that just because you want the earrings?"

She swatted at him with the magazine wrapping.

When New Year's Eve arrived, Finn and Petra found themselves together with no place to go.

"How about a bar," she said cheerily. "What about the Raccoon Lodge?"

"That would be insane, a crowd of noisy, sweaty drunks. Better to buy a bottle and stay home to watch the ball fall."

"Now I'm seriously depressed," she said.

"Aren't you the one who skipped town to *avoid* a party?"

"That's a little complicated," she said as if trying to curtail this conversation.

"How so?" he probed.

She sighed. "My mother is dying to set me up with a nice Jewish boy—really *any* nice Jewish boy—but this year there's one in particular, a family friend on break *from Princeton*. She just doesn't understand I..."

"I get it, Petra," he said and smiled affectionately. "You are who you are, even if your mother doesn't want to see it. In fact, maybe it's our contrasting tastes that allow *us* to be friends like this."

"You mean with no pressure."

"Precisely," he said, adding to himself, "and no judgment."

In the end they went up town together for falafels from a street vendor and the midnight show of *The Rocky Horror Picture Show* at the Eighth Street Playhouse. It was fun. She knew *of* the movie, like he did, but they were both unprepared for the level of audience participation. People mouthed dialog, some shouting out call-backs to the actors on screen. They threw rice at the wedding scene and spread newspapers over their heads and squirted water pistols in the air when it rained. Everyone got up to dance.

They got home at two in the morning, singing *Time Warp* together, which made it feel like a proper start for 1988.

Chapter Thirteen

It was January. Finn was glad to be back at work and busy. The missing watches were largely forgotten while everyone worked to build an ironclad case against GlobalX.

Because they feared the judge might resist granting an *ex parte* order against a company the size of GlobalX, Ainsley took the lead in arguing for the temporary restraining order. Fortunately, their judge was familiar with the Counterfeiting Act, and Ainsley convinced him GlobalX would destroy evidence if given notice before the seizure order was served. Finn liked to think his updated brief won the day, although Ainsely's gravitas certainly might have helped.

The raid would be noteworthy in hitting several locations of the same defendant: a warehouse in Irvington, corporate headquarters in Newark and a records center out in Knowlton Township. Victor would take Ray Bagatoni with him to the main offices. Ainsley and JT would cover the warehouse with Ray's partner. Finn would drive to the data center with Ted. Victor had arranged US Marshals to effect service with each team, so a government vehicle followed Finn's rental car.

It was important Finn was leading a team. It was his chance to prove himself after the debacle in Nashville. He would make the most of this opportunity, show Victor he could run cases by himself.

It took no time once they crossed the George Washington Bridge for big buildings to give way to blue sky. They passed stately old houses set back from the road, visible through trees mostly barren of leaves. Finn was reminded there were bucolic parts of New Jersey.

"This is my first time in New Jersey," Ted said, gazing at the natural contrast to Manhattan. "Jimmy said it was all factories and smog."

Finn chuckled. "That's on the highway west. But, you know, it *is* the Garden State."

"Do they grow a lot of flowers or something?"

"I think they came up with the term in the 1800s to advertise land to prospective farmers. But they do grow really good blueberries and tomatoes."

The receptionist at the GlobalX records center had a panic attack when Finn presented the order. Borderline hysterical, she refused to let them in until her manager arrived, looking ready to throw her wide body across the hallway if they tried to pass. The manager also resisted, but the marshal's game face and the manager's call to his legal department convinced everyone to calm down and cooperate.

The manager walked them to a large room where a young man was filing documents into binders. "This is Ingram, our chief file clerk," the manager said. "He'll be able to direct you to the files covered by the order." He paused, twisting his face as if thinking hard, and then added, "I'd like to say our records are computerized, but that's a project we just started."

Ingram was maybe twenty-four years old, thin and pale with blotchy acne scars. Finn reached out to shake his hand. "Looks like we've got a long day ahead of us, Mr. Ingram," he said. "We appreciate your assistance."

The young man was obviously pleased with the deference Finn showed him. "Call me Henry," he said cheerfully. "Happy to help."

The manager took Henry aside, pointing to the order and speaking in low tones.

Finn commented to Ted, "He's making sure the kid doesn't let us see anything beyond what's in the order."

Ted shook his head. "We'll have plenty to do with just the relevant records."

"But what we want will be buried in this mess, and Henry doesn't have to point it out. By the way, notice how the manager treats him like crap. We need to get Henry on our side."

Henry walked them to a shelf holding some fifty large binders. "The last ten years of import and sales records will be here," he said. "I'm afraid they're chronological and not sorted by merchandise, so you'll have to sift through to find the watch data."

Ted looked at Finn, perplexed. "Are we going to need more people?"

Out of the corner of his eye, Finn saw the manager grin as he took a seat at one of the long tables, apparently enjoying their bewilderment.

 Finn tried to maintain a look of confidence. "Thanks, Henry," he said. "Do you mind if we spread out on one of these tables?"

"Oh, no problem," Henry said. "Let me clear away my stuff."

"And where's the copy machine?" Finn asked, stifling a smile as the manager reacted nervously to this question.

Henry helped them move binders to the table, and Finn and Ted got to work.

The marshal approached Finn and said, "It doesn't look like there will be any trouble. Do you need me anymore?"

Finn and Ted looked at each other. "No," Finn said, "we'll take it from here."

Ted returned to the binders while Finn looked around the big room for anything else that might be relevant, not wholly trusting their hosts. When he rejoined Ted, they both kept up a friendly banter with Henry as they worked. Finn complimented the clerk's proficiency at organizing files, and Ted joked about what a thankless task filing could be. The manager did his own work, glancing over occasionally as if to supervise the review, but after an hour he was called away. Thirty minutes later Finn concluded the manager would not return, which left them free to befriend Henry and get his help with the documents. Finn wondered at the manager giving up the field, as if he had something more important to do than supervise lawyers ransacking his files. It brought to mind a lesson from raids and depositions, that winning sometimes depends on stamina. He smiled imagining G-pa riffing on Sartre: "It's your weakness gives them their strength."

"So, Henry," Finn said, "the manager introduced you as the 'chief clerk.' Do other clerks report to you?"

Henry scoffed. "That's a joke; there's no one else. They gave me the title last year instead of a raise."

Over the next hour Finn and Ted copied records showing importation of watches and identified two factories in Korea manufacturing them. But the merchandise was identified only by SKU numbers rather than brands, so as usual Finn and Ted would have to sort through it all later. For the moment they set aside a stack of reports to copy.

Henry offered to do the photocopying, but Ted suggested they work together. Finn soon heard them by the copy machine laughing and commiserating over the New York Knicks' disappointing season.

"Still a chance we make the playoffs," Ted said hopefully, "with Ewing and now Mark Jackson."

"Yeah," Henry replied, "but eighth place in the East means we'd face Boston."

They both groaned, no doubt envisioning lining up against Larry Bird and Kevin McHale. Finn smiled. Ted was getting the hang of real-world lawyering.

Nearing noon, Finn asked Henry what he typically did for lunch.

"The supervisors send out," Henry said, "but us chief file clerks go to the food trucks out front."

Finn smiled. "Well, young man, today is your lucky day. Why don't you find a menu, and we'll all order out, on Sanchi. You're certainly doing your part to help us wrap this up."

Henry's eyes lit up. It was obvious he wasn't used to praise at this job—or free meals—which was going to make it even easier to win him over.

As they shared an obscene amount of veal marsala and *ragù ala Bolognese*, Henry revealed he had graduated from Rutgers, hoping to go to business school, but took the clerk's job first to save up money. Ted commiserated, lamenting the pile of student debt he'd have to pay off before he could enjoy any fruits of his education.

Finn picked up on the conversation about the Knicks, as Henry listened intently and piled in more food than should have fit into his skinny frame. "We also have a site order," Finn said, "that protects the trademarks of all the musical acts that come to Madison Square Garden. We file declarations in this case describing each band's marks, and then investigators work on their own to enforce the seizure order around the venue."

"Wow," said Henry, "that's really cool. You just, like, just take the knockoffs away from them?"

"Yup, and serve them with a John Doe complaint. Of course, they're all fly-by-night and so default. But the enforcement limits infringing merchandise sales in the area around the concert, and theoretically boosts sales of genuine merchandise."

Ted also seemed fascinated. "Do we ever get to see the shows?" he asked.

"Not really, although I have stuck my head in to catch a few numbers when I really liked the band. Mostly, it's on autopilot once we give the investigators their instructions." He stopped to take a bite of his food, and laughed to himself. "Of course, it all blew up in our faces when the Grateful Dead came to town."

Finn paused for effect. "Our investigators enforced the order, as usual and next day brought us boxes of T-shirts. Problem was the shirts were tied-dyed, like so much Dead paraphernalia, but didn't bear any of the band's marks. That meant we had no authority to seize that stuff. We didn't know what to do, but next day these three guys showed up—tie-dyed head to toe. They followed the tour from city to city to sell this stuff."

"Holy crap," Ted said. "Did they complain to the court?"

"No, thank God. They just wanted their shirts back. So we returned the merchandise, with our apologies. And just then the snack lady passed by in the hallway ringing her bell, so we bought each of them a candy bar and a bottle of soda. That was all it took to make them happy, and they were off to the next tour city."

Henry looked at Ted with a big smile. "That's so funny."

"And the strangest thing," Finn concluded, "is these three Deadheads, who spent their lives following the band, had never met before that day."

Finn sensed Henry was enchanted by his story and the thought of having a job where he would see live people instead of being shut up alone in the archives. "You know, Henry," Finn said, "if you ever get into the city, I'm sure we could swing some tickets to the Garden, for a concert or better yet...."

"A Knicks game?" Henry interrupted.

"Why not? We can almost always arrange tickets, except maybe when Michael Jordan's in town."

Henry laughed, excited. "Oh, I'd love to see *any* game."

Soon after lunch Henry got a thoughtful look on his face and approached Finn. "You know," he said, "I've been thinking. You guys are all right, and what you're doing makes a lot of sense. I never really focused on the kind of crap GlobalX sells, but some of it's pretty troubling."

Finn put on his best look of empathy and gestured to go on.

"Well…" Henry looked around as if someone might overhear him. "Thing is, the watches are not the worst of it."

Finn waved at Ted to join them. The three leaned in close together.

"Another of our divisions sells airplane parts. I've seen invoices to the Navy listing those parts as coming from Boeing and Lockheed Martin, but they're really sourced out of Korea and rebranded here."

Finn and Ted exchanged looks of amazement.

"And there's a file," Henry went on, "about an F-15 that went down because of structural failure." Henry looked at both of them and bit his lip. "I'm pretty sure we sold parts for that jet."

Ted jumped up as if from an electrical shock. "How could they do that?" he blurted out. "Doesn't the military check its sources?"

"Even if they do, I guess it's possible to fake documentation. At least I think that's what happened, because after the jet crashed, a team of suits from the central office arrived here and removed documents from the archives."

"Removed them to…?"

"Destroy. They shredded lots of pages and even took the shredded paper with them."

"Did they say anything to you? You're supposed to oversee these archives, right?"

Henry laughed. "They hardly noticed me. I'm just a clerk."

Finn took hold of Ted's arm to get him to sit. "And were there other incidents like this?" he asked Henry.

"I think *so*. There was at least one other crack-up."

Ted's body tensed, but he remained seated, his eyes wide as he looked anxiously at Finn. Finn borrowed the GlobalX phone to call his office, but Victor and Ainsley were still out.

He had to decide what to do. Was this one of those moments—like when he stole the watch—that changed everything to follow?

"It would really help," he told Henry, "help us and help the Navy, if you copied anything about the crash or jet parts."

"I can do that," Henry said, standing up straight and looking proud of himself.

"And listen, this is not subject to our court order, but it looks like a crime, and one that may have killed pilots. You were right to tell us. Somebody needs to see this. We'll sort through what you give us and take it to the authorities, the police or the FBI or whatever."

"Will I lose my job?"

"We'll keep your name out of it, say we ran across this stuff in looking for the watch documents. For now we'll just copy the records and put them back so the company doesn't know we're on to them. The authorities will probably eventually want to talk with you, though, and maybe there's even a whistleblower reward. Don't worry. We'll figure that all out and make sure you get the credit."

While Henry looked apprehensive but excited, Ted's face had a look of cold determination Finn had not seen in him before. Clearly, the case had just gotten personal for his young associate.

"Just leave it to us," Finn said, "and keep working as usual. We've got the phone number here; does it ring straight through?"

"No, all calls to the building go through the receptionist."

"Well, we'll be in touch, but be careful about what you say over the phone. I'll also leave my card. You give me a call when you'd like to come into the city. Bring a friend, and we'll score those Knicks tickets for you."

At the end of the day, Finn and Ted packed up reams of documents and thanked Henry again. As they carried several boxes out of the facility, the ashen-faced manager resurfaced. Finn had warned Ted against showing any emotion and walked between him and the manager to make sure Ted kept his cool. Finn wished the manager and the still-trembling receptionist a pleasant day, smiling genuinely at the image of the two of them in front of a mug shot height chart.

This was the biggest day of Finn's career. This case would put Bolger & Plotkin on the map and make him a star in the legal world. But he wanted to get back to the office and dig into the documents before he told Victor what they found. He was not going to mess this up or hand it off to Ainsley.

"We should savor this moment, Junior," he said as they loaded the car. "Look for a pub along the highway, and I'll buy you a beer."

Ted looked apprehensive. "Shouldn't we go straight to the police, or the Navy?"

"No way. We've got work to do before we even show this to Victor. We'll need to sort through everything and connect the dots—before we show anyone. But I'm telling you, this will be great for the firm, and not so bad for you and me, either."

They found an old man's bar in a strip mall and sat across a Formica table from each other, sipping room-temperature beer.

"Henry was quite a surprise," Ted said. "Did you notice he seemed to grow two inches by the end of the day?"

"What a funny, little guy," Finn responded. "And *you* won him over."

"Well, he's a Knicks fan...."

"How did you end up rooting for a New York team?"

"As a kid I got used to shifting loyalties as we moved from base to base, but I loved watching Patrick Ewing at Georgetown, and when he came to New York, the Knicks became my team."

"Well, hopefully he can lift us back into relevance. And as to Henry, we'll have to see about getting him tickets. You said he lives with his mother?"

"Yes. And he rides a bike to work every day. It's like he's still twelve years old."

"Twelve years old and saving the world."

"It's true. We would never have found those materials without him."

"And don't minimize your role. I think this makes us genuine patriots."

Ted seemed to ponder this. "My folks will be proud, I guess," he said and then faltered. "And my brother...."

"Right, you said he flies fighter jets?"

Finn's smile faded. "I said he *used to*."

"He left the service?"

"He..." Ted said and stopped to gather himself. "He died; his plane went down on a training mission over the Gulf of Mexico."

"Oh, no. I'm so sorry. What happened?"

Ted shook his head and took in a deep breath. "They don't really know. The public explanation was mechanical failure, but Navy investigators insinuated there might also have been pilot error."

"Ouch."

"Yeah, that just about killed my dad, even though none of us believed it." Ted sighed and took a long sip of his beer. "I try not to think of it because it hurts too much."

"Listen, I understand, and I get why you are so invested in this case. I didn't mean to pry."

"No, you should know, particularly now." He took another long swig and squared his fists on the table. "Even beyond my brother, military service means everything in my family."

"Right, your grandfather and your father...."

"And it goes back farther than that. But the point is giving your life for your country is the most noble thing you can do. So, when my big brother crashed, we accepted this as his sacrifice to keep us all safe."

Ted paused, looking into his mug and gathering himself. "But if substandard parts..."

"Oh, shit," Finn said. "Could Global's parts have gone into your brother's plane?"

"Who knows? Maybe that's too neat an answer. What matters is the people serving our country deserve better."

Finn also appreciated serving justice, whatever that meant in this case, but to be honest he mostly wanted to stick it to the fat cats who always seemed to get their way.

By the time they got back to the office, everyone had gone home for the night. That was good. Finn was eager to dig into the documents, so he told Ted to order in dinner and started spreading things out on a conference room table.

When Ted joined him, Finn said, "Junior, this could be the biggest moment of your career. And we're going to make sure we get it right. Put aside the watch stuff for now; we'll get the legal assistants to help sort through that tomorrow. For now let's pull together everything on the jet parts: where they're made, what port they come through, how they're listed in the manifests, where they're packaged and branded. We also need to know how they're delivered to the Navy, who at the company and in the Defense Department signs off on the sales, how it's all financed, news reports about the crashes. I want to put a complete and coherent package in front of Victor."

They literally rolled up their sleeves and got to work. It was energizing to get hold of an important case for once, rather than another mauling of two-bit counterfeiters who wouldn't put up a fight. And Ted proved to be tireless and adept at culling information.

When the food was delivered, they ate as they worked. The cleaning lady came and went, and the hours passed. By two in the morning, they had sketched much of a scheme that laid blame for the crashes on GlobalX. They had more work to do, but things were pointing to a scheme to sell cheap, rebranded parts through a broker at Port Newark to a buyer for the Navy. An executive VP at GlobalX also took steps to disguise these deliveries after *two* jets went down in training exercises. An internal memo shortly after the first crash discussed steps to put the authorities off the company's track.

They had these bastards, for sure, but Finn would not move forward until they filled in all the gaps. And he didn't want Ainsley stepping in and taking over this case. He and Ted would keep working on this on the side while focusing on Sanchi during the day. When they had it all together, he'd lay it on Victor's desk—wrapped up with a bow.

"Okay, listen, Junior," Finn said as they straightened up the room and collected documents. "You did great work today—or at this point I guess it was yesterday. You should be proud of yourself. But we need to keep focused. We have to keep these documents locked up; chain of title will be important when we get to court. And it's crucial we keep it under wraps; tell *no one* until we get Victor involved."

"But we have to do something quick," Ted blurted out. "More pilots could die."

"I know, Ted, but we can't just announce this as if it will all be open and shut. These guys are for real. They're not going to lie down and take it unless we build a bulletproof case before we go public. Given how that guy at Luxe Watches went ballistic and his partner ended up dead, it's clear GlobalX will do anything to avoid bad press."

"And Victor?"

"Okay, so that's more personal. There's a lot they don't teach you in law school about how the business works. Doing great work doesn't get you a corner office. The rewards go to the rainmakers, the lawyers with clients. And one way to attract clients is to make a name for yourself by breaking a big case. If we hand this over to the firm before we have it all lined up, Ainsley will take the lead, and she and Victor will make it their own. That would leave you and me as bit players, stuck in the back office, like Henry ruling over his file room while his bosses screw us all and rake in the big bucks."

"Can't we at least bring in a legal assistant to help go through the documents? We could get Imani; she wouldn't say anything."

"She is the one person I *would* trust, except maybe JT. But there is real risk here along with the upside. We're tangling with big money interests that have shown they will strike back hard. You and I are in this to the end...."

"That's an affirmative, captain. We've got to hose those bastards!"

"Right," Finn said and laughed, thinking Ted probably resisted the urge to salute with that last outburst, "but there's no reason to put Imani at risk. There'll be plenty for her to do once the firm is on this."

"Okay, I get that," Ted said, showing some frustration, "but isn't it more important to protect pilots now?"

"We can't protect anyone by spilling it all before we're sure what we have. We'll do it all, Junior, but we have to do it right. Lock up the documents and then go home and get some sleep. In the morning we'll show Victor the watch stuff. That will keep Ainsley busy until we're ready to reveal everything. For now just remember, we have to tread very carefully and *tell no one.*"

Chapter Fourteen

Despite his late night sorting through documents, Finn was in the office early the next morning. He wanted an hour to work on the jet parts evidence before anyone else showed up. He focused first on the money trail from the GlobalX factory in Korea, through a series of brokers to the US Naval Air Warfare Center in Maryland.

As people started trickling in, Ted knocked on his door. Recognizing the papers spread on Finn's desk, he said, "Can we work on the jet parts this morning?"

"No," Finn said, looking up at the clock. "In fact, I need to put this stuff away, then we should get to work on the watch records in the conference room. What I've seen this morning tells me we'll need more time than I thought to nail down the jet case before we show anyone. We'll get back on that tonight. And I need to call our man, Henry."

The whole team met that morning to debrief. Ainsley reported she and JT had seized a load of knockoff watches and proudly displayed bogus GlobalX models they hadn't seen before. Finn was relieved, thinking this would put to rest the recriminations about the missing watches from Nashville and hopefully take any lingering pressure off Imani.

Finn followed up with records showing importation. This

was less dramatic than Ainsley's haul, but they all knew it would be even more important in calculating damages.

Victor then spoke in his glorious leader persona, unable as usual to keep from grandstanding. "Ainsley, Finnegan, great job. And the others on those teams, JT and Theodore, we pulled this one off with precision. We'll need to get cracking on those documents and develop a theory of damages because my visit to GlobalX headquarters may have paved the way for a quick settlement. The CEO and general counsel are sweating, afraid of bad publicity." His self-satisfied grin took a turn around the room, engaging each of them. "And," he went on, "I have spoken to Sam Eddings at the client. He is, of course, over the moon, and sends his thanks to you all."

Everyone beamed. Trademark enforcement didn't get any better than this.

"Ainsley," Victor went on, "put someone on sorting and inventorying the merchandise, and get that legal assistant—what's her name—who takes pictures to shoot some high-res shots. Then ship specimens of each of the models to Sam so he can have his engineers get to work breaking them down. And," he added with a momentary scowl at Ted, "let's make sure we get his title straight this time." Ted winced as Victor went on, "Remind the engineers we're looking for clues to subcontractors; where the components came from, which parts are substandard and why? And this time there *will* be nothing missing from the inventory. Are we all clear?"

Everyone nodded eagerly except Ted, who had shrunk down in his seat, apparently keeping his head low to avoid drawing attention to himself.

Victor continued. "Finnegan, you run the document review. You know what we're looking for: everything from production costs to distribution channels to damages. I will keep the CEO's feet to the fire, telling him we'll be ready to talk turkey in a couple of days and getting him to stipulate to the preliminary injunction. Jimmy, you get on drafting the stipulation. But one thing is crucial—and this goes for everyone—we don't let *any* information out, not yet and not a word. No one outside this room is to know anything. Keeping this out of the news will be our trump card here."

Finn was flying high. The client was happy, Victor was jubilant and even Ainsley was smiling. And Victor's timeline fit perfectly with Finn's plans for deciphering the jet materials while keeping everyone else busy on watches. Before long he would blow their minds with a way to take GlobalX down for good.

"Hope you didn't have any plans for tonight, Junior," he said in a quiet aside to Ted. "And let's order ribs; I need some red meat before we rip into these bastards."

"Roger that, captain," Ted said with a conspiratorial grin.

It was freeing to be ahead of any time crunch, and so Finn took a lunchtime walk. There was a chill in the air, but the day was bright and clear. He wandered through Rockefeller Center, stopping to marvel at the temporary model house a home design magazine had erected in the plaza and laugh at the awkward ice skaters. He even felt benevolent toward tourists; with the holidays over, the sidewalks near the big Christmas tree were no longer gridlocked, but any pack of half-a-dozen skyward-gazing visitors could still snarl the sidewalk.

He found himself walking down Fifth Avenue, pausing at the holiday displays in store windows. He marveled that no matter how seedy other parts of the city were, Fifth Avenue always remained a showplace, especially dressed up at this time of year. The cops even moved the homeless people off the avenue and chased away the squeegee guys. Soon he reached the flagship location for Charles Scribner's Sons. After Genevieve had reminded him of the great novels published there, he had done some research. It was far from an ordinary bookstore. One architectural historian called it "the grandest interior space" in New York, akin to Grand

Central Station—which was actually sad given that "grand" Beaux Arts train station's leaking roof, chipped stonework and crowds of homeless residents.

It occurred to him Genevieve might be at her job, so he stopped in. Satch was still infatuated, but he had told Finn he'd given up, that he had mistaken her camaraderie with a fellow actor for particular feelings for him. Anyway, after having read about the building she worked in, Finn really was curious to see the interior.

The store did not disappoint. He entered a long nave-like room with an ornately decorated ceiling some thirty feet up, resting on rectangular pillars. The floor was oak laid in a gorgeous herringbone pattern. A central staircase at the eastern end doubled back from a mirrored surface reflecting the entire shop, making the big room seem even larger. Second-story interior balconies ran along both sides, lined with cast-iron railings and ornamental moldings, above which were arched windows to the third floor.

As he slowly unbuttoned his overcoat and took in the view, he spotted Genevieve on the north balcony. She was reaching up to place a book. Her hair was tied back with a few strands loose. Stretching to the shelf showed off her athletic figure, hardly recognizable from the tepee costume she wore when he nicknamed her Puffy Dress Girl.

He stood still and watched until she glanced down and saw him. Then he gulped as her expression went from surprised to amused to...could it be conspiratorial? She gestured toward the stairway.

He gathered himself, walked to the back of the store and part-way up the stairs. She leaned over the railing. They were almost close enough to touch.

In a gold sweater that made her face glow, and wearing horn-rimmed glasses, she was a sexy librarian fantasy. But he squelched that vision. If his doomed pursuit of Dani had taught him anything, it was to keep both feet on the ground when he spoke with an attractive woman.

But why was he even thinking that way? Satch may have given up on her, but did that make her fair game? At any rate he had to laugh at how he disregarded his own advice, standing halfway up a staircase rather than remaining on the solid floor.

When her expression turned questioning, he was aghast that his long-overcome stutter returned. "I was out for lu-lu-lunch and remembered you work here."

She smiled, but he was humiliated. He had beaten back this infirmity long ago; why had it popped up now? He girded himself to speak slowly and firmly.

"Well," she said, as if she hadn't noticed. "I'm glad you came by. How do you like our little shop?"

"Dazzling," he said forcefully enough to overcome the stutter, but he wondered if she took his ardent tone to hint he was commenting as much about her as the store. This conversation was spiraling out of control. He needed to make a quick retreat.

"We've missed you at the club," she said. "The show is back on track. Are you still going to help out backstage?"

"Um," Finn stumbled. With all the drama at work, he had forgotten he volunteered. "Yeah, I've been out of town, but I will definitely get back to it. When do you open?"

"Dress rehearsal is Sunday, and—with absolutely no excuse— I'm still tripping over my lines. The director will have my head if I'm not off-book for the rehearsal tonight."

"I'm sure you'll be great," he blurted out. Again, he admonished himself to remain cool. This was an unscripted, friendly visit, not the *Romeo and Juliet* balcony scene. He had to stop making every encounter with a woman into a grand, dramatic interlude.

"Well..." she said, giving him an opening in case he had something more to say.

He sensed he was looking flummoxed when he wanted to

appear confident. "Right," he said. "Well, I really should be getting back."

"Back to hounding sad little shopkeepers?"

He laughed. "Yeah, I've got to go beat some more information out of them. But seriously, we just raided a big company, and it looks like we may have uncovered a major crime."

"That sounds dangerous," she said, suddenly concerned, and maybe impressed?

"Nah," he said, regaining some swagger from her reaction. "Law enforcement will do the real work once we hand them the case, but it could be a big deal for the firm and for me."

He sensed she was genuinely interested, but then she glanced around as if she needed to get back to work.

"Well, so," he said, confused at why he had bragged about the matter that was supposed to be a secret and feeling he had overstayed his welcome. "It was nice running into you. I'll see you at the club."

The team made a lot of progress over the next two days. They identified two of GlobalX's sources of counterfeits. The one supplying the cheap replicas was a familiar kind of broker in Korea whose connections to factories were hard to pin down. However, the documents revealed how some of these products came into the country using false documentation, or to be branded only after arrival.

The more troubling source of genuine, though unlicensed, product was a factory run by Sanchi itself. Surveillance by company security identified illicit operations in this factory; it produced Sanchi watches during the work week and over the weekend made more watches that differed from licensed product only in their falsified serial numbers. Sanchi shut down this operation, terminated the employees involved and took steps to improve internal monitoring in its facilities.

Bolger and Plotkin provided the import information to the

US Customs Service, which took steps to interdict shipments, effectively eliminating Korea for a time as a source of counterfeit Sanchi watches. This would limit the client's problem to the knockoffs already in the stream of commerce. In the view of Victor Bolger, that wasn't such a bad problem to have since it assured his firm continued enforcement work.

Late Wednesday morning Ainsley addressed the room. "We are bringing in a nice lunch for everyone, an extra thank you for the work you're doing on this case."

JT rolled his eyes at Finn and said, "In other words, she doesn't want anyone leaving until the job is done."

Finn just smiled. Ainsley was tough, but there was little subterfuge to her. You always knew exactly where she was coming from. Not that the legal assistants gave a damn; they were all about the free food.

Given Ainsley's less than subtle effort to push things forward, it was startling when she returned mid-afternoon and asked for everyone's attention. "We're calling off work on GlobalX," she said. "Victor is in talks we expect to produce a comprehensive settlement. All of you start packing everything up to send to the file room."

Ted shot a startled look at Finn, who shook his head almost imperceptibly. This should not affect the jet parts matter, since any settlement would be of the civil case between Sanchi and GlobalX, not a criminal prosecution instituted on behalf of the Navy. But it could be embarrassing to the firm and raise questions about how Bolger & Plotkin gained access to the evidence. Finn would have to get a look at the settlement agreement while it was being drafted.

Ainsley left the room. JT shrugged and followed her. The legal assistants smiled like kids let out early from school. Their primary interests tended to be simple; finishing up a job with praise from the boss was always a good thing. If they were much older than twenty-three or twenty-four, the prospect of a major job ending—thus putting in question if there would be more work for them to do—might have given them a more self-interested perspective.

For Finn, though, and Ted, this put a timer on finishing up with the jet parts evidence. They needed to lay this out for Victor before he cut a deal.

The office mostly emptied out in the late afternoon. It was Wednesday, and after closing the case, they had expected to be working on through the week, weekend plans took everyone's attention—everyone except Finn and Ted. They worked quietly in their respective offices, so as not to draw attention.

"You need a night out, my man," JT said, opening Finn's door as he half-knocked.

"No kidding," Finn responded, furtively covering up the papers in front of him.

"So why are you still chained to your desk? Come out and I'll buy you a drink. I cleaned up on the Super Bowl, so it's my treat."

"You had the Redskins?"

"And I could have given ten times the spread and still cleared a thousand bucks."

"Wow. How do you have the money to bet that big?"

"Not a problem," he said and grinned, "long as I win. And so what about it? We hit some hot spot and find us some babes?"

"No, man. First, I'm exhausted. And then I also have to deal with the sanctions motion Hune & Buchanan filed in Nashville about our threatening their clients with deportation."

"Oh, dude, I heard Big Niccolò dumped that on you because of the gun thing."

"How did you hear that?" Finn wasn't sure if he was more angry or embarrassed. It was bad enough the boss came down on him for a mistake anyone could make, and in the end didn't really hurt anyone, but it was insufferable to become fodder for office gossip.

"Shit, dude, everybody knows."

Finn let out an exasperated breath. "That's why you're the only cluck who thinks I've got time to go out to the bar?"

JT rested his hand on Finn's shoulder. "This, too, will pass, dude."

A moment after his friend left, Finn thought about changing his mind and going out for a drink. Things were going to start popping once Victor knew about the jet parts, and then there would be no time for socializing. But he couldn't let up now; he had to keep focused and finish the presentation before Victor finalized a deal.

There wasn't really anything Finn needed to do on the Nashville case that night. He was just waiting for the office to clear out. Once everyone else left, he asked Ted to come to his office. They laid out the documents together and continued going through the evidence. They were close to putting together a convincing story, showing each connection in how substandard parts led to crashes.

As they worked Ted became more and more incensed. "Jail time is too good for them," he said of the GlobalX executives and the middlemen. "They should have to face the families of the dead aviators and then be buried in some dark hole for the rest of their lives. We *are* going to hold them accountable, right?"

"Yes, Junior, we'll make those suckers pay."

Finn believed what he said, although Ted was so angry Finn needed to calm him down. His young associate seemed to think of all military personnel as family, but they needed to treat this matter dispassionately, objectively.

To be doing what was right—for its own sake—was an unfamiliar motivation for Finn. He had mostly gotten past his childhood compulsion to seek retribution from the wrong-handed world, always grabbing for all he could get, but that didn't turn him into some kind of crusader for justice. He chased infringers, which was at least arguably a noble calling. But with GlobalX he could really make a difference, have a positive effect on a world apart from any self-interest. This was no time for philosophizing about legal realism, or considering whether the Korean executives and their American facilitators had difficult childhoods or struggled to make ends meet. This was a straightforward matter of foreigners defrauding America and service members dying.

As he gathered the papers on his desk into a large envelope, Finn was hit with a fear something might go wrong. Ainsley's sudden talk of settlement before completing the damages calculation was jarring and suspicious, and he hadn't seen anything in her manner to explain it.

He needed insurance against everything going south, and so took the envelope of critical documents to the duplicating machine and copied the most important pages. He'd take the copies home for safe keeping, just in case.

It was still early when Finn got home to the loft. Lance was rehearsing. The insulation of his studio was good but not absolute, so the windows shook a bit.

Petra was at an easel at her end of the dance floor, apparently oblivious to the music and hard at work on her "Somatic Complements." Finn had yet to see the finished painting of his left hand, but his favorites so far were the seductive eye with the pyramid and another unfinished image of a woman's perfect rear end.

At that moment she stared as if transfixed at an empty canvas, and he thought maybe he should leave her in her creative zone. But they were friends now, and it had been days since he had seen her, so he decided to say hello.

"Finding Lance's music inspirational?" he said with a smile.

"What," she said softly, as if coming out of a trance. "Oh, hi. Haven't see you in a while."

"Yeah, things have been busy." He stepped over to her easel. "What's the new painting?"

"I was thinking. I've never done a piece showing more than one person, and always work from live models, but I feel a need to speak out about what's happening."

"What's happening?"

"AIDS," she said impatiently, as if surprised he was thinking of anything else. "I'm going to paint two hands shaking, based on the photograph of Princess Diana with that AIDs patient in London."

"I saw that on the news," he said, again drawn into how seriously she took her work, even if painting isolated body parts and "correlated" images had up to then seemed a bit abstract for his taste. "I understand the Queen wasn't happy."

"Well, the Queen...I guess she's living in another time."

Then she snapped out of her ponderous expression and gestured toward another easel. "How do you like this one," she said with a smile.

"Whose elbow?"

"A friend from the restaurant. Do you like it?"

"Very shapely. How come I never see your models?"

"I schedule them that way on purpose—ever since you harassed my nude model." She laughed and playfully punched his arm.

"All I did was ask for her phone number."

Petra shook her head with a smile.

"Have you seen Satchmo?" he asked.

"Think he's in his room," she said and turned back to her canvas.

He found Satch reading on the threadbare couch in his room.

"You talking to yourself again?" Finn said with a grin.

"Just the man I wanted to see," Satch said, sitting up. "How's about running lines with me? I have to be completely off-book tonight, and I can't get it down."

Genevieve had also been anxious about learning her lines before that evening. Finn mulled over saying he had seen her, but this wasn't the time. Satch needed to concentrate. Was there something in Finn's feelings about Genevieve that should bother Satch?

"I'm all yours," Finn said, hoping that helping out would assuage his strange sense of guilt. "What do I do?"

"Here," Satch said, handing him the script. "In this scene Raskolnikov's friend, Razumikhin, is courting his sister, Avdotya Romanovna Raskolnikova."

Finn laughed. "Gotta love those Russians and all their names."

"Yeah, well we mostly use her nickname, Dunya."

"Right," Finn laughed. "That's easier, though not as lyrical as Puffy Dress Girl."

Satch paused with a questioning grin and then went on. "This is our big scene together. Just read the Dunya part."

"Sure. Should I take my voice up an octave?"

Satch shook his head, clearly in no mood for humor. Finn wondered if it nonetheless would help if he put on Genevieve's hundred-watt smile, but instead he just read the words with all the feeling he could muster.

They ran through the scene twice, Finn correcting Satch where he missed lines. When they finished, Finn said, "You seem to have it almost memorized."

"I know, but Gen will have it down pat, and I hate to look like a hack when I work with her."

"You've got to relax."

"What do you mean, about the play?"

"The play, well, and also about Genevieve. She seems to make you nervous, which can't help anything."

"Well, she does that, for sure."

"Are you still resolved to move on?"

"Like I have a choice? You've seen her. She's just nice and always upbeat, but I'm afraid she only thinks of me as part of the cast."

"Um..." Finn said, struggling to find words for what he wanted to say. "Satch, I've got to be honest with you."

"You think I was wasting my time."

"No, well, maybe; I don't know. But that's not it."

Satch looked over inquiringly. "Then what?"

Finn wanted to be forthright but stumbled over how completely truthful he could be. Satch was a good friend to him and deserved faithfulness in return. Yet, a feeling was growing inside Finn; he wanted to get closer to Genevieve, to give them both a chance to see if they might mean something to each other. "I don't know," he said again, realizing he had to say something. "It's nothing; I was just going to mention...I saw her on Monday."

"Saw Genevieve?"

"Yeah. I was out for lunch and passed Scribner's, and she was working."

"You talk to her?"

Finn nodded. "For, like, two minutes. She asked how I liked the store and if I was going to help out with the show."

"And all this means...?"

Finn let out an unsteady breath, girding himself. The last thing he wanted to do was hurt Satch, but there was a truth here and hiding it would help no one. Given his new, noble resolve at work, he couldn't slide back into a personal life where he rationalized taking whatever he wanted. Satch didn't deserve any part of Finn's sociopathic need for retribution against the world; he had only been good to Finn. Still, Finn couldn't bring himself to confess he thought he might really like Genevieve.

"Nothing," Finn said, "except I agree with you that she's amazing. And I'm sure your scene together will be great."

Satch squinted at him but snapped back to the matter at hand and asked to go through the scene once more. As soon as they finished, he packed up his knapsack and headed for the theater. But he stopped as he went out the door and turned back. "You *are* going to help backstage, right?"

Finn was almost startled. He had been pondering what there really was between Satch and Genevieve. They seemed... was *comfortable* the word? Friendly, certainly, but not passionate, or even intimate. "I'll be there for whatever you need," he said, feeling duplicitous.

Chapter Fifteen

Finn couldn't wait to get into the office the next day to show Victor the GlobalX evidence. This would make up for his screw-ups with the gun and the Sam Eddings declaration. And it would eliminate any doubts the boss had about giving him more responsibility.

He was behind his desk by eight o'clock, waiting for everyone else to arrive, rearranging the documents and rehearsing his presentation. Too much coffee had his head buzzing. But as he paged through the papers, he realized they were missing evidence of where GlobalX applied the false branding to the parts. There might still be a way to pin this down, but a simple story would always be best, so he called Henry.

The receptionist put him through to the file room.

"Files," Henry said.

"Henry, it's Finnegan Alger from Bolger & Plotkin. I'm glad I caught you at the office."

"Are you kidding? Where else would I be?"

Finn laughed. "You and me: just cogs in the machine, right?"

"Yeah, I guess."

In a short conversation, Henry explained how the counterfeit trademarks were applied to the parts at the Irvington warehouse. "The work orders don't identify trademarks; they say something like 'branding for delivery.' I think I saw a memo about this, but it may have been removed from the archives."

"Is there a copy somewhere?"

"I don't remember. I'll take a look this morning. How can I get it to you if I find it?"

"What do you mean?"

"Since you were here, everyone is jumpy. It might not even be a good idea to call me through the switchboard."

"Understood. For now, you can just FedEx any additional documents to me or Ted. We'll reimburse you. If we need to talk again, I'll call you at home. And Henry, we really appreciate you standing up for the truth, for everything, for your country."

"Thanks," Henry said, with little emotion.

"And hey, Ted will call you about basketball tickets, get some dates from you. Boston's coming town in a couple of weeks."

"That would be awesome," Henry said, enthusiasm replacing reluctance.

At almost nine-thirty Ainsley walked by Finn's door and said good morning.

"Ah, Ainsley," he called out. She stopped and poked her head into his room. He hadn't wanted to tell anyone about the jet parts until he could meet with Victor, but he was anxious to move this matter along and ached to tell someone. Anyway, Ainsley would certainly be brought in on this case, and telling her first might win some points with her. "Have you got a minute?"

"Sure," she said. "Just let me put my stuff down. Why don't you come to *my* office."

Ainsley had a notion of power that required them always to meet in *her* office. But she was the boss, or soon would be when they made her a partner, and he didn't care where they spoke as long as they were not overheard.

He took a big envelope with the most important documents to Ainsley's office. She had removed her coat to reveal a red suit with big silver buttons. She looked incredible.

"Nice suit," he said. "Is it new?"

"What," she said absently, as if his comment had gone right by her, though he believed she collected compliments like the deal toys on her credenza. "Relatively new, but what did you have to tell me?"

Finn laid out what he and Ted had found at GlobalX. She was astounded and visibly excited, for once letting him talk without interruption. But then she turned cautious and started probing for holes in the case. She questioned various points, and he relished being ready with answers and evidence. The late nights he and Ted had put in had been well spent.

"Have you shown this to Victor yet?" she asked.

"I'm waiting for him to get in."

She bit her lip and pondered. "Well, here's how we'll handle it. Leave these documents with me. I'll get with him as soon as he comes in and let him know what's coming. That way he'll be prepared for you. You know he met with the CEO when we raided the executive offices, and then guess who showed up the next day representing GlobalX?"

"Don't tell me...."

"Yes, the esteemed counsel at Hune & Buchanan have appeared once again to throw a wrench into the discussions. With their motion for sanctions in Nashville court, it's like those guys are hounding us. But at least now their involvement makes sense; they took on the flea market vendors because their real client is GlobalX. But all this is just to say you need to give Victor time to think through this new angle before you answer his questions. You know he'll have questions."

"Sure, I understand. But shouldn't we go to him together? I mean, it's not like I'm expecting him to make decisions on the spot."

"No, trust me on this. I've known Victor a long time. It'll be better if I introduce the subject so he's prepared to discuss it with both of us."

Finn's mistake hit him in the face. He had fumbled the ball on the goal line and Ainsley scooped it up. He was such an idiot.

"And who else knows about this?" she asked.

Who else? Why would she ask that? "Just Ted and me," he said uneasily. "Well, and our guy who showed us this stuff."

"You have an informant at GlobalX?"

"I wouldn't call him an 'informant.' He's a records clerk who had a crisis of conscience while we were there."

"Just coincidentally?" she said suspiciously.

"We may have encouraged him a bit."

She nodded in a way to compliment his resourcefulness. "What's his name?"

"Ah," Finn said, uncomfortable about sharing everything he knew. "I don't recall his name. I've got it back in my office."

"Okay, get everything to me right away. And besides you two and the clerk, who else?"

"That's it. Victor said the defendant was paranoid about publicity, so we kept it quiet."

"Okay, good. You leave that envelope and send me that clerk's contact info, and I'll shoot a message to Victor that we need to meet on this first thing."

Finn returned to his office without the documents, feeling taken. He was such a dope. He had spent three days poring over evidence and checking details. Wouldn't they need him to connect the dots? Could Ainsley cut him out of this?

Ted was waiting for him in the hallway.

"Morning, Junior," Finn said, trying to hide his disappointment.

"Morning, captain. What's the news?"

"Ainsley's got the documents, and I'll meet with Victor and her this morning."

"They going to make you a partner?"

Finn laughed humorlessly.

Finn suffered through a long morning. It was small comfort knowing he had the extra copies in his briefcase; he had not wanted to leave them lying around at home. He'd just hold on to those documents or find someplace secure to stash them.

Victor's secretary finally called and said to meet him in his office at eleven. The clock on his desk said ten. He dreaded another hour of waiting and couldn't sit still and so walked around the office making small talk. He ended up in the kitchen with yet another cup of coffee, pretending to read the *New York Law Journal*.

"You see the big boys are upping starting salaries again?" JT said, entering the kitchen to fill his New York Rangers mug.

"What," Finn said, distracted. "Oh, yeah. How come we don't get any of that?"

"Swing a job at Cravath or Skadden."

"Or Hune," Finn said and chuckled. There was a clear demarcation between the big firms, which paid top dollar to associates, and places like Bolger & Plotkin, where the senior partners did quite well but felt little need to share the wealth.

"Did you hear about Jimmy the Greek?" JT said.

"No. Was his Super Bowl prediction off?"

"No, not that. The guy knows football—though I don't really trust Vegas bookmakers. No, the news is he said something about how breeding practices during slavery made Blacks superior athletes, and CBS canned him."

"What an idiot."

"Yeah, I think he was also convicted of something back in the '60s. Still, he's done well for himself."

"Until now."

"Right, until now. It always catches up with you in the end, right?"

Talking with JT distracted Finn for a few minutes, but then he panicked, thinking he had forgotten the time. He looked at his wrist before remembering he had given away his Sanchi and should get his old Timex out of his drawer.

JT's eyes fell to Finn's wrist. "Good thinking not to wear your watch in the office."

"Actually, I don't have it anymore."

JT's eyebrows went up. "You didn't sell it, did you?"

"Gave it away," Finn said, taken aback at the suggestion he would sell a counterfeit. "I wasn't comfortable wearing it after all those others disappeared."

"Dude, you've got to have more confidence. No one's going to trace those things. That's a done deal, especially with the shitload of merchandise we got from the raid."

"Yeah," Finn said, shaking his head. "I get it, but still...."

JT looked smug. "What falls off the truck is salvage, me bucko."

Finn was not amused or comforted and said he had to go. He returned to his office for his notes and headed for Victor's office.

"Come in, Finnegan," Victor said. "Take a seat."

"Thanks for seeing me, Victor."

"You are the star of the moment; it is my pleasure to see you."

Finn smiled and nodded, not comfortable with Victor's unctuous tone.

"I am impressed," Victor went on, "with how you have turned things around. You appear to be ready for a more senior role."

"Well, thank you, Victor. I'm trying." Although it was great to hear praise from the boss, Finn was eager to get to the substance of the meeting and show his mastery of the evidence. "I assume," he went on, "that Ainsley gave you the short version of what else we found GlobalX?"

"Indeed. Though even the short version takes some time to digest. And we need to talk."

Finn waited. This wasn't going as he expected. And where was Ainsley? She said they would discuss the jet parts with Victor together. He was sure she had maneuvered herself into a starring role and so should be at this meeting.

"First," Victor began, "I want again to express my admiration for your work on the watch case. Helping the client uncover the goods going out the back door of its factory was especially important. And the documents you brought back give us all the leverage we need to drive a settlement."

"But why did you call off everything before we finished calculating damages?"

"Not necessary. GlobalX is so eager to settle, we just need to name a number."

"That's a new twist. What's our demand?"

"Not your worry, not now. What I really need to talk with you about is this other thing, this matter of jet parts."

Then there was a turn in Victor's tone from personal to serious. This was like any interview where one person has all the power to set the agenda, be it a police detective with a suspect or a despot surrounded by toadies. After he put you at ease, there was always this moment of setting aside the trivial for a man-to-man discussion.

Now they were getting to it. Finn sat up straight.

"You know, of course" Victor said, "that seizing those records exceeded the court order?"

"Sure, but..."

"And that could lead to having any case thrown out, as well as sanctions against the firm?"

"Yes, I know, but we're talking about a crime here; those bastards are killing people."

"Well, we don't know that for certain. And whether they do or not, or did or did not, it is beyond our prerogative to call it out. We had no right to look into this. And we have no authority to spend the client's money policing someone else's trademarks."

"But we didn't go looking for this, and it didn't cost Sanchi anything; Ted and I haven't billed for the extra time. And the

GlobalX employee volunteered it all. He's a whistle-blower. All we need to do is help him get to the authorities."

"You're not hearing me, Finnegan. The airplane shit is not our concern. And Henry Ingram is not our concern...."

Finn knew he had held back Henry's name from Ainsley, sensing the kid might need protecting. How had she identified him so quickly? Was his name going to get out now? Had Finn lost Henry his job?

"Point is," Victor went on, "we got what we were after, what the court order permitted us to pursue, and the airplane angle is just another reason why GlobalX will bend over for it. You know, of course, that Hune & Buchanan has come in for GlobalX; they assure me the company—like the vendors at the flea market—will sign a consent judgment and permanent injunction. Sam Eddings at Sanchi is overjoyed. That marketing moron, Frank Jones, will have his ceremony and run over a mound of counterfeits, and we will walk away with a success bonus and a solid client going forward. Since you are one of the heroes of this story, I'm making you our primary liaison with Sanchi."

Finn's mind swirled. Victor was congratulating him, even promoting him, but ignoring dead pilots. What was going on? "Don't you think," he said, "that exposing the traffic in bogus parts would be great publicity for the firm *and* give us entry to clients from the aircraft industry, the companies whose parts were copied?"

"Again, Finnegan, we were hired by Sanchi to destroy the counterfeit watch trade. Boeing and Lockheed Martin have to deal with their own problems—or hire *us*."

Victor's phone buzzed. "Yes," he said peremptorily. "Tell him I'll call back in five minutes. And cancel my lunch for today."

He hung up and looked closely at Finn. "You're at a crossroads, Finnegan. You've done good work and are due a reward. Now you need to keep moving forward. This is no time for distractions. We do our business, and we're damned good at it, and now you've reached a position where the game starts to come to you. The partners have their eyes on you."

"Yes, sir."

"I want you to help Jimmy on the sanctions motion in Nashville, since everything seems intertwined with the appearance of Hune & Buchanan. I'll keep you abreast of the GlobalX talks. As to that other thing, I've asked Ainsley to collect all the jet materials so we can be sure they are secure. I don't want you wasting any more time on that, and we'll need to make sure none of this gets out. Ainsley will talk with Ted to make sure he's on board, but I want you to see that he gets this message. All papers and all attorney notes are to be collected. Is there anyone else who knows about this?"

"That's about it," Finn said. Victor and Ainsley had already found Henry, so that really was everyone. Still, he was troubled Ainsley had gone around him to identify the GlobalX clerk. Finn saw that he'd better call Henry to warn him things could get hot.

Ainsley called out to Finn as he left Victor's office. "I just spoke with Ted," she said. "He's collecting any notes or other materials he has about the jet parts."

"Okay, good. You've got the essential materials in what I gave you. I'll check my office for backup documents and anything else."

"But one thing," she said, catching hold of his elbow and looking at him earnestly. "Ted seemed reluctant, almost belligerent, like he didn't want to give me the documents. It was out of character for him. I'm concerned he might have some hidden agenda."

"Oh, he's just conscientious. The whole connection to the military makes it personal for him."

She looked at him thoughtfully and said, "Okay, so look around and make sure nothing's left. We need to keep all these materials together."

Confused by her tone and what she clearly was *not* saying, he replied, "Yeah, sure."

"And talk with Ted. He needs a pep talk, a little help understanding the situation."

She walked off, leaving Finn uneasy. He understood Victor didn't want to proceed with the jet parts matter, and his reasoning made sense—at least from *his* perspective—but now Ainsley didn't trust him and Ted to toe the line. Finn had been at this job for five years and knew how this worked. And while Ted was new, he was a team player. So why was she concerned?

Still, Finn *had* copied the evidence in case of...what? Something seemed very wrong about this whole thing.

Finn knocked on Ted's door. The young lawyer was in his cramped office collecting papers.

"What the hell?" Ted said.

"My reaction, too."

"Are we just going to drop the whole thing?"

"Sounds like. I take it the Ice Queen told you to gather all the evidence?"

"She made that more than clear. She wants everything on her desk in half an hour."

"I got the same orders."

"And the copies you made? Didn't you take them home?"

"Yes; I mean no; I mean I did take home copies, but I brought the package back in with me. Listen, this is important. Those copies were never made. Got it? They never existed."

"Sure, boss. But what are you thinking?"

"I'm having trouble thinking right now. But I know we've got to preserve the evidence regardless of what Bolger & Plotkin does."

"I have to say I'm relieved to hear you say that. You know I'm on board all the way."

Finn left Ted's office wondering what he should do with the

copies. Carrying them in his briefcase was foolish, and leaving them at home also seemed risky, although there was zero chance anyone would find them at the loft. Could he ask Imani to file them away somewhere where no one would look, hide them in plain sight? No, this whole case was becoming a dumpster fire, and he would not involve her.

If his withholding evidence blew up in his face, he didn't want to take her down with him. And what about JT? He would certainly help Finn keep this stuff from Ainsley and Victor, but was it smart to share information about the jet parts after Victor said not to tell anyone?

"Hey, man," JT said, grabbing Finn as he walked back to his office. "Seems like some gnarly turmoil going on here. Can I give you a hand?"

"Ah, no. We just have to gather some GlobalX stuff for Ainsley."

"She taking credit again?"

"Hard to tell," Finn said, trying to fake a conspiratorial laugh but thinking her motivation was for once far from clear.

"Well, let me help."

"There's nothing to it. I just have to gather a few papers."

"You giving her everything she's asking for?"

It was out of character for JT to care what Finn gave Ainsley, or how to-the-letter he carried out her instructions. He normally would joke about her imperious attitude, how she expected everyone to jump at her command. Or, realistically, he'd be glad to be out of her crosshairs and would steer clear of the whole thing. But instead he was trying to insert himself into the matter. And Ainsley had told Finn to keep everything to himself. Was that meant to include JT? He was on the GlobalX raids and working the case, but he shouldn't know anything about the jet parts, not unless Ainsley or Victor told him.

"You know," Finn finally said with a grin, "there's no way to hold out on the Ice Queen." He returned to his office and gathered all the extra copies of documents and a few pages of notes on GlobalX. Once he had handed them over, he told his secretary he was going out to get lunch. He didn't want to raise suspicions by bringing his briefcase, so he folded the envelope with the evidence copies into a newspaper and carried that instead.

On the street he walked aimlessly for few blocks, wondering what to do with the copies. He unconsciously ended up at the post office.

He took the envelope from within the newspaper, set it on a table and opened it. Shuffling through the papers, he wondered if he had all the essential pieces of the puzzle. Henry had talked about some kind of smoking-gun memo about rebranding, and he realized he hadn't copied it because Henry had sent it to Ted. He assumed Ted turned that over these over to Ainsley, which was unfortunate, but at least Finn had the basic materials, and he needed to keep this set safe. In the postal system, no one would be able to get hold of these copies—at least until they reached the addressee.

But where to send it? G-pa wasn't around anymore, and he couldn't think of a friend who would understand the situation and help him and yet not be close enough to him to draw suspicion. It made no sense to send it to Satch or Petra since then the package would be delivered to Finn's building.

Then the late night after SOBs sprang into his head. In his mind's eye he saw Genevieve's building, the darkened windows of her fourth-floor apartment and the number thirty-eight on the door, which he remembered because of his family's crash on Route 38.

Could he mail the package to her? What would she think? He hardly even knew her. She'd have no idea what it was, but she also had no connection with him, so no one would suspect she had it. If he could just trust her—but of course he could trust her. He hadn't known her long, but with some people you knew from the start. If he just scribbled a note saying these documents were important and asking her to hold them and tell no one, she'd certainly do that. And it wouldn't be like he was putting her at any kind of risk. All she had to do was hold the envelope until he retrieved it.

She had some French last name he couldn't remember, and so he just addressed the envelope to "Genevieve." He knew the building was on East Seventh Street because it was on the same block as McSorley's, and he guessed the front fourth floor apartment would be 4A. A paperback guide told him the zip code.

He scribbled a note on the back of a post office handout about bulk mailing: "Genevieve: I'm sorry to impose like this, but it's really important. Please hold this package until I ask for it, and don't mention it to *anyone*. Thanks a million, Finn Alger."

Before he sealed the envelope, he pondered. This didn't mean he was going to turn these papers over to the police; he was only keeping his options open. It was insurance against something going wrong. And Genevieve? Well, she would never need know what this was about, or be mixed up in it at all. She was just an acquaintance who he was sure would help.

But thinking he needed to avoid scaring Genevieve, he tore up his first note and tried again. This time he wrote simply that the envelope held confidential legal documents, and he would explain later if she would please hold them for him.

When he handed the envelope to the clerk, who affixed postage, a weight lifted from his shoulders. He was confident now he could face whatever Victor and Ainsley were cooking up. Walking back to the office, he realized he was also hungry and so picked up a dish of chicken over rice from a halal cart. Carrying the food in would not only satisfy his hunger but also give him cover for why he had gone out.

At the office Ainsley again intercepted Finn, this time barely inside the front door.

"Sorry I missed you earlier," she said. "I was thinking we could get lunch."

This was only the second time in five years Ainsley had suggested eating a meal with Finn when they were not on the road together. He tried to mask his surprise, though, and simply said, "Sorry. Had some errands and so brought something in."

"Really? What kind of errands?"

Finn was getting spooked. Why was she all over him? He fumbled for an answer, cursing himself for not having a cover story ready and paranoid about lying. "Just picking up a prescription and stopping for a shoeshine."

He followed her gaze to his shoes, obviously some days away from a shine.

"Right, yeah," he laughed. "My guy was out today, so I decided to wait. Still, it was a nice day to get outside."

"Uh huh," she said and squinted at him suspiciously.

As he turned to go, she asked, "Have I got all the documents now from GlobalX?"

"I'm pretty sure you do. You have everything from my office, and I think Ted finished up from his end this morning."

"Okay, good. And you made sure Ted understands his orders?"

"Yeah, sure. You know him. Following orders is in his blood."

Now she definitely looked askance. Then she said, as if the thought had just occurred to her, "I really would like a chance to talk with you outside the office. I won't interfere with your lunch—which smells delicious, by the way—but how about dinner tonight...my treat? Things will be slow now for a while. We could get out of here early."

Finn's head went into a spin. For five years he would have stood on his head to go out to dinner with Ainsley, but now it felt like this was all about something else.

She seemed to sense his hesitation and said, "You've been

doing great work, especially on GlobalX, and I haven't really acknowledged your contribution. I've reached a position in the firm where I need to do more of that. Call this a small way to make it up to you. And I think I can get us into a fantastic spot—really exclusive; you'll love it, and we'll keep shop talk to a minimum."

"Okay, sure. Just let me know when you want to go."

Chapter Sixteen

Finn didn't know which way to turn. He thought he had triumphed in uncovering GlobalX's criminal enterprise, but Victor shot him down. Yet, Victor still made him the new point attorney for Sanchi. Except for uncovering the jet parts scheme Victor wanted to bury, he hadn't done anything exceptional to deserve this. Was his promotion a payoff to keep quiet?

And Ainsley! For years he had fantasized about breaking through to her but gradually reduced his goal to getting along with her at work. Then she started acting all nice, especially after G-pa died. And now she was taking him to dinner? Something duplicitous was going on; he was elated but suspicious. He didn't feel safe.

And there was his obligation to Henry at GlobalX. The kid had put his job at risk to do the right thing, and Finn had promised to protect him. He closed his door and called.

"GlobalX," a woman answered.

"May I speak with Henry Ingram in archives, please?"

"Mr. Ingram is unavailable," she said with no hesitation. "May I direct you to someone else?"

"No, that's okay," Finn said quickly. "Thanks."

He felt like kicking himself. Henry had cautioned him against calling the GlobalX number.

"Those fuckers," he said out loud as he pulled a slip of paper from his wallet with Henry's home number.

The phone rang but no one answered. Finn stared at the receiver in his hand. Something was wrong. Was Henry legitimately busy and couldn't come to the phone? But how would the receptionist know that without checking? More likely that bloated manager found out Henry was helping them and moved him to another job, or shut him off from outside calls. Finn couldn't believe Henry would suddenly decide to leave GlobalX on his own. Or did he?

Finn asked Ted to come into his office, and said, "Did you give Ainsley all the Global documents you had?"

"Of course. But, oh yeah, there's one thing...."

"What?"

"That Transfers folder: the one I told you was at home when I collected things for Ainsley...."

"Where is it?"

"I still have it."

"Well, look," Finn went on, "keep that someplace secure. I just tried to reach Henry to tell him to watch his back, but all I got was he was 'unavailable.' "

"What does that mean?"

"I don't know. He was clearly unhappy working for those dirtbags. But would he quit?"

"I doubt it, not Henry. And not this fast. What do you think happened?"

"All I can imagine is they discovered he turned over the records and kicked him out. I can't see him just getting fed up and leaving."

"So what do we do?" Ted's expression said he was distressed and looking for guidance. That was only right, since Finn was the senior lawyer and had given the orders that got them into this mess. Finn owed responsibility to this kid.

"Hold tight," Finn said. "I mailed off the copy of the evidence, so it's safe for now. And I'm going to meet with Ainsley later. I know she'd do anything to get ahead, but she can't go along with Victor in covering this up. Maybe I can get her to talk to him. And we should both keep trying to reach Henry at home."

"All right," Ted said. "You're the boss. But we can't let this go; I'm just saying. There's no way we can let GlobalX mess up F-15s and not do something about it. It's sabotage...treason even."

"We'll straighten this out. Don't worry. I'm sure Ainsley will help."

Soon after Ted left Finn's office, Ainsley appeared. She had changed into a dress too short and too tight in all the right places to be appropriate for work. She stood in his doorway, coat draped across her arm.

"Are you ready to go?" she said.

"Um, yeah," he managed to get out, a little dazzled by her outfit. "Give me two minutes."

He started to gather his things and then decided he didn't need his briefcase and just put on his suit jacket and grabbed his coat.

From the moment they left the office, Finn was swept up in a swirl of emotions. The GlobalX case was foremost in his mind. Ted was right; they had to expose this fraud. But it was hard to think about that when Ainsley had transformed from a humorless, overbearing boss into an alluring woman who took his breath away. He could make no sense of any of this.

"Thank you, sir," she said with a playful smile when he held the taxi door open for her, implying with that "sir" something completely different from what Ted meant by it.

Once they were headed across town, she said out of nowhere, "You grew up in the Midwest?"

"Chicago, and then Missouri."

"There's something solid about people from the middle of the country, don't you think? A sincerity you can count on."

"Oh, I don't know."

"No, really, Finn. I sense that in you. You're the kind of guy who would stand by a friend or help an old lady cross the street."

"Well, you're certainly not old, but I'd be happy to escort you across the avenue."

Her sly smile sliced through him like an electrical charge.

"So where are we going?" he asked.

"Oh, this will be a treat. I managed to pull some strings and get us a table at Rao's."

"I thought you had to inherit a reservation to eat at that place."

"Well, you do...normally. But a friend loaned us his table for the night. That's why we need to go early."

Finn had heard of this restaurant, up against the FDR in Spanish Harlem, but had never seen it. When the cab dropped them off, he was surprised at the fire-engine-red exterior, and that there were only ten tables, each with a white tablecloth. The walls were crowded with framed photographs of celebrity patrons. Leftover Christmas decorations framed the fireplace and a small bar.

Ainsley and Finn ordered drinks at the bar but were quickly shown to a corner table. Seeing his left arm would be bumping up against her right arm, Finn asked to reverse their seats. The host grasped Finn's gesture of holding up his left hand and deftly rearranged the couple.

In this room, sitting close enough to the new incarnation of Ainsley that her scent wafted through the tempting aromas all around, Finn felt like one of the stars in the photographs. But he hardly had time to take it all in before a waiter in a zebra print vest and bow tie was asking for their order. The waiter looked first to Ainsley. When it was Finn's turn, the waiter interrupted him in a tone of authority. "Those will not really go together. Why not try the veal *francese* with a vintage Chianti Riserva?"

Finn accepted the waiter's suggestion; he was happy to go along with anything. And the food and wine were excellent.

Throughout the meal, Ainsley joked and laughed as if this were the most natural of settings. She seemed so unlike the rigid, relentless litigator he saw day to day. Even her voice took on a throaty, timbre that swept him up. With her luxuriant blond hair loose upon her shoulders and a sultry look in her eyes, it felt like he had never really seen her before. When dessert came with more wine, his head swam in Mediterranean waters, and he wished he would never wake up.

A privileged table at Rao's did not entitle them to linger into the next seating, and they soon found themselves in another cab.

"They can be a little abrupt when they want the table back," she said as they headed downtown. "But it's still early. Why don't we stop at my place for a drink?"

He could not have imagined a better idea. And when the cab pulled up at an Upper East Side apartment building where a uniformed doorman opened the door for them, the dream continued.

Ainsley's apartment was modest, if you could call a spacious, modern one-bedroom with oil paintings on the walls and a balcony view from the thirtieth floor "modest." Finn had to stifle a laugh at how she would react to his loft, full of severely downtown roommates and wildlife prowling the corners.

She handed him a snifter of cognac and took a seat beside him on the sofa. "You know, I thought it was unfair how Victor lit into you about the flea market. We've all made the same mistake, and this is the first defendant I ever heard of actually pulling a gun."

This work talk jarred him back to a reality he had almost put out of his mind.

She continued. "And the mix-up with the papers was really Ted's fault, regardless of how new he is. You were more than honorable in taking the blame for that."

"Well, I should have checked his work."

"Maybe so, but it only mattered because of that wimp at Sanchi."

"Sam Eddings," Finn said with a sneer. "But I agree, Victor could have been a bit more chill about it all."

Her lips turned into a smile, but her face went hard. "Victor has not made Bolger & Plotkin successful by being nice. In fact, he can be a real bastard at times."

This turn in the conversation took Finn by surprise. He had always seen Ainsley as in lockstep with the boss, but there was a real edge to her comment. He couldn't help saying, "I always thought you...."

"I what?

"Well, Victor's your rabbi, right? I mean he's everyone's boss, of course, but he's obviously your main supporter."

She sipped her drink and looked away, tight-lipped, before turning back to him. "Things are not that simple, Finn. Just because Victor is my ticket to partnership does not mean I agree with everything he does, or has done, or what he thinks about things."

Finn wished he understood what she was saying; this was so unlike anything he'd heard before. Maybe it was her tone or maybe it was the liquor talking, but he sensed her vexation had nothing to do with Nashville or the mix-up about the declaration. Could she have some other annoyance with Victor that might pull her over to his side?

"It sounds like you've got a beef with Victor," he said cautiously.

She flinched but quickly recovered. "We don't need to go into that; leave it as we have our personal issues. What's important now is Ted. Do you think he has the makings of a good lawyer? Can we trust him?"

"Oh, yeah. He's a great kid. Works hard, takes direction well."

"*That* might be the most important point."

"What? Taking orders?"

"Exactly. Especially when we find ourselves dealing with a company willing to go to any lengths to protect itself. Going along on things he lacks the experience to understand could save Ted a lot of grief."

It took no genius to understand Ainsley was talking about the jet parts. She wanted Finn's assurance Ted would fall in line and follow Victor's orders. But Finn feared Ted would never agree to bury the matter, which was not what Ainsley wanted to hear, so talking about it could derail their evening. Finn wanted to get back to the elaborate seduction.

He laughed to try to lighten things. "Like I said, he's a great kid. I'm sure he'll do what he's told and focus on the work."

She paused, looking closely at him. "He will he keep quiet, then, about GlobalX?"

Well, that put it all on the table. Struggle as he might, Finn saw no way to avoid answering a direct question. He had hoped he might sway Ainsley to the view he shared with Ted, that this fraud was too important to let go. But this was sounding more and more like Ainsley pushing the party line and demanding his cooperation. A sudden realization that it was probably Victor who arranged the table at Rao's drained all the sensual energy from the room.

"I...just don't know," he said. "The kid has strong feelings about military pilots. And he's not like us, well into our careers and aware things like this have consequences."

"That's troubling," she said and went quiet.

Finn cursed himself for painting Ted as an intractable problem. But the kid was right, and Finn had to make her understand.

"Look," he said, "Ted is not wrong about this. GlobalX is rotten; they sold defective parts and people died. And this is probably still going on. How can we let them off the hook just to settle a case?"

Ainsley's seductive look turned almost threatening. "But we represent Sanchi, not the aerospace industry, and this is a total win for our client, and us, and you...and Ted. I understand Victor put you in charge of the client, which jumps you past Jimmy, in case you didn't notice."

"I get that, and appreciate the opportunity—though I hate to think it comes at JT's expense—but it's more important that people have died, and it may have been Global's fault. Who else will be hurt if we don't follow up?"

"We all feel bad about plane crashes, Finn, of course." Her expression relaxed as she reached for the bottle to top off his glass. "But look, we have no way of knowing if Global's parts caused accidents. That's all speculation on our part. Yes, they may have put false marking on goods, and that's where we normally come in, where we fill an important role—*for our clients*. But we're not the worldwide trademark enforcers, and we are not the FAA. We don't stumble across a counterfeit and pursue it on our own; that's for the trademark owners to do, or for them to hire us to do *for* them. Imagine if we stopped to prosecute every bogus mark we saw. We'd never make it down the street."

"I hear you, and in most any other situation I'd agree. I'm not looking to make the world secure for brands. But how do you get past dead pilots? And how do we expect Ted to accept this? You know his brother died when his fighter went down, and Ted is convinced it was a mechanical issue."

"I..." she said and paused. "I knew about the military connection, of course, but not about his brother. That's awful."

"Even beyond Ted's brother, there's a clear right and wrong here. Don't you see that?"

She became quiet and sipped her drink. He watched her, wondering if he was getting through. It felt like too much to remind her about the jeans case where she had supposedly skirted ethics to win a case, since he didn't really know the facts. But maybe hearing about their young associate's sense of justice would lead her to reconsider. Besides, Ted going public after Bolger & Plotkin tried to bury this would prove disastrous for everyone.

She resumed. "We still have to think about ourselves. In copying those materials, you overstepped the seizure order. That could land you, and us, in big trouble. And convincing a file clerk to assist you may be grounds for Global to allege you induced a breach of contract and violated its privacy. But now I understand what you're saying about Ted, and we'll have to find a way to convince him. The important thing is to keep this in house until we come up with a path forward that will satisfy him—and you—and Victor, of course—and make us all comfortable with our roles. For now," her smile became slightly flirtatious, "let's forget about work and not let GlobalX ruin the evening."

It did not seem they had settled anything. There was no solution to assuaging Ted's furor or, for that matter, Finn's reluctance to overlook GlobalX's crime. But as he took another sip of cognac, Finn became more absorbed with whether Ainsley was trying to seduce him. If so, he was more than willing to go along, work issues be damned. This could be the culmination of years of fantasy.

She took his snifter from his hand and placed it on the coffee table. His breath shortened as she took his hand.

"I want to show you something," she said and rose and pulled him to his feet.

He thought she was leading him to her bedroom, but instead she pulled open the sliding door to the balcony. He followed her outside. On the narrow overhang, a stiff wind blew her hair out behind her. She looked like the heroine of a Manhattan film from the forties.

"You see this?" she said, waving an arm at the thousands of buildings lighted against the night.

"Yeah. Great view," he said, thinking the next view he'd like to see was from her bedroom.

"Do you know how this was all built, what makes it work?"

"I'm thinking you're going to tell me," he said, wondering if the seduction scene had turned into something else.

"Riding the current. Rising to the top without getting washed aside."

"What does that mean?"

"It means, Finnegan, that the world is here for the taking, but you need to play ball."

She left him to take in the view from the balcony alone and went to the kitchen. When he came back into the apartment, the atmosphere had changed. She handed him a glass of sparkling water. "Just to put this whole thing to rest," she said, "you *are* going to keep the jet parts matter quiet, correct?"

"It would be much simpler, for sure. But I don't know. I feel like I have to try Victor once more. And Ted—I don't know what to do about him."

She took in a hissing breath. "Well, convincing Victor would change everything. I wish you luck with that, I really do, but don't get your hopes up. There's something behind this rush to settle, and I don't know what it is. But I'm pretty sure he has made up his mind, and he's calling the shots. And as to Ted, well, he's going to have to fall in line too if he hopes to keep his job."

The switch from cognac to sparkling water mirrored the altered mood. Where Finn wanted to get to know Ainsley in a more corporeal way, he suddenly sensed it was time to leave. She handed him his coat with a look that said they both knew all along Finn would not be staying; the point of the evening being instead to simply confirm their understanding.

Finn cabbed home to a dark loft. Everyone was asleep—although Mandy might not be home yet. He poured a glass of milk and sat at the kitchen table digesting the past eight hours. How was it possible he had just spent the evening eating and drinking with Ainsley? He guessed this date would not be repeated. If she was interested, her time to act just passed. Or was it possible she genuinely liked him but wanted to take things slowly? What would that even look like, he and Ainsley together? No, that was never going to happen. She took him to dinner because Victor told her to nail down his cooperation. There was no more to it than that. The Ice Queen was still way out of his league and playing a game he hardly understood.

But the evening had given him a peek beneath Ainsley's veneer. She did have a conscience and was not entirely comfortable with Victor's hard line about GlobalX. And she had some kind of grievance with Victor he had not sensed before. What could that be about? He always saw Victor as her mentor, who brought her up through the ranks and relied on her. According to JT's story, that all started when she went along with him on the jeans case, and she had made the most of it and never looked back. But she still needed Victor. Could their "personal issues" nonetheless shake her loyalty to him?

More importantly, what was he going to do when he got back to the office? He would risk losing his job if he pushed the jet thing too hard, but if he didn't, he'd have to live with letting GlobalX get away with murder. And even if he listened to Victor, how could he get Ted to keep quiet?

G-pa would be ready with an aphorism. Finn had no hesitation as a teenager rationalizing stealing the cost of a Thanksgiving turkey as just getting what he deserved, what the wrong-handed world owed him. But when it all blew up in his face, G-pa quoted Kant about how we should act in a way that might safely be made a law for the whole world.

At seventeen Finn had pushed back, blaming his hard life in a backwards world. "Conflict," G-pa responded, "is the underlying nature of being. And the first and best of all victories is the victory over oneself, as being defeated by oneself is the worst and most shameful of defeats."

Finn could never win an argument with G-pa. But now he faced off only against himself. There was a right and a wrong here, and his grievances against the world were not relevant to the decision he had to make. Could he justify hiding the truth? Did the magnitude of harm undercut a lifetime of justifying his wants as overdue payment? He had no personal hold on justice. The world owed him nothing, and yet he had made one withdrawal after another from its natural balance as if he could mold morality to fit his childish sense of entitlement.

He was trapped in a roundabout with exits shooting off toward differing measures of sanctity or ignominy. It was too late to go back to prior turns, where the consequences of choices all seemed innocuous. His path had led him here, and now he had to choose.

Chapter Seventeen

Finn's headache Saturday morning might have resulted from too much cognac at Ainsley's apartment, but the throbbing felt more like a reflection of the confusion roiling his mind. He rolled over and went back to sleep.

Lights flashed, brakes screeched and the night exploded. He was closed in, crushed. Then he lay face up on the highway, snowflakes falling on his face, and again he awoke with a start.

He wouldn't let himself drift off again. Better a headache and his quandary with Ainsley and Victor than a return to that too-familiar nightmare.

In the course of one day, he had presented his evidence to Victor in triumph, been shot down, and been promoted, feted, fed, seduced and sent packing, leaving him no closer to making a choice between self-preservation and justice.

He looked up at an old blood stain on the ceiling from a mosquito he had killed one hot summer night. Everything was sucking the blood from him these days. But at least life and death made sense.

After a cup of coffee, he suited up against the cold and went for a run. The sun was shining and, after a mile along the East River, he warmed up enough to lose himself in the rhythm of the steps and music from his CD player. In the afternoon he watched a rerun of the Knicks' win over the Trail Blazers. He guessed JT must have bet on the game, as he seemed to be doing more and more. Finn wondered how he made out. It was sad he no longer felt close to his colleague, one of his few real friends in the city.

The television at the loft was set up on the stage, at the end of the dance floor opposite Petra's easels. As he watched the game, Finn glanced over at her, hard at her painting. He was impressed, as always, with how she lost herself in her art. At halftime he walked over to see what she was working on.

"I see you're back on the elbow," he said, "with, what is that, a compass?"

"Yes, the elbow enables movement and so symbolizes adaptability and flexibility in your spiritual journey. The same way the joint permits your arm to move in various directions, a compass leads you to the ever-changing currents of life."

Finn smiled, thinking how symbolism in art went right over his head.

"It's correlative," she went on, scratching her head with the back of a paint brush, "but I think it lacks drama."

"I should buy it and hang it my room. My life has entirely too much drama."

"You mean working on Satch's play? I thought it was a comedy."

"It is, and that's not what I meant. That farce is probably the most intelligible part of my life right now—although tomorrow will be the first time I actually help with a performance."

"What do you mean?" She put down her brush and tilted her head.

"I'll be working backstage."

"That's not what I'm asking, dumbo. What's so crazy about your life?"

"Ah, Petra, I'm not gonna unload my problems on you, but I appreciate your concern."

"Maybe it would help to talk about it."

He shook his head. "Talking won't solve anything. But hey," he said, purposefully putting on a smile, "don't let me darken your day. You've got art to do."

She glanced at her elbow painting and back at Finn, squinting as if trying to determine if he was poking fun. Apparently convinced he was not, she shrugged and turned back to her work.

On Sunday Finn was glad to be able to go to the theater with Satch. He needed to do something social, where people worked toward a common goal that had nothing to do with law or crime—although that was funny given the play was based on *Crime and Punishment*.

He found himself caught up in the electric atmosphere. Everyone was busy setting up for the first performance before an audience, although this was still a dress rehearsal, and the house would be filled mostly through the club's invitation to a social desk at the United Nations. Instead of members and their guests, the seats would largely be filled with staffers and their families from around the world. The ushers at the door would not check off the name of the member who had invited each guest, as usual, but instead the country the guest represented. While any ordinary theater troupe might think of this audience as important, the crew of *Crime* saw them as merely strangers helpful as a sounding board. The real test would come when they performed before the other members.

There was so much to do. He helped Derk again move a heavy light bolted to the ceiling, following an actress's meltdown about speaking her most impactful lines "in the dark." Then he vacuumed the rug on stage and helped put down extra chairs for the full house expected that night. Finally, he joined Satch behind the canvas flats, where a young man sat at a sound board and an older man with thinning hair barked instructions through a headset.

The man with the headset turned to them, looking for an explanation.

"Finn," Satch said, "this is Brad. He's our stage manager and a grizzled veteran of the footlights. Brad, this is my roommate, Finnegan. He signed on as your grip."

"Great," Brad said. "And none too soon. We definitely need your help."

A woman interrupted. She held up two vases, confused about which should be on stage. Brad instructed her and then turned back to Finn. "I need a few minutes, and then I'll show you what to do. Why don't you pop upstairs for a cup of coffee."

"Sure," Finn said, thinking the way Brad was buzzing suggested he might be a little over-caffeinated himself. He went up to the kitchen, hoping to find Genevieve.

"Oh, hi," she said when he found her in the Green Room. "I'm so glad you came. You'll see; it's really fun."

She was in her big, frumpy costume and theatrical makeup, so he was not too distracted while he said what he needed to tell her.

"I took a big liberty," he said, "and I hope you won't mind."

She paused with a coffee cup halfway to her mouth and tilted her head in question.

"There's a case at work —I think I told you—that might be really serious and involves sensitive documents."

"Yeah," she said, her interest piquing.

"Well, I need to preserve a copy of these documents. So I mailed an envelope off...to *your* address."

"*My* address?" she said, her usual smile turning to concern.

"I know it sounds crazy."

"And pretty random."

"Right," he said and grimaced. "You see, there's been some trouble about this case, and things have gotten weird. I didn't know if the documents would be safe at my apartment. I went to the post office to put the package in the mail, but I needed someplace to send it...."

"And you chose *my* apartment?" she said, now beginning to sound disconcerted.

"Well, I remembered your address from that night Satch and I walked you home. The number, thirty-eight, well, it means something related to my family, so it stuck in my head. And you told us you were on the fourth floor. Whether it made sense or not, I mailed it to you at Apartment 4A."

"It's 4F, actually," she said somberly.

"Yeah, and I didn't remember your last name either, so it's just addressed to 'Genevieve.' I hope it gets to you."

"It should. The mailman and I are pretty tight. Though I still don't get choosing me. Don't you have lawyer friends who would help?"

Finn had made a mistake. Genevieve was clearly confused, and who could blame her, being dragged into something she didn't understand and he wouldn't explain? But there was no way to call the letter back; he just had to try to ease her apprehension. "It probably won't arrive until Tuesday or Wednesday," he said. "And look, I'm sorry about this. When I realized I couldn't send the package home, I had nowhere to turn, and then your building popped into my head. I figured no one from work would be aware we know each other. You don't have to do anything; just hold the letter."

"Well," she said, her misgiving seeming to ease. "I haven't received anything yet. If do, I'll bring it to the theater."

"No, just hold it, please, I mean, if you don't mind. Again, I'm really sorry. If you could just put it aside, I'll pick it up, and that'll be the end of it."

Her curiosity seemed to edge aside her befuddlement. "What will you do with it?"

"That's up in the air. Maybe nothing. I just sent it when I wasn't sure what I would do."

"Well, okay," she said hesitantly, still looking perplexed. "Give me your number, and I'll call when I get it. Now I need to see Sylvia about my costume, and I assume you have work to do."

"Right. I have to get a grip on something."

She nodded, turning her attention back to the performance about to begin, and left the room.

Just then Brad came into the room and ran Finn through his duties. At five minutes to "places," everything was finally set. He only needed to open the curtain when Brad gave the signal and then stand by. Just before intermission, he would go upstairs and, on a cue in the script, sprinkle artificial snow through a trap door. "The play is set in Russia, after all," Brad said. During intermission he would sweep up the snow while the audience was upstairs drinking coffee, and then set the stage for act two. A half-hour after opening the curtain for the second act, he would have to use a large fan offstage to blow off Raskolnikov's hat in a storm scene.

"Will that actually work?" Finn asked, nervous he'd do it wrong and ruin the scene.

"Not to worry," Brad told him. "This is only a dress rehearsal, and the actor knows to lose the hat himself if the wind doesn't do the trick."

Finn wished he had had a dress rehearsal before his failed scene with Victor, but he had been so sure his boss would applaud him for uncovering the GlobalX plot, and turn the whole litigation effort to taking this company down. GlobalX deserved the condemned fate of Raskolnikov in the book, not the musical sendoff he got in the club's farce, where justice had to bow to larger concerns.

Even though the audience would never see him, he felt stage fright until the curtain went up. Then everything started to fall into place, and he drew confidence from the people around him. It felt like when everyone at the firm pulled together on a case, part of why he enjoyed working on a litigation team. With nothing to do twenty minutes before he had to make it snow, he stood with Sylvia, trying to stay out of the way.

Genevieve came down the back stairs and entered the stage from near where Finn stood. But he stepped back, thinking he should give her space. She wouldn't have noticed him, anyway. Like the other actors, she was detached, as if she were no longer of this world.

As the play went on, he also felt transported, consumed with creating a spectacle for the audience. Genevieve was right; he enjoyed this.

There was a tense moment in the second act when it came time to blow off Raskolnikov's hat. Brad had cautioned him it would take a couple of beats for the fan to power up and the noise had to be masked by the sound of thunder and wind, so it was important to be precisely on cue. Also, everything depended on the actor standing on his mark and Finn hitting the hat and not the large mural backdrop.

Finn's hands sweated as he waited. Brad finally waved Raskolnikov on as he started the storm noise. Finn saw the actor rush to his mark as he cranked up the fan.

To his relief, the hat *did* blow off. As scripted, Raskolnikov grabbed to catch it ineffectually, and the crowd cried out in laughter with a splattering of applause.

"Can't beat slapstick," was Sylvia's snide aside, but Brad gave Finn a thumbs-up with a grateful smile.

Finn felt like he had actually contributed something to the show. And best of all, his concentration on the performance transported him from his troubles; it made him think he might be happier if he just did what Victor told him to do. It was *his* firm, and he was right that Finn was paid to take orders and represent the firm's clients, not prosecute crimes. Finn would make one more attempt on Monday to convince him they should hand the matter over to the authorities, but then he would go along with whatever the boss wanted to do.

When Finn returned home to the loft, he found a message from Petra taped to his door: "Victor Bolger's secretary Alice. Meet Jimmy Henderson tomorrow at 8. You have a ticket on the 11AM flight to Nashville for a hearing."

Finn knew the hearing on the sanctions motion was the next day, but he didn't expect to appear to argue the motion. He had helped draft the opposition, as the new lead lawyer for Sanchi, but JT was still handling the flea market case. Why did Victor ask *him* to handle the hearing?

He suspected Big Niccolò was trying to distract him from the jet parts or maybe punishing him for wasting time on issues that didn't involve the firm's clients. In any event he had no choice. If the boss sent him to Nashville, he had to go, even if it meant putting off the parts matter for another day.

It was late but Finn called Ted to make sure he wouldn't panic and precipitate something while Finn was out of town.

"What does this mean for GlobalX?" Ted said, plainly impatient.

"It's just one day. I need to talk to Victor again. He might still listen to reason."

Ted replied, uncharacteristically, "He damned well better."

Chapter Eighteen

"**W**hy is Hune & Buchanan pushing this sanctions motion if it intends to settle the flea market cases *and* the case against GlobalX?" Finn complained. He sat in the large conference room sipping coffee as JT brought him up to speed on the hearing scheduled for that afternoon in Nashville.

"Who the hell knows why those guys do *anything*," JT responded, "other than make our lives difficult?"

"And why," Finn asked, "is Victor sending *me* to this charade instead of *you*? You filed the case. You've made all the court appearances."

"Strange as it may seem," JT said sarcastically, "Big Niccolò did not share his reasoning with me."

The receptionist buzzed and said, "Raymond Bagatoni is here. Says he has something to drop off."

They looked at each other. "More exhibits for Orchard Street?" JT said.

"Counselors," Ray said as he entered the room, placing a litigation bag on the table and shaking their hands.

"Did we have a meeting?" Finn asked.

"No," Ray replied. "This is strictly social." He opened the flap on the bag, while Finn and JT exchanged amused smiles.

"Merry Christmas," he said, handing each of them a foot-high, black bird statue.

"The Maltese Falcon?" Finn said.

"Bingo," Ray said and handed each a videocassette of the movie of the same name.

"Bootleg, of course," JT said.

"Nabbed at a factory in Jersey," Ray said with a smug smile. "We cleaned them out last week."

Ray was never one for legal niceties. On the way to the first raid Finn worked with him, he had commandeered a cab from a tourist couple by flashing some kind of badge—which went back into his wallet before they could examine it—implying, without saying, that they were on police business. They all knew Ray used strong-arm tactics and sketchy friends to gather information. So it was not surprising he gifted them the fruits of a raid conducted by another law firm.

This brought Finn back to his philosophy of law. What exactly was "justice," and who got to decide? He smiled, picturing Ray as the model for legal realism, where the law is inseparable from the discretion of judges—or in this case Mr. Justice Bag-a-Donuts. He had to claw with his left hand up through the mean streets of Brooklyn, so he was entitled to anything not nailed down. It made Finn a little sick to see how the philosophy Finn had often used to justify his retribution against the wrong-handed world put him in the company of Ray Bagatoni.

"I already gave Victor and Ainsley their gifts," Ray said, "but wanted to catch you guys so I don't have to lug these statues around. Oh, and Finn..."

"Yeah, Ray."

"Victor said you're going to Nashville today."

"That's right." Finn wondered why Victor would share this information with Ray. "Just a stupid sanctions motion."

"Well listen, could you do me a solid and deliver a statue for me?"

"What do you mean?"

"I got a client there, and I don't want to ship it."

"And you want me...?"

"You don't have to go out of your way. Just carry it on your flight. A guy will meet you at the airport. Bada-bing, bada-boom; that's it."

This was odd, even for Ray. Finn picked up one of the falcons on the table. "It's one of these?"

"Yeah, they're all the same, but I boxed his up to travel."

He placed a wooden box on the table.

"I guess," Finn said reluctantly.

Deplaning in Nashville after a long nap, Finn spotted a man in a leather jacket holding a handwritten sign bearing his name.

"That's me," he said to the man, who had the slick, slightly asocial look of one of Ray's friends. "Are you here for the package?"

"That's right," the man said, reaching for the box in Finn's hands. "And the boss said I should carry y'all wherever you want to go. Any other bags?"

"No, this is it."

"Okay, good. I'm Ed. The car's just outside."

The two men made their way to a parking lot where Finn was surprised to find Ed drove a private car rather than some sort of livery vehicle. But nothing about Ray's associates should have surprised him.

"So," Ed said, "Any holdup with the package?"

"Hold up?" Finn said, thinking this a strange choice of words. "Why should there be?"

"You carried it on board. Anyone ask what was in the box?"

"No one seemed to notice. I can just imagine telling them it was a falcon. But no, there was no problem with security, even though it's pretty heavy."

"No problem; that's good," Ed said with satisfaction, "we heard you was a professional."

Finn smiled. "Right, a professional delivery man."

Ed put an unlit, half-smoked cigar in his mouth and removed it again to say, "The boss man will be very happy."

"Who *is* the boss?"

"Mr. Arkadin; thought you knew that. He said to tell you he appreciates you making the delivery."

"Like I said, no one even noticed. But it was so heavy I pushed it under the seat instead of putting it in the overhead."

"Right. Smart."

Finn paused, wondering at this odd conversation. "And you work for Mr. Arkadin?"

"You might say that," Ed said, unnecessarily inscrutable. "I do odd jobs when he needs me."

Finn laughed, adding to himself, "Like when he needs someone to pick up a Maltese Falcon." Then he asked out loud, "What business does Mr. Arkadin do?" He had really lost interest in Ed and his employer. He was just making conversation to put off the pre-hearing jitters he always felt.

As expected, the hearing was a non-event. Before the judge appeared, an impeccably dressed gentlemen introduced himself and his young associate to Finn as the Hune & Buchanan lawyers for Luxe Watches. He suggested Finn agree to adjourn the hearing in anticipation of his firm withdrawing the motion—if the main cases against the flea market defendants and GlobalX could be resolved.

"No sense bringing up unpleasant allegations of professional misfeasance," the attorney said, leaning into an unctuous Southern accent. Finn wondered if he always talked that way or if he was trying to make the point that they were on his home turf—he played golf with the judge and attended the same church. The judge only had to agree with his good buddy to hear the baseless motion in order to make Finn waste a day coming down from New York when he really needed to be in the office.

"No sense," Finn agreed, disgusted at the waste of time and expense Hune & Buchanan had cost everyone.

The case was called, and the Hune lawyer advised the judge the parties anticipated resolving the motion by agreement. Finn quickly found himself back in a cab to the airport, hoping to catch an early flight home. The way this trip had gone—with no real reason for Finn to appear—confirmed his suspicion that Victor just wanted him out of the office while he resolved the GlobalX case.

Chapter Nineteen

Finn got into the office late the next morning, tired out from his pointless trip to Nashville. When he opened his office door he froze.

An envelope sat squarely on his desk. This was not normal. He kept his door locked; his secretary never entered with his mail until after he arrived.

And his visitor did more than leave an envelope. Papers he had worked on Friday were not where he left them. A file drawer was slightly open, the one he *always* closed, having once ripped his pants on the edge.

Someone searched the room and they must have been looking for GlobalX materials. Why else? This kind of thing didn't happen at a law firm!

He turned to the envelope. Inside was notice his annual bonus had been deposited in the bank, for *twice* what he expected. In any other circumstance he would have done a rebel yell. Now he was unsettled. This was payment for his silence.

But why didn't Victor trust him? Finn hadn't squawked when Ainsley collected the documents. Despite how unprecedented that was, Finn had cooperated and so had Ted. Pushing the firm to pursue the case didn't mean they would disregard Victor's orders. He was king; he dictated the bonuses; he made and broke careers.

He didn't need to check to know his orders were followed. So why had he followed up this time, by freaking breaking into his office? Why was he so convinced Finn was holding out on him?

Finn, of course, *was* holding out—though he called it preserving evidence. Maybe that meant Victor was smart to suspect him, smarter than Finn. It wouldn't be the first time. Still, there was nothing to find in Finn's office, so hopefully the search got him off the boss's radar. As to who conducted the search, it wouldn't be Victor; he'd send someone. Clearly it wasn't Ainsley; she was too polished for that. There was the new legal assistant who had been kissing up to everyone, but would Victor trust a new kid with a dicey job like that?

While he waited for Victor to see him, Finn tried again to reach Henry Ingram at home. There was still no answer. He called the phone company but was told there was nothing wrong with the line.

Feeling too anxious to sit at his desk, he went to the kitchen for a cup of coffee and then stopped by Ted's office. He was not in, which was surprising given how energized the kid was to move this matter forward. But maybe this was good; Ted wouldn't be shaking things up while Finn tried to reason with Victor.

As he turned back toward his own office, he ran into JT.

"How did it go?" JT asked.

"Like you expected. They said they'd withdraw if we settle the two cases, so we adjourned."

"Well, at least you got to enjoy an afternoon of sunshine and Southern belles."

Finn nodded and sighed. "So what were you working on?"

"Ah," JT said slowly, as if buying time to come up with an answer. "Just same old same old. The consent judgment, and..." He looked both ways in the empty hallway and lowered his voice, "Big Niccolò asked about the inventory from the Nashville raid, you know, the missing watches."

Finn gulped, feeling the weight of the fake Sanchi on his wrist as if he still wore it. For a moment, he pictured the Rasta from Times Square flashing the watch as he channeled Bob Marley.

"Do you still have the one you took?" Finn said.

"No, I dumped that," JT said and paused. "You got rid of yours, too, right?"

Finn looked him in the eye. JT knew Finn had given his watch away. And his friend's conspiratorial tone was offensive. Finn had only taken that throwaway watch at his goading. Now he was acting like they were partners in a heist gone bad.

"You know," Finn said, refusing to join the conspiracy fantasy, "I don't know, really, *what* you're talking about. Is this concerning the box of watches that went missing—and are probably back in the market by now?"

JT looked disgusted, shook his head and walked down the hall. Finn gave him a moment and went to his own office, closing the door behind him. He thought again about the watch he had taken and given away. Why had he stolen it to begin with? He had to admit he enjoyed wearing it; it got noticed. But how had he convinced himself he was some hotshot man about town just because he wore a replica of an expensive watch? As he rubbed his wrist, missing the weight of the knockoff, his perplexity turned to anger at JT for getting him into that mess.

Then he called Ted's home number—just to make sure he would keep quiet for the time being. There was no answer.

At nearly eleven o'clock, Victor passed reception and Finn's open door with his usual bluster. Finn put on his suit jacket, took a deep breath and followed to Victor's office.

"Good morning, Mr. Alger," Victor's secretary said, the familiar sour expression on her face.

"Morning, Alice. I need to see Victor."

"I'll check," she said, as if this was a bother. "If you'll just take..."

"Send him in," Victor called through the open door.

Finn entered and closed the door behind him.

"All right now, what's the emergency?" Victor asked without preamble.

Finn girded himself. This would not be pleasant. He had to be forceful enough to convince the boss without closing off a possible compromise. He wanted to do right, but he did not want to find himself out on the street without a job.

"Victor," he said, "we need to talk."

"We're talking. So talk."

"We have to turn over what we know about GlobalX."

As soon as he said this he knew he had gone too far. He should have appealed to Victor's sense of justice, not told him what to do. He wished he had one of G-pa's axioms to make his point in a way inoffensive and irrefutable. But Victor's reddened face made clear Finn had stuck his foot in it.

"I get a little tired," Victor said, "of people—particularly people I pay substantial salaries to—telling me what we *have* to do. You seem to be confused about who gives the orders at this firm."

"It's not a matter of orders," Finn said, scrambling, "or firm policy...."

"Oh, well, given your wealth of experience running a law firm, just what is it, then?"

"Well, legal ethics to start, and morality."

Victor laughed derisively. "And let me understand: *you* are going to lecture me about legal ethics?"

"What do you mean?"

"Well, we could start with the watch you stole from the Nashville raid."

It was a gut punch. How did Victor know about that? JT was the only one who knew. But there was no time to think. Should he just say he had no watch, which other than the old Timex in his desk would be true? What sense would that make when Victor already knew?

"Victor," he said, deciding it best to just change the subject, "you gave me this job; you taught me how to run a case..."

"I've shown you what it takes to build a successful practice, to represent *our clients* rather than going off half-cocked to save the world."

Finn had to bring this conversation back to the point. Victor couldn't care less about one knockoff watch, and Finn wouldn't let that divert him from why he was there. Overcome with emotion and dispensing with diplomacy, he said, "Those bastards sold defective parts and pilots died. How can we bury that?"

Victor sat back and folded his arms. It looked as if his blood was about to burst through his face. His gaze bored a hole in Finn's scull as he cleared his throat and said menacingly, "Enough of this bullshit. Are you going to drop this?"

"I can't, Victor. And given Ted's family, how can we expect him to let it go?"

Victor rubbed his hand across his chin. Finn could feel hatred radiating across the space between them. "There's something else you better consider," he said, suddenly and eerily calm.

Finn turned out his hands in question.

"I'm talking about your delivery to Nashville."

"Delivery?"

"To a representative of a Mr. Arkadin?"

"What, the falcon? You knew about that?"

Bolger sneered. "Knew about it? Of course not. I didn't know a thing. But I heard a disturbing report and now I find that you... Well, let's say I'm astonished and disappointed—devastated really, given you work at my firm—that you would be involved in something like that."

"Something like what!?" Finn was losing control of this confrontation. Victor had the upper hand and seemed to be taking sadistic pleasure in toying with him.

"How much cocaine was packed in that statue?" Victor said,

now conversational. "And what was your cut for moving it across state lines?"

"What are you talking about?"

"It was clever using an attorney headed to a federal court hearing as a mule. And a seemingly respectable attorney wouldn't draw attention flying in and out the same day to deliver a box. But the plan went bad."

"What do you mean?"

"I mean, the whole operation in Tennessee. Arkadin and the others, including your contact, I'm told his name is Ed Wilson...?"

"Wait, my what?"

"The man you delivered the drugs to. The police caught up with him and busted the whole gang. They are out on bail but face serious charges. We arranged counsel for them, and we were able to convince Wilson not to reveal who brought the drugs in."

Finn couldn't believe what he was hearing. This could not be happening. Ray set him up? Victor arranged counsel for drug dealers practically before they were arrested?

"And," Victor went on, "I dare say, your take for delivering—what did you call it, the 'falcon'—nicely padded the generous salary I already pay you, as well as the bonus you earned for being such a vital part of the team. But I understand you made the beginner's error of simply depositing your payoff, where was it, in the Bank of Missouri?"

Finn was speechless. He had not had enough distance from G-pa's death to monitor the Missouri bank account. With direct deposit from that one annuity, he could easily have missed an anonymous deposit, especially if it just happened. Was that possible? Could someone simply put money into his account? And how could this happen so soon after he delivered the statue? Everything was wrong about this.

"I believe your account in Missouri is secure. But you should not overlook the tax consequences of accepting that payment; we wouldn't want you getting into trouble with the IRS. Also, you probably shouldn't access those funds to defray legal expenses. That really wouldn't be smart since you might have to turn it over as restitution."

Finn was stunned. This bastard—or someone—had set him up to control him. But how could they make this charge stick? He simply delivered a gift for a work friend; he had no idea what was inside; Ray said it was a statue. And how could they even show he carried it on the plane?

"I can see the wheels turning," Victor said. "Let me fill in the rest of the picture for you, in case you have any doubts."

Victor threw an envelope on the desk. "Go ahead," he said, "take a look."

Finn wanted to get up and leave the office. Bolger's machinations disgusted him. But he had to know what he faced. In the envelope were photographs—taken from a distance—of him arriving at the gate at Nashville International Airport carrying the box that held the falcon, meeting Ed, the driver, and handing over the box.

Finn was silent, thinking through whether these photos put him at risk.

"These arrived anonymously first thing and look like they show you delivering the 'falcon.' Who knows where they came from? Oh, and there's also an audiotape about how you had no trouble with the authorities taking the package on board. You don't need to hear that; you were there, after all. But you can be sure a jury would eat it up."

Finn seethed. He wished he had that statue in his hands so he could crack it over Victor's head, squash him like the poisonous reptile he was.

Victor rose from behind his desk and gestured Finn toward the door.

"I am on your side, Finnegan, as always, but I think you can see this scandal of yours promises no end of trouble if you pursue it. If GlobalX's lawyers get their hands on this evidence—

that's assuming it didn't come from them—you know they'll use it. "Or..." he said, pausing to fix a stare into Finn's eyes, "we can resolve the case and all come out heroes."

Finn couldn't believe what he was hearing. The office swirled around him.

"You go have a good think about things, Finnegan," Victor said, his tone now repulsively paternal. "I'm sure you'll see a good job, a fat bonus and a promotion to run Sanchi look pretty damned good compared with five-to-ten upstate, even with time off for good behavior."

Finn stumbled back to his office. It was impossible to believe what had just happened. Victor, or someone pressuring Victor, had set him up to make him bury the jet parts scandal? What kind of manipulative monster was he working for?

He needed to get away from the office and think. A wrong move now would ruin his career, if not put him in jail. And what was the alternative? He could play along, hold his nose, go on doing his job and forget about GlobalX. Could he live with that?

He grabbed his briefcase and headed for the elevator.

"Off to a meeting?" Imani said.

He turned to her, almost startled. She looked so innocent. But she sensed something was wrong.

On one hand he wanted to bring her into his office and explain it all. In this place where everything suddenly felt threatening, she was one person he could trust. But it was bad enough he had brought fire down upon himself...and Ted. The relief he'd get from sharing his troubles with Imani was not worth getting her involved. "Yeah, I've got to deal with some personal stuff," he said. "I'll see you later."

"Okay," she said, looking askance. "But...could I just see you for one minute before you go?"

"Sure," he said haltingly and led her back to his office.

Once behind the closed door, she said, "I know what you and Ted found at GlobalX."

"What?" He suddenly felt exposed but tried not to reveal anything. "What did we find?"

"About the jet parts. C'mon, Finn, I'm telling you, I know. You and Ted are keeping it under wraps, but there are some precautions I could show you about late-night photocopying."

"You found...?"

"Yes, I found your documents, and after that it was hard not to notice the glances between you two and the unusual hours you've been putting in."

"But you haven't told anyone?"

Her hands went to her hips as her chin and chest thrust out. He saw he had underestimated both her intelligence and her fierce loyalty.

"I'm sorry, Imani," he said. "I didn't mean to question..."

"Never mind that. You should know you can count on me. I'm disappointed you didn't pull me in to help."

"That was to protect you."

"I don't need your protection, Finn. And I want what is right here as much as Ted or you or anyone."

"And if it's not our place to enforce the law here, and we exceeded the court order and any legal justification for seizing this evidence?"

"That doesn't mean diddly-squat. There's a right and wrong here that has nothing to do with who we represent or what's best for Bolger & Plotkin."

Finn smiled sadly.

"What?" she said, catching her breath after this unusual outburst.

"Nothing, it's just...my grandfather would have loved you."

Arriving home Finn found Petra painting a shoulder of a young woman seated before her, her sweater pulled partly down her arm.

Petra looked up in surprise. "You're home early," she said brightly.

The model looked over with an impassive expression and returned her vacant gaze to the windows. He looked past her to the painting of his hand set up on another easel, the space above the hand for Petra's "correlative" image still blank—like her current model's face. "Yeah, uh, hi," he said absently. "I had some things to take care of."

He was too dazed by the day's events to even pay much attention to the attractive model. He excused himself and continued toward the back of the loft, where he found Satch eating in the kitchen.

"Oh, hey," Satch said, putting down his sandwich. "What did you think of the dress rehearsal?"

"What," Finn stammered. The play was the furthest thing from his mind. "Yeah, it was good. I enjoyed helping out."

"You did a good job running the big fan. We weren't sure it could actually blow off Jack's hat."

The show, make-believe on a grand scale, seemed so foreign to the chaos in his life that he hardly knew what he was saying. He couldn't think about play-acting, not now. He needed to be alone to think, to work out his confrontation with Victor.

Satch finished his sandwich and went into his room. Finn retreated to *his* room, closed his door and collapsed on the couch without removing his coat. He looked up at the mattress on the loft and wished he could be in bed, pull the covers over his head and wake up realizing this had all been a dream. But he lacked the energy to take off his clothes and mount the ladder, so he just lay back and felt the minutes tick by.

The one adornment to his room was a bookshelf he brought home from G-pa's house with a collection of paperback novels he had read over the years. His gaze fell on a few titles, and he tried to recall the story from any one of them to give him an escape from the chaos of his life.

But that was futile. Just like the play, this was not the time for made-up stories. He needed to decide on a course, regain control. Ted was as straight a shooter as there was, and he was hell-bent on exposing this scandal. Finn had to get hold of him, get control over him. He could not let this thing explode in their faces.

The drug charges wouldn't stick. That was so clearly a setup. They just happened to record it? It was such bullshit. And a recording wouldn't prove anything, anyway. What had he said except he had no trouble getting on the plane? What did that prove? And who would have access to those photos and the tape unless they were trying to entrap him?

But still, staying out of it, staying safe—and remaining employed and able to pay his rent—might still be possible. He just had to make sure Ted understood this was a good thing for him, for them both. They had to tell the same story.

Satch poked his head into the room, dressed for work. "What's got you on edge?" he asked.

"Crisis at the office," Finn replied. "Everything's a mess. We stumbled on some really bad guys, but my boss wants to ignore it all."

"Well, he's the boss, right?"

"Yeah, he pays my salary."

"And he decides who the firm goes after?"

"Yes, but..."

"And like you said, he pays you...and quite a lot, I might add."

"Okay, I hear you. It's just more complicated than I can explain."

"Well, I've got something to take your mind off it. You could come in and grip for the show again. Brad told me the guy who signed up for Wednesday and Thursday got sick, so he's scrambling for a replacement."

"Oh, man, I can't, not now. There's just too much..."

"No worries. We'll figure it out. I just thought you could use the distraction, and everyone said you did a great job at the dress rehearsal."

"Thanks," Finn said, thinking with grim humor that he might look for work as a stagehand after his legal career collapsed.

Satch headed out, and Finn continued his train of thought. Where were all his roommates in the grand scheme of making their way in New York City? Satch's job neither challenged him nor paid him very well, which left him living for his acting. Lance was even more adrift. Yes, he had produced a record, but realistically he was never going to be a rock star; his main employment was subletting rooms. Mandy was just a lost cause, with no telling how long she could keep up her consumptive lifestyle. And even Petra, so genuine and talented, and yet forced to wait tables and dodge her mother's attempts to fix her up with a husband she didn't need or want.

Compared with them, Finn had a good life. His work was sometimes interesting and the pay, while not astronomical, was more than enough for now and certain to go higher over time. If he could just get along, keep his head down and do the work, maybe he could overcome his obstacles and build some kind of life in a real apartment in a residential part of town, with friends and a girlfriend—especially a girlfriend—to push back the loneliness. There was a philosophical adage to cover this dilemma; he was sure of it. Where was G-pa when he needed him?

Chapter Twenty

Tuesday morning Finn went to work still unsure what to do about GlobalX. But whatever he ultimately decided, he had to give every appearance of going along with Victor.

One big wild card was Ted. Finn hadn't been able to reach him the night before but really needed to find out what he was going to do. This was when Finn needed guidance from a more senior lawyer, someone with the wisdom of experience. That's how it was supposed to work. But he couldn't talk to Victor, Ainsley was clearly working with the boss, and he didn't feel close enough to any of the other partners to approach them. Just like life in general—which he now faced without G-pa—he had to navigate this ethical maze on his own.

He brought a cup of coffee to his office, wishing he had stopped on the way in for a bagel or a scone. Then his phone rang.

"My God," Ted said breathlessly, "I'm so relieved to reach you."

"What's going on? Where are you?"

"I just left the office; I'm in a phone booth on Fifth Avenue. But listen. I got through to Henry Ingram's mother."

"And?"

"Henry's dead."

"What?"

"He was killed, a hit and run while he was riding his bike home from work."

"My God, that can't be."

"Yeah, well, it is. When I found out I bolted. You think this was because of us?"

"I don't know. It's nuts. But keep calm. We'll figure it out."

Finn didn't want Ted to hear how rattled he was. This could *not* be a coincidence. That poor kid was killed because he told them about the jet parts, he was sure of it. And it was Finn who got him mixed up in this. And what would happen next? Were any of them safe?

"And one more thing," Ted added. "What should I do with that Transfers folder?"

"Just, keep it with you. You get home. We'll talk later."

This decided it. Finn couldn't be guided by Victor or whoever was giving the orders. Ted was only a brand-new lawyer, but Finn should have followed his lead all along. Now Henry was dead and that was probably GlobalX. It was up to Finn to stop this.

He still wished he had more support. JT had been at the firm longer than Finn and could have been some kind of mentor, but he never took much interest in that role or in the big issues like legal ethics. Besides, he had been acting so odd lately. But Finn felt out of options and so knocked on his friend's door.

"Hey, Finlandia," JT said, looking up from his desk. JT's office was configured much like Finn's, although the walls were decorated with sports posters, and boxes of documents and folders took up much of the floor space.

"Can I ask you something?" Finn said. "I mean seriously, can I trust you to give me the truth?"

"Are you high? What's this about?"

Finn closed the door and sat.

"You look rattled," JT said. "What's up?"

Finn took a deep breath. This was a friend; he'd understand. "Ted and I found a big pile of shit at GlobalX."

"I heard: the watches we took were genuine, out the back door of the Sanchi factory."

"No. This is something else, something much worse."

JT's expression turned uncharacteristically serious. "What are you talking about?"

"They're selling counterfeit jet parts. Ted and I found evidence they sold parts to the Navy, and there were crashes."

"You're shittin' me. But wait, are you investigating jet parts?"

"Exactly what Victor said. When I told him about the evidence, he said to bury it; it's not our client and not in our interest. Ainsley is in on this, too. I mean, I spent a lot of time talking to her Friday night, and it's hard to say what she really thinks, but that's for another time."

"Wait. What? You...and the Ice Queen. No way!"

"JT, just focus. I'm not talking about getting laid. I'm saying..."

"What? You got laid?"

"No, I did *not* get laid. She took me to dinner and pumped me about what I planned to do with the information. And on top of pressure from her, and direct orders from Victor, someone rifled through my office—and Ted's."

"Looking for what?"

"Documents we didn't turn over to Ainsley, I guess."

"You're kidding. Are there any?"

"Not really."

"You mean you didn't really turn over everything?"

"That's not the point because it gets worse. I think they killed the Global clerk who gave us the information. This guy disappeared from the earth, and we just found out he died in a hit and run."

JT missed a beat at this but then scoffed. "You can't think Victor and Ainsley would be involved in killing someone. How do you know it wasn't an accident and some scared driver just took off?"

"I *don't* know, not really, but it's way too convenient. And scary. Shit, I might be next!"

"Oh, settle down, dude. That's crazy. You told Bolger you'd go along, right?"

"I did, but..."

"And you meant it? I mean, there's really no reason for anyone to come after you?"

"No, not any reason that makes sense. But then there's Ted...."

"What the hell's his problem? He's been a lawyer for, what, ten minutes, and you're taking your lead from him? Does he think he's Captain America or something?"

"In a way. But I'm starting to think he's right. If they're ready to kill people over this, maybe this *needs* to get out."

"Dude, you can't let vague suspicions make you psycho. If these guys really mean business, it would be best to go along. It can't be worth dying over."

"That's just the point. People have died...are dying!" He grimaced and shook his head. "I have to get out of here."

"Okay, look, first you should make damned sure you gave Ainsley everything she was looking for. And you better keep your mouth shut, and rein Ted in or else this thing will blow up in all our faces. And maybe you should make yourself scarce while things settle down. I'll give you my keys; you can use my place."

"Thanks, but I can't go anywhere they'll look."

"Okay, but if someone is really looking for you, where can you go?"

Finn considered his options. No one would come after him in a public place, like a café or a library. But Henry was killed on a public road. No, better to get out of sight, someplace they wouldn't look. He could leave town, but then what would happen to Ted? He needed to stay in the city, anyway, to retrieve the package from Genevieve.

"I think I have a place," he said, half to himself.

"Where?"

"My roommate acts at this private club. I helped out backstage on Sunday. No one would connect me with that."

"Oh, that place you told me about, some kind of stand-up club?"

"Not stand-up, but yeah, it's a clubhouse in Murray Hill."

"That's fine for right now, but shouldn't you call someone? Get hold of Ray's friend, Detective Vulpe. Ray said he's at Midtown South."

"Yeah, maybe I'll give him a call."

"You want me to do it?"

"No, I'll call him now, and then get out of here. And JT..."

"Yeah?"

"Thanks for your help. I really needed someone to talk to."

Finn returned to his office and called the precinct number to reach Vulpe. He started to explain about the evidence, and that Henry may have been killed, then hesitated.

"Go on," Vulpe said. "What else?"

It occurred to him that Ray obviously was in on the drug setup. And if Ray was dirty, his good friend Vulpe would be, too. That made it a big mistake to call the detective. And suddenly he realized how strange it was that JT suggested calling Vulpe. Were they all in on this?

He needed to cut this conversation short without raising any suspicion, if he hadn't already hung a target on his chest.

"Okay," Vulpe resumed, "you don't need to give me the whole story over the phone. Tell me where you are so I can send a car to pick you up. We'll sort it all out once you're safe."

"Great," Finn said, convinced he needed to stay clear of anyone connected with Ray or Victor. "I'm leaving the office right now, and I'm scared. I'll come straight to the precinct house."

"No," Vulpe said, a little too emphatically, "not the precinct. Meet me at the southeast corner of the park, by the fountain in front of the Plaza."

"Right," Finn said. "I'll be there in ten minutes."

Finn hung up and tried to gather his thoughts. First, he called Ted's apartment.

"Lucky you caught me," Ted said, sounding nervous. "I just got in."

"What's wrong?"

"My apartment door was pried open. Someone broke in."

"I can't believe this."

"Yeah, I know. I looked around, and it didn't seem like anything was missing, though it's hard to tell with all this mess."

"They were looking for the evidence," Finn said, "but why did they think there was anything at your apartment?"

Ted was silent for a moment and then blurted out. "It was my notes! I gave Ainsley notes I took about the branding documents; I think I even labelled the last page Transfers folder. So stupid!"

"They know you still have that folder, and that's just what we need to make the case airtight."

"You've got the rest of it?"

"I have, though I don't have it in hand. I mailed it to a friend. She should have the package in a day or two. But how can I get the folder from you?"

"I've got to wait here for now. I called the police to report the break in, and they're sending someone."

"I also called Detective Vulpe, but then realized he's probably in on the coverup. He said to meet him at the Plaza, but I'm not going there. You didn't mention his name to the cops, did you?"

"I did," Ted said reluctantly. "I thought Ray's connection would get quicker results."

"Yeah, but not the result we want. You shouldn't wait around for the police."

"You think *all* the cops are bad?"

"No, but who knows what pull Vulpe has? We just can't tell. And if you gave his name, they're sure to loop him in."

"This is all getting scary. I'll bring the folder to your apartment or...maybe not. You think Vulpe will search your place, too?"

"Probably. But I can get there before him, though we'll still need a place to meet, somewhere public or better yet where they won't look."

"Or both. Along the esplanade in Battery Park there's a World War II memorial; it's an eagle statue that looks out over the bay. I'll meet you in front, on the walkway, at say, four o'clock."

Finn rushed out of the office and into the subway station. The entire side of one downtown local car read "TIME IS NIGH" in orange and black letters, as if G-pa's spirit was still annotating his life with aphorisms.

He took the train down to Chambers Street and hurried home. But stepping off the elevator into the loft, he was struck by stillness. Petra wasn't working at her painting. There was no sound from Lance's studio or his sleeping space up by the ceiling. Stranger still, Bogart wasn't there to greet him. Where was the dog?

He heard faint scratching. In the kitchen he saw that all three bedroom doors were closed, which would be typical if Satch and Mandy were out. But the sound came from behind Satch's door.

He knocked and heard a deep bark. Bogart! When he opened the door, the dog looked up at him, as if asking Finn to explain his imprisonment.

"Hey, buddy," he said. "I didn't lock you in there."

Bogart squeezed past him and headed for his water bowl. Finn looked quickly into Satch's room and closed the door again. He was trying to imagine how Bogart could close himself into Satch's room as he opened his own door.

It looked like a tornado had blown through. Books and clothes lay strewn everywhere. And since there was nothing in the room worth stealing, this could only be about the evidence.

It was odd there was no mess in the rest of the loft. Was it too big to search, or were they just trying to scare him? Either way, the message was clear. Henry was dead, and he could be next. He had stumbled onto something incendiary. He needed to keep his back to the wall and sense where trouble might be coming from.

Maybe he could still assure these people he was no threat. They knew now—or thought they knew—he had turned everything over to them. If they just believed he wouldn't make trouble, could he still get back to his life? What other way was there out of this mess?

He'd have to convince Ted that patriotism was not worth dying for. First thing, though, was to get the rest of the documents from him, so he'd have everything in hand in case he needed to bargain. Then he could assess their options.

There were footsteps out in the apartment. He froze to listen and then peered out his door. It was Petra. She was carrying a portfolio and humming to herself.

When she saw him, her smile melted. "You look wasted," she said and stepped toward him. "Are you okay?"

"Yeah. No, not really. Do you know where Satch is?"

"I'm sure he's at work, either that or at his theater."

"Oh, right." Finn was trying to stay calm. "Petra, listen you've got to do something for me."

She looked suddenly wide-eyed. "What's going on?"

"I can't explain. It's even best you don't know. I'm gonna grab some stuff and get out of here. The police..."

"The police?!"

"...or someone else may be looking for me. Anyway, they already broke in this morning; they locked Bogart in Satch's room...."

"They what?" she exclaimed.

"Oh, he's fine. And believe me, I've done nothing wrong. The cops, or whoever they are, are bad news, really corrupt. But you shouldn't get into that; you're completely outside of this. If they come back before I leave, just stall while I duck down the fire stairs. You can say you saw me earlier, and I rushed out, but you have no idea where I went."

"Which will be true."

"Exactly."

"I understand. I've got this. But if these bastards locked up Bogart, we'll both have to hold back from going at them."

He looked startled and started to caution her.

"But no," she said. "I understand. I will act sweet and oblivious, and I'm sure the dog will go along—although I wish he'd learn to bare his teeth."

"You're an angel, Petra. Just go about your day. You know nothing."

He grabbed his passport and the cash still hidden behind his sock drawer, put on a Yankees cap and looked around for what else he needed to take.

The door downstairs buzzed, freezing them both. Hard knocking followed. Petra looked at Finn in alarm, gulped and moved slowly toward the front windows to see who was at the door.

Finn didn't wait for her to confirm what he knew in his gut. With a grateful look, he grabbed his coat and shot through the fire exit back by the restrooms.

The hallway at street level led from the front door through to a door at the back, which opened onto a narrow strip of dirt and weeds along a wire fence. Finn waited, afraid his heart was pounding so loud it would betray him, until he heard the front door buzz open and two heavy sets of footsteps clomp up the stairs to the loft door. He used the sound of their knocking to mask the noise of unbolting the back door, and he ducked out.

At the end of the dirt patch, he climbed a concrete wall and the chain link fence above it and dropped into the service entrance of the big building spanning the east end of the block. From there he moved quickly onto Reade Street, cap pulled low over his eyes. He turned south and strode purposefully, but not fast enough to draw attention, toward the subway.

Chapter Twenty-One

Finn walked down State Street, checking over his shoulder that he wasn't followed. He wanted to enter Battery Park at its eastern end, which was normally quiet. Paths laced from that gate through the park, mostly parallel to the Upper New York Bay shoreline.

To keep out of sight, he stuck to pathways under cover of trees. The monument where he was to meet Ted was hard to miss. An imposing statue of an eagle stood with wings upraised, looking out through two rows of granite pylons toward the Statue of Liberty. Finn stepped slowly past the eagle and stood behind one of the pylons to look for Ted.

He stayed out of sight and cursed leaving his old Timex in his desk drawer. But Ted soon approached from the west, walking along the railing that traced the curve of the bay. Finn waved to get his attention. But Ted didn't see him; he just kept walking. Then he stopped, directly in front of the memorial. He looked backward and forward along the esplanade but not toward Finn.

Finn was about to call out when Ted suddenly turned and they locked eyes. In a subtle but vehement gesture, Ted warned Finn to stand back. Something was threatening, and Ted was imploring him to stay put.

A man in a long overcoat and a fedora pulled low over his eyes approached from the west. Was this what spooked Ted?

Finn waited for the man to pass. But he didn't walk by; he stepped right up to Ted. In a flash Ted went limp, and the man helped him to the ground up against the railing.

What just happened?

Finn instinctively stepped forward but then pulled back. Who was that man? What did he do? He looked like he was helping but then he...was he reaching into Ted's jacket?

Passersby rushed toward the two men. A woman shrieked. Another woman with a no-nonsense manner kneeled beside Ted and waved others away.

Finn hurried forward but paused to see where the overcoat man went. If he came back, Finn would have to defend them both, but with what?

But the man disappeared. Finn realized he couldn't even describe him, except for the herringbone coat and the hat.

Finn squatted down beside the woman, who was taking Ted's pulse and holding his side. "Is there something I can do?" he asked. "Are you a nurse or something?"

"I saw the whole thing!" a young man volunteered. "It was a man in a long coat and a brimmed hat; he ran into the park."

A jogger ran to call an ambulance. Someone else said she'd look for a police officer.

"A doctor," the woman replied to Finn without turning her head, as if this should have been obvious.

"Oh, wow. Well, I know this man."

The doctor glanced at Finn.

Finn wanted to be sure Ted would get to a hospital, and this woman seemed capable of arranging that. But he also needed to keep his head on a swivel. It made no sense to offer himself as a second target. He had to get out of the park, melt back into the city streets.

"Will he be okay?" Finn said to the doctor. "What happened to him?"

She looked into his eyes with condescension and gestured at Ted's side. She pulled his coat open. A dark red stain was spreading on his shirt.

Finn looked at the woman in panic.

She shook her head softly. "You friend has been stabbed. Find something clean to hold against his side."

Finn pulled the handkerchief from his back pocket and pressed it inside Ted's shirt, against his wound. That made Ted wince, as if he wasn't already in enough pain. Looking into Ted's vacant eyes, Finn's thoughts careened from Ted to Henry to his own safety. What had he gotten them all into?

Ted momentarily came to. Through half-open eyes, he looked at the doctor, and then found Finn's face.

"I'm here, buddy," Finn said, holding Ted's limp arm, at a loss for what else to do.

"The...." Ted said and coughed.

"Don't speak," the doctor said.

A siren approached down Broadway.

Ted tried to reach into his coat.

"Lie still," the doctor said.

The GlobalX evidence was meaningless with Ted lying in his own blood. Yet, the kid was obviously searching for the folder that was no longer there. With his life in the balance, he stuck to their purpose.

That jerked Finn back to why they were in this park. There was work to do. There had to be a way forward without the folder. He would find that way; he had to find it for both of them. He kept hold of Ted's arm and nodded at him.

Ted's face showed a moment's understanding but then his eyes rolled back in his head and white bubbles formed on his lips. The people around him backed off, but the doctor kept her eyes on Ted's face and held his hand. Finn again scanned the crowd for the man in the overcoat.

"Look," Finn said to the woman. "I can't stay. His name is Theodore Cummings, and he works at Bolger & Plotkin here in the city. You got that?"

The doctor half turned to Finn. "Crandall, ah...."

"No," Finn interrupted, "Cummings, Theodore Cummings, Junior."

"It's okay," the man who had seen the incident said. "I'll tell them, and give the cops the description of that guy."

Finn rose to his feet and nodded appreciation at the young man.

"But who are you?" the doctor said.

"A friend," Finn said. "I'll also contact the police...later." He turned and looked nervously about. "Right now I have to find that man. Thank you both. Please take care of him."

A Bellevue Hospital ambulance pulled up, drawing a bigger crowd. Finn slipped through the granite pylons and back under the trees. He realized there was no sense searching *for* the assailant; it was more important to get away from him.

Chapter Twenty-Two

Finn rushed up to Duane Street. He wondered if Vulpe's guys were still at his building, but he had to go somewhere. They had already ransacked his room and found he wasn't there; why would they stay—and how many of them were there, anyway?

Rounding the corner to his street, he saw a black car parked in front of the loft, two men in the front seat. He stood for a long moment watching them, and realized it had started to snow. Zipping up his coat he turned away, trying to think of where else to go. Then he remembered Satch's clubhouse.

He turned back to City Hall and dropped into the subway. At the front of the uptown platform, he stood behind a column to keep out of sight, just in case. It was unlikely anyone was following, but his sense of danger was almost overpowering.

He was responsible for putting his roommates and Ted at risk from whoever was behind this. It had to be GlobalX, or someone protecting that company. But how did Victor fit in? There was no doubt he'd turn a blind eye to Global's crime to protect his business; at the end of the day, he cared only about himself. But surely he wouldn't condone killing his own people.

And Ainsley might have had no choice about cooperating. She had worked eight years to become a partner at the firm and could not succeed without Victor's support. Did that outweigh any sense of morality? Apparently it did, given the Rao's charade to ensure his cooperation. Still, it was hard to believe she knew how far GlobalX would go. Could she condone attacking Ted?

G-pa loomed large in Finn's thoughts, as always in times of crisis. His grandfather had from the first acknowledged Finn's attraction to the glamour and excitement of living in New York but never bought Finn's preference for anonymity over living among neighbors who knew and cared about him. He always wanted to know about Finn's friends, not just girlfriends but the community he found in the city. Did his grandson have the support of people he could count on? Would they be there for him in time of need, the way folks in Lebanon pulled together after a tornado or snowstorm? Finn should have appreciated the wisdom in those questions, given how he had lost any foundation of family or friends at such a young age. Now it hit him how rudderless he was in this savage sea.

Leaning against a grimy pole at the far front of a subway stop, he breathed in the faint smell of urine and gazed into the dank, dark tunnel ahead. He tried not to see this grimy shaft—with a rat scurrying between the tracks—as a metaphor for where he was headed, but that was the direction his train would take and the sense he had about his future.

There was too much to digest, and it was clear he wouldn't make sense of it standing on a subway platform. The task at hand was to get away from Vulpe and whoever else was working for Global, go to ground, catch his breath.

All hope was not lost. He had friends he could trust. Satch and Petra, at least, would stand by him, and maybe he could count on JT, although it was JT who suggested he call Vulpe. And then there was Ted, but what had Finn's friendship cost him? Did his stabbing have to be part of this? Should Finn reach out to the police, tell them what he suspected? But what could he tell them, and how could he trust them? Cops had already banged on his door, maybe the same ones who already ransacked his room, and for what? What had he done that justified the police coming after him?

A rumble signaled the approach of the 6 Train. When the brakes stopped screeching, the doors opened on the first car, which was tagged from front to back, "CRIME IN THE CITY."

The train pulled out. Inside the windows were almost completely painted over in black spray paint. Finn leaned back against the door and lost himself in the rhythm of the tracks. In the summer, he would never get into a subway car with open windows because that meant the air conditioning didn't work. But opaque windows didn't trouble him, and he took comfort riding up front, close to the train operator in his locked compartment.

A boy maybe six years old sat with his mother across from Finn. As the train rattled on, the kid stared at Finn's left hand holding the pole. Finn looked over and saw blood on the pole and his hand. It was Ted's.

He thrust his hand into his pocket. There were also spots of blood on his right hand but not enough for anyone to notice. He shuffled across the doorway to hold on with his right hand instead of his left. The kid kept staring, and then pulled at his mother's sleeve, talking dramatically and throwing glances at Finn.

Finn adopted a commuter stare into the middle distance. The woman looked at him and then turned her son's face away.

When the train stopped at Bleecker Street, Finn leaned out the door and looked back along the platform. Seven or eight cars back a man got off the train, saw Finn and moved toward him. As the doors started to close, the figure jumped back on the train five or six cars behind Finn's. The station faded into a blur through the window, but Finn retained the image of a long coat and a fedora.

He watched the door between train cars nervously. He had stopped believing in coincidences; the man in that coat carried a knife, he was sure of it. The train was full, so it would be hard for the man to pass between cars while it was moving, if that's what he was trying to do. But Finn still had to get off before that man made it to the front car. Then he could melt into the crowd on the platform and find a way up to the street.

But at these local stops there would be only one way out, toward the center of the train, which meant he was trapped. He struggled to think of a way to fight this man off or get away. If the man was armed only with a knife, Finn could defend himself by keeping away from him, keeping someone else between them.

At the busy 14th Street stop, he poked his head out the door again. Overcoat man had moved up to two cars behind Finn's and leaned out the door watching him, one arm blocking the door when it started to close.

A muffled announcement came over speakers inside the car, and the doors opened again and started to close but once more popped open. The man again stuck his head out, as did Finn, and they locked eyes.

As the doors started to close, Finn stepped onto the platform, his move mimicked by the pursuer, but Finn quickly hopped back into the car. Herringbone man did the same, and then as the doors closed, Finn once again jumped onto the platform. The doors stayed closed, and the train pulled out.

Finn caught a quick look at a hard, seething face as Herringbone man passed. With a satisfied smile, Finn pulled up the hood of his coat and fell in with people rushing toward the station exit.

Garbled announcements pierced the air. A guitarist seated on a small amp played the Hendrix tune, *Hey Joe*. He was afraid to get back on the subway because his pursuer could be waiting at the next stop, so he walked the rest of the way to 36th Street through snow accumulating on the sidewalks.

Finn's feet were wet and cold, and it was close to curtain time when he reached the clubhouse. He was surprised when he opened the door to find Derk in a resplendent turquoise tuxedo holding a clipboard. Inside was a world insulated from the storm, peaceful and yet bubbling with excitement, but most importantly safe.

"Hey, man," Derk said, reaching out to shake hands.

"Ah, yeah," Finn stammered, keeping his bloody right hand in his pocket while gripping Derk's proffered hand with his left.

Derk looked at their joined hands with a peculiar expression but then snapped back to a host's smile. "Get caught in the blizzard?"

"Pretty much; it has really picked up out there." Finn stamped his feet and brushed off his coat.

"Well, it's dry in here. Are you working tonight?"

"I'm not on the schedule, but I came by to see if anyone needs me."

"Great. I'm sure Brad will put you to work. The house is filling up, so go up here," gesturing at the stairs to the second floor, "and down the back staircase."

As latecomers in the prescribed formal attire crowded in behind him. Finn headed up the stairs.

Derk called out from behind him. "And hey, Finn, thanks for helping out."

Finn paused for a moment. If anything, the club was helping him, giving him a safe haven. He wondered if he should tell them he was on the run but decided it was best for everything to stay as normal as possible.

Upstairs he passed through the curtain closing off the workroom and ducked into the bathroom. He pulled off his coat and saw blood had stained not only his hand but also the coat near the pocket and the sleeve of his shirt. He washed his hands and tried to clean the shirt sleeve with water and paper towels, giving up in the end and rolling the sleeves. He then tried to wipe the blood off his coat sleeve and hung the wet coat out of the way at the end of the room.

When he returned to the workroom, Sylvia, the costume

lady, was helping an actress with her dress. She looked over with as much of a gruff smile as she could manage with pins in her mouth. An actor stood behind the bar gesticulating and speaking to himself. The light operator was sipping tea and reading a paperback. But Satch wasn't in the room, and Finn didn't know what to do with himself. He kept thinking he needed to stay calm and look like he belonged.

A pang of hunger reared itself. He hadn't eaten all day, and he hungrily eyed the plate of small sandwiches on the coffee table.

"Go ahead," Genevieve said, coming out of the hallway from the dressing rooms. "They're for the cast and crew."

"Genevieve," he said, relieved to see her smiling. He wanted to say more, to hopefully rebuild whatever it was they almost had, but the situation was dire. "Have you seen Satch?"

"He's getting dressed. You should report to Brad, or maybe Sylvia could use a hand?"

They both looked over at the costume lady. She pulled pins from her mouth and said, "Not now, but I will need help in act two with the puppets and police costumes."

"Sure," Finn said. "I can do that."

"Good," she responded. "Just come down to stage left a half hour after intermission."

Sylvia returned to pinning the dress. Genevieve looked closer at Finn. "You've been running?"

"Yeah, sort of. But excuse me; I really need to talk with Satch."

She waved him toward the men's room, which opened onto the dressing room. He found his loftmate seated before a mirror affixing a false mustache.

"Satch, man, I've got to talk to you," he said.

"Hey, what are you doing here?" Satch said. "You're not scheduled, are you?"

"No, I came here to hide."

"Hide from what?"

"Okay, this is going to sound crazy, and I don't have time

for details, I told you I found some shit at work that points to a crime, stuff my boss said to ignore. Well, it looks like he's in on some kind of cover-up. So my associate—that kid I told you about from Minnesota—he was trying to bring me evidence when he was attacked."

"Attacked?! What the hell? Is he all right?"

"I don't know. I couldn't stay to find out. But the guy also took the evidence. I freaked out, afraid he was after me, too. That's why I need to stay out of sight."

"You think they're after *you*?"

"It would make sense. Ted and I are in this together."

"Shouldn't you call the police?"

"I did call a detective I know, but I think he's in on it too. I don't know who to trust."

"Okay...I think. Well, you're right: no one will look for you here. You stay out of sight, and I'll warn the ushers just in case."

Brad knocked on the dressing room door and stuck his head in. "Five minutes," he said and looked surprised to see Finn.

"Thank you, five," Satch said. "And hey, Brad, Finn needs to stay backstage tonight. Can you use him?"

Brad looked confused. "*Needs* to stay backstage? What are you talking about?"

"Well, he isn't properly dressed to sit in the audience, and..."

"No matter," Brad replied and looked at Finn. "We've got a new grip tonight; you can show him what to do."

Finn made his way downstairs just before Brad raced up again calling out "Places," and the actors descended the stairs to wait offstage. Satch pulled Finn by the elbow to get him out of the way, and he found himself standing by Sylvia.

She eyed him suspiciously. "If I didn't know better," she said, "I'd say there's more drama going on backstage than front stage tonight."

Finn gulped and turned his attention to two actresses talking together.

"Quiet, ladies, please," Brad whispered forcefully. "The curtain speech is about to begin."

The house lights dimmed and went dark. A spotlight lit a tuxedoed man on the far side of the stage. "Welcome," he said in a loud stage voice, "to the one hundred and fourth year of consecutive performances by the Amateur Comedy Club...."

As the speech went on, Geneveive squeezed down the stairs in the oversized dress she was trying on when Finn first met her. Sylvia turned to her and began adjusting the buttons in back, rotating Genevieve to face Finn. He thought about the Puffy Dress Girl nickname, which seemed so foolish when he was running from killers.

"Having fun yet?" she said playfully, but Brad shushed them. He looked at her, wondering if he was falling for the same general affability that had led Satch to mistake her intentions.

As the curtain speech dragged on, she leaned into him and whispered, "Some of the old guys who give the curtain speeches won't give up the stage until we get out the vaudeville hook."

When the speech ended and the curtain went up on the first act, Finn found a spot where he could see most of the play. Mostly he tried to say out of the way of actors preparing to go on and the stage manager giving signals to the sound operator by his side and through his headset to the man in the light booth out front.

On stage, Raskolnikov soliloquized, "To go wrong in one's own way is better than to go right in someone else's."

Those words sounded like actual Dostoevsky, and something like Finn's philosophy of defiance against a wrong-handed world. But in the ACC version of the story, where the protagonist was trying to justify dodging a late fee at the library, the line got big laugh.

Similar moments followed. Finn watched as Satch went on as Raskolnikov's friend, and Genevieve made her entrance as his sister. With accompanying recorded music, the two of them sang a bouncy number about taking new steps in life, deconstructing the novel's woeful story.

At a scene change, the curtain closed, and Finn helped the grip move furniture on and off the stage. Then he was backstage again. He held a light for Sylvia while she pinned the hem of a dress. Satch passed by without seeing him and went up the stairs, returning dressed as another character with muttonchops in place of the mustache.

Finn then went upstairs to help the grip with the snow. They laughed about the idea of just opening the window over the spiral staircase and letting real snow blow in. At a cue from the script they shared, they quietly opened the trap door in the floor of the workroom and readied two bags of white confetti. At the next cue they started sprinkling. From above the effect was impressive, until a twist in Finn's plastic bag caused a large lump of confetti to break loose.

"Oh, shit," Finn called out, loud enough to be heard on the stage below and the first few rows of seats.

He watched the clump fall, as if in slow motion, at the same time seeing his future as a stagehand vanish along with any goodwill he might have earned from the cast and crew.

The clump bounced off Roskolnikov's head. Finn was mortified, but his fellow grip burst out laughing, along with the audience. When the actor looked skyward with daggers in his eyes, there was another raucous laugh from the crowd.

Back downstairs Finn dreaded Brad's reaction, but the stage manager lifted the microphone from his mouth and said, "We're going to add that to the performance from here on."

Genevieve appeared then, in a different dress. She threw him a smile that said she knew the snow mishap had been his fault, but it was all part of the fun. Then she focused on the stage and made another entrance, along with Satch, for their big scene.

"We sometimes encounter a person," Satch's character said in a bad Russian accent, "even a perfect stranger, who interests us at first sight, somehow suddenly, all at once, before a word has been spoken..."

Despite the schmaltzy accent, Satch was convincing. Finn knew this was because he was not *acting*; he was speaking those lines to Genevieve. And it was easy to see why his loftmate had fallen so hard for her. She was genuine and pretty and full of life. But Satch was also expressing exactly what Finn felt about Genevieve. But now, even though she had rejected Satch, she'd probably avoid him as well.

And what was he even thinking? A man with a knife was chasing him, and dirty cops were looking for him. He had no business involving Genevieve, or anyone else, in his life. The kindest thing would be to stay away from them all, leave town, find somewhere far away to hide. When this was all over and the dust settled, it would be clear if Satch had a second chance with Genevieve. Or not, and then maybe Finn could make it up to her? Until then, he had to concentrate on getting the evidence to the authorities.

When the curtain closed for intermission, Finn helped sweep up the confetti and change the set for the second act, which took only five minutes. He then went upstairs to where the actors were changing costumes, reading over their lines and noshing.

Satch pulled him aside to ask what was going on. As Finn started to explain, Genevieve joined them.

Finn gave the short version of the facts, concluding, "When I told my boss, he said it wasn't our business. He half convinced me to keep quiet...."

Genevieve flinched, which made him stop and think how that sounded. He realized he cared more about her opinion of him than about the danger he was in. Was she seeing the truth here of what was right, the way Ted had? Was he still so mired in recrimination and rebellion against the world that he had lost any sense of morality?

"But I was torn," he said. "I mean, we're obligated to represent our client, not be the police, and the court order gave us no authority on the jets parts thing." Genevieve's urgent expression kept willing him to do the right thing. "But still," he went on, "people had died, were dying, and so I pushed back. But I also screwed up and told my boss my colleague would never let this go."

Both Satch and Genevieve seemed stunned.

"Well, I thought that might convince my boss to reconsider, because he couldn't be thinking only of the business when people were dying. But I was wrong. Then Ted was attacked this afternoon trying to bring me evidence. They had other ways to pressure *me* but must have concluded Ted wouldn't be convinced and so had to be eliminated. And now...I don't know, they might be out to remove me as well. Anyway, they grabbed papers we need to bring to the police. And from all that's happened, it looks like I'm in their crosshairs. I came home to find they had broken in."

"They got into the loft?" Satch said, enraged.

"And locked Bogart in your room."

"They didn't hurt him," he said, seething, "did they?"

"No, he's fine. And it looks like they didn't mess with anything except my room."

"Damn," Satch said.

"And so you came here," Genevieve said, as if everything was beginning to make sense to her.

"Right," Satch said, "of course you did, as you should have. As soon as the show is over, we'll get help. Until then you'll be fine; no one will look for you here."

Brad came into the room saying, "Places," which Satch and Genevieve echoed, and everyone headed downstairs for act two.

When the curtain went up, Finn was back in the wings watching the show. Raskolnikov had pushed the bursar—Satch—out the window to end act one, so the drama now ratcheted up. But this was a farce, and soon another musical number brought a flurry of activity as actors streamed on and off.

Brad told Finn there'd be twenty minutes before he had to show the other grip how to run the fan to blow off Roskolnikov's hat. He decided to take the time to check out the view from stage right, where he was less likely to be in the way. He went up the back staircase, through the workroom and down the spiral staircase to the other side of the stage, musing about how much of his life he had wasted on the distinction between left and right.

He peeked through a frosted window—actually many times repurposed plexiglass. The house looked full, and he saw Derk at the back, seated just inside the curtain that closed off the theater from the front vestibule. Suddenly Derk got to his feet and spoke with someone pushing through the curtain. Words were exchanged, and Derk and the man disappeared behind the curtain. A minute later Derk came back into the house and spoke into the ear of the other usher. He then signaled to someone across the house. A tuxedoed man rose from a seat and approached Derk. They spoke quietly and looked up at the stage.

Finn's attention turned back to the play. Whatever was going on at the door, he wanted to see Genevieve perform.

But two minutes later Derk came down the spiral staircase, an anxious look on his face.

"Two sinister dudes showed up," Derk said. "They said they were police and had to talk with you, though they didn't show any ID. I told them the dress code was black tie, and they'd have to wait upstairs in the Green Room. I said I'd get word to you to come up as soon as you were offstage, but they said not to bother telling you, and they'd wait upstairs. Is this what Satch was talking about?"

Finn panicked. "I can't explain," he said, "but I have to get away from those guys."

They crawled under the windows in the canvas flats to stage left, where Genevieve was waiting to go on. Squeezing Finn's arm with an anxious expression, she said, "There are men—cops or probably not. They're upstairs."

Then Satch came off the stage. Seeing their serious faces, he also looked concerned.

"I'm clearly missing something here," Derk said.

Genevieve looked urgently at them all. "They came through the dressing rooms. I don't think they'll wait. They'll be down here soon; I know it."

"What do we do?" Derk said, leaping into the fray.

Genevieve looked at Sylvia, who was watching them with hawklike eyes. "Wait," Genevieve said suddenly and led Finn by the hand to the costume lady.

"Sylvia," she said urgently, "we need you to make your magic. It's a long story, but Finn needs to hide. Can you put him in a police costume?"

"You mean now?" Sylvia said, incredulous.

"I mean before the closing number."

"But there are no extra costumes."

"He can use mine," said Satch. "It'll fit okay, and it's hanging right here."

Sylvia didn't miss a beat. She grabbed Satch's costume and sized up Finn, while Genevieve stepped part way up the staircase to position herself as a lookout or maybe a barricade. Brad watched this commotion while keeping one eye on the stage and barking out cues. He had no idea what was going on but didn't care as long as nothing interrupted the play.

Sylvia and Satch helped Finn put the costume over his clothes and fitted him with a mask. Then two more actors in police costumes came down the stairs, and Sylvia handed each a life-sized puppet on a pole, dressed in a police costume.

Satch came in close to Finn and said, "Just follow the others on stage, and stand in line holding a puppet. When the song starts, sway back and forth with them. Don't worry about singing. I'll chime in from here, but it won't really matter, the audience will be laughing so hard no one will be able to tell. Just keep your mask on, and after the curtain closes and opens again, take a bow with everyone else."

Finn was breathing hard, trying to listen to the directions and make sure his costume was secure but also agonizing over what to do after the bow. He looked at himself in a mirror hanging on the back of one of the canvas walls. The mask hid his face, but if those men were there for him, how long would they be fooled? What would happen when the show was over and he had to drop the mask? How would he get out of the theater?

All his life, from the time his wrong-handedness had caused his stutter to his current job of arguing in court, he had suffered from fear of public speaking. Now, going on stage felt like nothing; the challenge would be getting off the stage.

"Who *are* you?" he heard Genevieve say on the stairway, forceful annoyance in her voice. "You can't come down here."

"Police," a man's voice responded forcefully. "Step aside."

"You're on," Brad said to Finn.

Finn followed the other two actors with puppets onto the stage, leaving behind the commotion on the stairway.

Behind him Sylvia croaked, "Break a leg."

Chapter Twenty-Three

Finn couldn't see the audience beyond the stage lights, just vague silhouetted shapes in the dark. Was this what enabled actors to ignore reality and inhabit the world of a play?

He followed closely behind the two police actors with puppets, but the second one stepped aside and nudged him into the center of the three. He gestured for Finn to hold the puppet in his right hand instead of his left and nodded encouragement. It felt like the entire cast and crew were pulling for him, as if this were all part of the show.

Each policeman held a puppet pole in one hand and waived the other in a pantomime of directing a crowd. Finn mimicked this, while also watching backstage out of the corner of his mask.

His attention was pulled several ways. In front of him Raskolnikov confessed to losing his head and pushing the bursar out the window. Yet the actor dressed like a judge absolved him, saying, "The man who has a conscience suffers whilst acknowledging his sin. *That* is his punishment."

At the same time Finn sensed a disturbance in the wings and saw a sinister figure looming over Brad, who ignored him and continued to call out cues. Finn's impulse was to bolt the other way, but at stage right he saw another hulking figure.

He couldn't tell if these men recognized him, but both

stared at the actors in masks, so clearly they were narrowing down their search.

He wanted to blend in with the other two actors as long as he could and so kept an eye on how they moved and aped their movements. The voices of the actors at the front of the stage were almost drowned out by the beating of his heart as he struggled to think of a way out.

The judge's last line cleared the way for the closing song, which began with the main actors and was taken up by the puppet officers. The actor next to Finn nudged him to join the other two marching in place and pumping the puppets up and down. Then the stage cops joined in the song. Finn could hear Satch singing from offstage.

The audience roared and clapped in time with the music, and the song continued as the curtain closed. Then all the actors came on stage and positioned themselves in a tableau. The puppet officer to Finn's left guided him into position, and the curtain opened again as the music got louder. The audience rose, applauding. The actors bowed and Finn followed along. But when the two puppet officers dramatically lifted their masks, he left his in place.

The goons lurking in the wings now looked only at him. One checked what looked like a photo in this hand.

As the cast took another bow, Finn handed his puppet to another actor and edged toward the front of the stage.

The curtain remained open as the house lights came on. Hugging each other, the actors moved toward the wings, while audience members in their tuxedos and gowns stood and gathered themselves.

The goons pushed past actors on both sides of the stage. There was only a moment. Finn had to run.

He ripped off his mask and jumped into the blinding stage lights. He fell into the first row of chairs. People moving up the aisles looked back, aghast. He stumbled to his feet and pushed past them, not looking to see if someone was chasing him.

They would run him down on the sidewalk and the snow, particularly with the bulky costume over his clothes. He needed to buy time.

In the vestibule he threw open the street door as a feint, then made a sharp turn into the cloak room. The woman handing people their coats was startled.

"Sorry," he snapped as he squeezed past her.

The cellar stairs at the back of the cloak room were steep and narrow. This was his first time down this way, and he might have fallen had he not grabbed the heavy rope bolted to the wall as a banister.

Derk had said this cellar connected through a crawl space to the back cellar, so he rushed away from the stair, immediately tripping over a trash can. He got up and raced in semi-darkness along the narrow passage between shelves piled deep with props. He pulled over a tailor's mannequin and a box of electronics behind him to block the way and cursed at being slowed by his costume.

At the end of the passageway, he saw a deep-black opening, which had to be the way to the back cellar. He climbed over a wooden stile, catching his pants on a nail but ripping free. He was careful not to hit his head on the beams he remembered hung low on the other side.

Feeling his way in the dark, he kicked a table. Pain shot up his shin. Then behind him there were loud crashes and curses. After one more turn in the dark, Finn felt for the wooden ladder he and Derk had used to descend to the back cellar. He climbed up far enough to reach the trap door and started pushing it open.

"There you are," Satch said, lifting the door and offering Finn his hand.

"They're right behind," Finn said breathlessly as a loud curse sounded from below.

Satch let the trapdoor slam shut with a loud crash, saying under his breath, "Trap closed." He then led Finn to where Genevieve stood behind the canvas walls stage right. She looked distressed as she started stripping off Finn's costume.

"Two of them followed you," she said, "and another is upstairs, but there's a fourth man out front."

"How do I get out of here?" Finn said, out of breath and out of options.

"I'll move something onto the trap door to close in the rats in the cellar," Satch said and rushed off.

"And I'll distract the man outside. You go out here," she said, pointing to a big crash door he had not noticed before, "then wait behind the gate at the front of the mews until I get to him."

"Will you be able to occupy him?"

She flashed a look at him as if the question insulted her ability.

He replied with an apologetic smile, wishing there was time to say more, but then in anguish said, "Oh, shit, I left my coat upstairs."

"You can't go back," she said. "There's no time."

Derk overheard this and handed him a hooded sweatshirt lying on top of a piano. "Take this," he said. "Just shake out the sawdust; it'll keep the snow off your head."

"I can't take your..." Finn started to say.

"Hush," Genevieve said as they heard angry banging on the trap door. "Just scoot."

Finn pulled on the sweatshirt, glanced back with a grateful look and left.

In an instant he passed from the hustle and chaos of the theater into a jarringly serene scene of a snow-filled carriageway between converted stables. But the door banging behind him spurred him to move up to the low, metal gate that closed off the mews from the sidewalk. He leaned over the gate to look toward the front door.

Couples and small groups were emerging from the clubhouse, chatting and laughing in the swirling snow. But one man stood alone at the curb, watching the door as if waiting for someone. Genevieve came out to the sidewalk and spoke to him. He stepped closer, she gestured inside, and they both entered the building.

Finn pushed through the metal gate and rushed down the hill toward Third Avenue, slipping on the snow-covered sidewalk. At the corner he looked back and saw the lookout return to his post. He didn't wait to see what happened next.

Finn couldn't remain on the street. He didn't know who might be following, so he suspected everyone. Besides that, the snow had picked up, and the cold cut through his sweatshirt. Instinct said not to double back across Lexington to the subway, so he walked east to Second Avenue. Fortunately, he had change for the bus and caught one going south.

He watched out the window for danger but saw none and so focused on catching his breath. A siren made him jump, but he calmed himself; the people coming for him would not use sirens. His pursuers were insidious and hidden, like the cockroaches in the loft. He needed to rest, but first he needed to stay ahead of them.

He pulled the hood tight for warmth and leaned against the grimy window, secure for the moment, or at least warm. Despite the faint musty smell of the seats, he kept thinking of those sandwiches at the clubhouse. Why had he passed up his last chance to eat?

And how had they found him? Did they know his loftmate was acting in the show? Did something at the loft tip them off?

He hated to think they had gotten to Petra. She'd push back, wouldn't tell them anything, but who knew how that might have played out. She shouldn't have had to go through this at all; it had nothing to do with her. But once again he brought danger to someone he had come to care about.

How else could they know about the clubhouse, unless...? Finn had told his "friend" JT he might hide there. Could he be in on this too? Was that even possible? JT worked for Victor, of course, and he was never held back by scruples, but would he betray Finn? And why?

Finn returned to the search of his office; could *that* have been JT? He was in unusually early that day. And it was JT who said to call Detective Vulpe!

No, JT wouldn't do Victor's shit work, not if it hurt Finn. But Victor knew Finn took that watch! He could only have known that if JT told him. Was Victor holding the theft over JT, too? Maybe even of that whole box of watches?

It was alarming to think his friend would betray him, no matter what they offered him, or how they threatened him. It shattered Finn's faith in his instincts about people. If his main drinking buddy turned on him, who could he trust?

The raid in Nashville came to mind. JT tempted him to steal that Sanchi. He was just like Matt Handy at the supermarket, a devil leading Finn to perdition. And he considered what he knew about JT: his cynical view of authority, his crude comments about women, the gambling. JT could have lost big on a bet—it wouldn't be the first time—and have to make it up somehow. But would he stoop to helping Victor? Against a friend? To the extent of an attack on Ted? That was too hard to accept.

Whatever JT's part was in this mess, one thing was clear: Finn could not risk trusting him now, precisely when he needed help inside the firm. The package he had mailed to Genevieve held solid evidence, but it wasn't the whole story. He needed the folder Ted had been bringing him. That would be in Victor's hands by now, or else Ainsley was running this shit show for him like she did all his other work, but either way Finn couldn't get hold of it—if it even still existed.

The bus turned east. By the time he got off at Catherine, Finn was confident no one was following. It was a short walk to the loft, where he could get something to eat and come up with his next step...if no one was watching his building. Having chased him up town, maybe they'd be gone.

But after losing him at the theater, would they return to the apartment? And where else could he go?

Chapter Twenty-Four

Finn came at Duane Street from the north and huddled behind the *Tilted Arc* in Federal Plaza, across from his building. The massive steel sculpture was ice cold, but at least the curved wall blocked the wind. Still, Finn was frozen through after walking only a few blocks.

As he feared, two men sat in a parked car in front of his building. While he watched, a police officer walked up and leaned in the window and then continued up the block.

It would take at least another day for the package to reach Genevieve, and he couldn't surface until he had the proof in hand. But now he had to deal with this weather, get inside somewhere. Where to spend the night was the problem, but first he needed to get warm.

He backtracked away from his building, keeping hidden by the wall. Eventually, he found a bar up on Lafayette. Inside he brushed the snow off his sweatshirt, drawing stares from the people seated at a few small tables.

"Cold out there," a grinning man on a bar stool said, less in jest than in question of why Finn was out in this weather so lightly dressed.

Finn smiled and acted like nothing was unusual. He ordered hot whiskey at the bar and asked the bartender for change. When he had thawed out, he found the public telephone at the rear and called the loft. Petra answered.

"It's me," he said.

"My God, Finn, what's going on? Those men are still parked out front."

"I know. They found me at Satch's theater. I got out—with a lot of help—but when I got back to the building, I saw the car."

"What are you gonna do?"

"Well, I can't come home; that's clear. What I really need is my coat."

"You don't have a coat? You had one when you left."

"I had to run from the theater without it. All I've got is a sweatshirt a friend loaned me."

"But it's snowing."

"No kidding. The sleeves are frozen stiff."

"Where are you?"

"In a bar on Lafayette. Listen, I know I've already asked too much of you."

"Don't be stupid. What can I do?"

"I'm gonna freeze out here unless I find a way to get warm. Is there any way you could get me my parka?"

"But those awful men would see me."

"Right, and they'd be suspicious of you carrying a coat."

The phone clicked and a recording told Finn to deposit another twenty-five cents. Then Petra hit on an idea. "What if I take Bogart for a walk. Regardless of the weather, he needs to go out."

"Yeah, and so..."

"I throw your parka over my coat. It's so big, it'll fit easy."

"It will look strange."

"Sure, but who's going to notice in this snow? Those men will likely be watching Bogart."

"He won't scare anyone."

"Well, they don't know he's a marshmallow. He's big; that's

all they'll see. And I'll find his leash and pretend I need to keep a tight hold on him."

"Of course, these could be the same bastards who stuck Bogart in Satch's room."

"Maybe, but he's still imposing, and the point is to distract, not scare them."

"Okay, so you walk out, and I meet you around the corner on Elk Street."

"Perfect. Just stay out of sight until you see me. If they're following, I'll continue on and turn down Centre Street, and we can try again at the corner of Chambers, or I'll just leave the coat and come home. They can't follow me and stay with the coat at the same time."

"Sounds good. You're a lifesaver, Petra. I'll wait for you on Elk."

"Give me five minutes."

Finn hurried to the meeting place and found a doorway out of the wind with a view of the corner Petra would walk around with the dog. In a few cold minutes he saw her with Bogart. The leash idea was smart; she looked like a regular person walking a dog, her coat and the dog a bit oversized. And the cops—if that's who they were—had no reason to hassle her for Bogart being off leash.

She paused to look back before turning onto Elk Street and then hurried along, scanning the buildings. When she had nearly reached him, he stepped from the doorway.

"You've saved me," he said. "I'm frozen through."

She didn't bother with a greeting. She just dropped the leash, pulled off the outer coat and handed it to him. He was so relieved he almost stopped shivering. But as he zipped up and reached in the pocket for his woolen hat, a man's voice shouted, "There he is!"

One of the goons was at the corner, yelling back toward the car. Then the man ran toward them.

Finn spun on his heels, slipped on the snow and started running.

Before the man reached Petra, she picked up the leash and turned toward him. He tried to pass between her and the dog but tripped over the leash, yanking Bogart and Petra almost off their feet.

As Finn ran big dog barks shook the buildings around them. He glanced back to see the man rising from the snow and backing away from Bogart, and his partner racing around the corner.

Finn practically ran out of his wet shoes, sliding down the sidewalk. He knew his pursuers would be after him again in a moment and strained to think of a way to lose them. When he heard a train pulling into the City Hall stop, he bounded down the subway stairs. Someone pushed open the exit gate, and Finn ran through it onto the platform as the train doors opened and people streamed off and on.

He rushed along the platform and up the stairs at the opposite end. If anyone was following, he hoped they would jump on the train.

Up on the street he ducked behind a tree to watch the subway entrance. There was nothing suspicious.

He headed west as quickly as he could in the drifting snow. After a few minutes he warmed up, except for his wet feet. The main issue was his pursuers; they certainly would try to pick up his trail again. He needed somewhere warm to hide. Then the solution sprang to mind, and he hurried across town.

Chapter Twenty-Five

The Raccoon Lodge sign glowed like a beacon in the swirling snow. Finn looked ahead and behind. Except for a cab on Church Street and a couple kissing in a doorway, the street was deserted.

He entered and walked to the end of the bar, keeping his hood up and avoiding eye contact. It was a slow night. Only a few of the usual suspects were drinking or playing pool. *Wild Thing* blasted from the jukebox.

He brushed off his coat and sat on the last stool against the wall. The bartender finished pouring a beer for another patron and approached, stooping comically to look under the edge of Finn's hood.

"Haven't see you in a while," the bartender said, his curious look turning into a smile. "You incognito?"

Finn forced a humorless chuckle. "Yeah. Hiding from the paparazzi. Let me have a beer, please. And is Bridie around?"

"Where else *would* she be?"

"I need to talk to her."

While he sipped his beer, Finn recognized a couple of regulars who always showed up in suits to mingle with the blue-collar crowd, even now when they also wore hiking boots. But he turned away when one looked about to call out to him.

He was halfway through his beer when Bridie came out of

the back room, casting a proprietary look around the bar with her usual stony expression. She walked up to his stool.

"My man says you're lookin' for me," she said in her deep, raspy voice, with an eyebrow raised in question.

"Yeah, Bridie, look, I've got to..." He hesitated and looked around to make sure no one could hear. "I need a favor."

She waited two beats and blurted out, "Jesus, lad, I'm not about divining what you have in mind. Might you not just spit it out?"

"Any chance I could sleep here tonight?"

She guffawed and then paused, apparently seeing he was serious. "Listen, Finnegan lad," she said impatiently, "it's a grand thing you feel at home here, but this is no hostel. Don't you have an apartment for sleepin' in?"

"I do, Bridie, of course, but..." He paused, again looking around suspiciously. "Could we talk in your office?"

She looked skeptical but curious. In the three years he'd been coming to the Raccoon Lodge, he had never asked for any kind of favor—except to let Bogart sit at the bar with him. He almost wished he had the dog along now; Bridie wouldn't deny *him* anything.

In her crowded office, Finn laid it out. "I'm in a jam, Bridie. At work I got hold of some stuff that's going to put powerful people into a world of pain. So I need a place for tonight—until a package reaches a friend—and then I can bring it all to the cops."

Her look of rapt attention turned into a smile. She shook her head. "You'll be pulling my leg, now, isn't it?"

"No, Bridie, I swear. This is some serious shit."

He explained about the counterfeit parts and the cover-up. "These bastards don't mess around," he said. "They've already trashed my place and chased me around Murray Hill."

"Aye," she said, "I remember readin' about a jet goin' into the ocean. It was some time ago, but it struck me because one of the navy men had relations where my people are from in County Mayo."

Finn could see she was about to let him stay and so didn't mention what had happened to Ted, for fear of scaring her off from helping.

Her look became piercing, as if she were looking right through him. "You're talkin' straight, now?" she said. "This isn't at all about your girlfriend kicking you out of the apartment? We're talkin' factually here?"

He nodded and heaved a sigh of relief, seeing he had come to the right place.

"Well, it's for *one* night, mind you," she went on. "And you'll have to be lockin' up when you leave in the mornin'.'"

"You're a life saver, Bridie."

"Aye, that's me," she said sarcastically, "Saint Bridie, patron saint of vagabond heroes."

She paused, pursed her lips and went on. "If someone's looking for you, best you keep in here. You'll just be makin' yourself comfortable, and I'll be back in a few and set you up with a blanket."

Finn asked if he could use her phone.

"Long as you're not bringin' your troubles to my door," she said and left him alone.

He called Bellevue Hospital, said his friend Theodore Cummings had been taken in by their ambulance and asked about his condition. But all the receptionist would tell him was Ted had been admitted. It was hospital policy to share patient information only with family members.

He tried to take that as good news. Ted was alive and getting medical attention. That wasn't enough to say if he'd be okay, but Finn had to hope for the best.

He cleared space on a couch, assessing it to be the only place to sleep, though it was a least a foot too short and had a musty backroom smell. There was no letup in the music pulsing through the walls, so he wouldn't get to sleep anytime soon, in any event.

The important thing was to stay hidden. He pulled up his hood and tried to block out the noise while he went over his plan. The package should arrive the next day, so he could pick it up at Genevieve's and take it straight to a police precinct downtown, where Detective Vulpe wouldn't get wind of it until it was too late. Then the cops would protect him. At least he hoped they would.

Bridie came back with a blanket and a beer. "I was thinkin' you'd need a bit of sustenance," she said. Her suddenly maternal air surprised Finn and was more comforting than he could have imagined.

She left and he settled in. The beer was welcome, he was thirsty, though he'd have traded it for something—anything—to eat. But the Raccoon Lodge didn't serve food, not even peanuts or chips. His stomach rumbled loud enough to hear over the music. He smiled, thinking how Satch called that sound "borborygmi."

Hungry and still cold, he concluded it would be easier to stretch out on his coat on the floor rather than the short couch. But sleep still came hard. His stomach growled, music shook the walls and his thoughts raced from what had happened to Ted in the park to the bedlam Finn brought down on the comedy club.

And then there was Genevieve. Was she going to be okay holding the package for him? She sounded more or less willing, but she couldn't appreciate the danger involved. Was it fair to involve her in this mess? But without her—and Satch and all those people at the clubhouse—he would never have made it out of the building. It was a wonder how they rallied around him, as if he were one of them. Maybe this was the community G-pa always wanted for him. He only hoped the thugs chasing him caused no further disturbance at the clubhouse. If he ever got through this dilemma, he would have to make it up to those people, send them a check or sign on to the work crew, or perhaps even join if they'd have him.

He smiled. His life might be a subway wreck at the moment,

but somehow he thought G-pa would finally be proud of the boy he raised. Maybe that wasn't fair; regardless of all the lessons in ethics and morals, his grandfather had always looked for what was salvageable in Finn. Only rarely, and with complete justification, had G-pa shown disappointment in him. What quotation about nobility or fortitude would he pull from the shelf for this situation?

And another thought crowded out the others: could he convince the authorities to move against GlobalX without the evidence Ted was carrying?

Chapter Twenty-Six

Finn woke up on the floor, sweating from his car crash nightmare.

He looked around and remembered he was in Bridie's office. How long had he slept? What time was it?

There were quiet sounds through the door, which must have been what awakened him. But he was grateful for anything that pulled him out of that dream. Why did he have to relive the crash over and over? Wasn't the scar on his cheek and the permanent numbness in his hand enough to remind him of the night that changed his life forever? When would the wrong-handed world let him live in peace?

G-pa told him Sigmund Freud wrote that all dreams were wish fulfillment. If that were true, why would he keep experiencing the worst moment of his life? Surely this was something he wished he could forget.

He shook off these thoughts and reached for his shoes. Bending over he noticed a clock on the desk. It was nearly ten o'clock! How had he slept this long? He had to reach Genevieve before she left for work.

He put on his shoes, still moist, and picked up the phone, certain Bridie wouldn't mind a couple more calls. Genevieve had written her number on a matchbook. He pulled it from his pocket and dialed. After four rings her ebullient recorded voice said,

"I'm out and about. So sorry I missed you. Please leave a message, and I'll be sure to get back to you."

"Ah, Gen," he said. "Listen, this is Finn—Finnegan Alger, you know, the guy you broke out of the clubhouse last night? I was wondering if my package arrived...." He paused, debating whether to say more, but the machine beeped and the recording stopped.

He tried NYU again. The receptionist confirmed Ted was a patient but would provide no further information. He slapped himself for forgetting to impersonate Ted's brother or father. It was a relief to know his friend was being treated, but Finn still didn't know how badly hurt he was.

He didn't relish the idea of sneaking around the city until he could pick up the package from Genevieve's apartment. What was he going to do? He couldn't push things with Bridie by hanging around here. And how could he even be sure Genevieve would be at home to receive the package?

He stepped out into the bar. The room, dingy in the bright light of day, was empty except for Patrick, one of the long-standing bartenders. He stood at the front door dealing with a delivery.

"Hey, Finn," Patrick said, more amused than surprised to see him, and went back to moving crates and stocking the bar.

Finn went to the men's room and saw one reason for Patrick's grin. Finn looked like hell. His hair stood up in choppy waves, and a deep crease across his right cheek almost matched the scar on the left. He tried to flatten down the hair, took off Derk's sweatshirt to wash himself, and then put it back on. With that, and his parka, he was presentable enough to hit the street without drawing attention among the strange characters on the sidewalks of Tribeca.

Another call going to Genevieve's answering machine told him she must have gone into work, so he headed uptown. He didn't really need to see her; he could just wait or try to call her at Scribner's. But he was anxious about standing still when people were chasing him. Anyway, Bridie would be happy to see him on his way. He could blend into the city if he just kept away from his apartment and his office.

Bright sunshine lit the city digging out from its day of pure white grandeur before the snow started coalescing into blackened mounds. On the subway he kept his hood up and didn't meet anyone's eye. This left him feeling paranoid, but it was better than chancing someone might recognize him.

He took the Number 1 Local all the way to 50th Street and walked across to Fifth Avenue. The morning rush was over, but the sidewalks were still busy. The day was much warmer than the night before—*and* he was wearing a coat—making his biggest obstacle the slush at the intersections, which kept his feet wet and cold.

When he reached Scribner's, the store had just opened for the day. He paused outside, looking up at four busts on medallions decorating the façade. One looked like Benjamin Franklin, but he couldn't guess the others. What qualified you for a memorial like this? Could it be giving up your job and putting yourself at risk to save lives?

He found Genevieve on the ground floor of the store, again shelving books. She was a picture of quiet diligence, focused on her task through big horn-rimmed glasses.

"Gen," he said from behind her.

She turned with the general smile intended for whomever had addressed her. But when she saw Finn, her expression turned to concern. "Finn," she said, "are you okay? What happened last night? You should have called us."

Called us? It had not even occurred to him to call back to the clubhouse. Should that make him feel bad about leaving them worried, or happy they cared? He looked around to confirm no one could hear. "I got downtown, but they were watching my building."

"So where did you go? Where did you spend the night?"

"The reward for a life of dissipation is being friends with the owner of the Raccoon Lodge; she let me sleep on the floor."

"Oh, no," she pouted. "You poor thing."

"No, it was fine," he said, waving it off. "But just...did the package arrive?"

Spectacularly calm, she gestured for him to follow her behind one of the large pillars. He sensed none of the resentment he expected for dragging her into something he hadn't even tried to explain.

"It didn't arrive yesterday," she said. "Probably today, but who knows?"

He was sure she caught his admiring gaze, but she acted as if she didn't notice.

"Well," he said, "when do you get home?"

"Meet me at my building about five."

"Okay. That's perfect. And Gen...."

"Yes?"

"You're...amazing."

"Oh, stop. This is nothing. But will you be all right wandering in the open all day?"

"I'll be hiding in plain sight, with a little help from a few million friends."

With Genevieve on his side, a plan in place and the package on the way, he felt more hopeful than he had in days.

It was no trouble to stay out of sight. He walked downtown, bought a sandwich and coffee at a deli and sat in Bryant Park. Sunshine warmed the air. There was a good ten inches of accumulation on the grass where the snow still looked pristine, the way snow was supposed to look. The sight brought him back to the bucolic countryside around Lebanon, a memory that belied his delusion that everything about growing up had been miserable.

The park stretched out behind the main public library. In the '70s people called it "Needle Park" because of all the addicts and drug deals, but things had started to turn around under Mayor Koch. The city was building new stacks for the library under the central lawn, which would be torn up soon. At any rate, Finn sensed nothing threatening—couples strolled and hustlers lured passersby to chess boards set up in the sunshine. It improved his mood to relax on a bench and finally get something to eat with clear sunshine cutting through the chill in the air.

After finishing his sandwich, he contemplated how to spend the day. Then he realized he was sitting on top of a world-class collection of research materials. So rather than just killing time he entered the library, found the periodical room and submitted a request for magazine articles about GlobalX.

None of the stories touched on the company's illegal activities. They were mostly fluff pieces about an enormous conglomerate with tentacles reaching across countries and industries. But the size of this company was daunting. Its broad reach and economic muscle brought home again the kind of resources it could devote to avoiding scandal...and finding him. Fear again took center stage.

He walked downtown, in the general direction of Genevieve's apartment, but he was way early and so stopped at The Strand, thinking this store's famous "eight miles of books" could contain something the library lacked about GlobalX. He didn't find anything about this company but picked up a paperback of *Crime and Punishment*. With the comical version so tied to his great escape, he wondered if he might have forgotten some humor in the novel. Somehow he doubted it.

A half-hour before the appointed time, he took up position in a doorway across from Genevieve's building. He emerged only when he saw her coming down the street. When she greeted him, her warm, slightly crooked smile filled him with hope. But her mailbox held only a flyer for an off-Broadway play and a phone bill.

"I'm so sorry," she said, as if this were her fault. "Maybe tomorrow?"

"It better be," he said glumly, thinking he had probably used up Bridie's patience for sleeping at the bar.

Genevieve invited him upstairs to get warm and off the street. Up four flights, her apartment was small but livable. The bedroom faced the street and a living room-kitchen took up the back, with access to a fire escape overlooking a narrow side yard.

"Excuse the mess," she said over her shoulder as she brewed tea.

He sat on a worn but clean sofa, laughing to himself that she thought *her* apartment was messy when his bedroom still looked like a disaster site.

With two steaming cups on the coffee table, she said, "You can't sleep on a pub floor again. You'll stay here tonight."

"No. I'm already imposing, getting you mixed up in this."

"Balderdash," she said and giggled. "I've always wanted a chance to use that word. But really, the sofa is comfortable—my sister spent a week on it in the fall and never complained, which is not normal for my sister. I don't have to be at work tomorrow until noon, so we can have breakfast and plot out a strategy."

"What time does the mail arrive?"

"Late morning, usually. Around eleven?"

"Well, okay. Twist my arm. But can I go get some food for dinner?"

"Sure, if you think it's safe."

"You have a performance, right? What time do you have to be there?"

"We're meant to sign in by seven, but it's no big deal. That's really for the actors who need to be there for fight call."

"Fight...what?"

"We run through all the action scenes before each performance. Not just fights, but dances or stumbles, anything that requires choreography. I'm not in those scenes, so I just have to do my makeup and get in costume before eight."

"When do you eat dinner?"

"I usually bring something to eat while I get ready. Tonight we can grab some takeout and eat at my place before I head uptown. You need to keep clear of the theater, so you should wait here."

"But I don't want you getting mixed up with…"

"Don't be silly. No one's going to find you here. And you will *not* spend another night in the bar. That image is too icky."

He was speechless but sure she could see how grateful he was. He assured her it would be safe for him to go out in her neighborhood, so together they picked up burritos from a food truck and a sixpack of beer from a bodega and brought it all home. In the apartment they ate off the coffee table, he on the sofa and she cross-legged on the floor.

"I can't sit up straight like that," he said. "You've got incredible posture."

She looked almost embarrassed but also pleased.

When she rose to clear away the dishes, he stopped her.

"You get going. I'll clean up here."

"That's nice of you."

"Are you kidding? Here I am acting all Anne Frank in your place, and you think I'm doing you a favor?"

"Well, don't overdo it, Finnegan. It's just a sofa for the night."

"Which is everything right now."

Sitting alone in Genevieve's apartment, Finn got antsy. He still needed to find out what was happening with Ted and give the police a description of the assailant along with his suspicion that it was all tied to GlobalX. But he was scared Vulpe would be able to trace any call he made to the cops.

He telephoned the hospital again and said he was Ted's brother. They put him through to a nurse's station where a woman said Ted's surgery had been successful, and he was sleeping. Finn wondered if he should go see him but was afraid Vulpe's goons would be watching the hospital.

He wished he could remember exactly what he had copied and put in the mail so he could be sure what was missing. Did he absolutely need the records Ted was bringing him? If he did, he would have to find another way to fill in the blanks.

As he thought about the evidence, he kept his hands busy by cleaning up the dishes from dinner. When he put the leftovers in the refrigerator, he saw she had very little food. She had left the door key, so he put his hood up and descended to the street to find a grocery store. He picked up salad fixings, chicken and vegetables, thinking he should cook some healthy food for her to eat; she obviously wasn't cooking for herself, running from her job to the theater every night.

Back in the apartment he cooked the chicken and a pot of broccoli and found plastic take-out containers to pack a few meals into the refrigerator. While the food cooked, he passed the time straightening up the living room. He then borrowed a towel to take a long-overdue shower, putting his same clothes back on. After that he passed the time sipping a beer and reading his new Dostoyevsky. With all the focus on the play, he had forgotten how bleak the novel was, such a contrast to the new energy he was feeling.

At almost eleven o'clock he heard footsteps on the stairs and opened the door before she reached it.

"What a treat to be greeted when I get home," she said with genuine warmth that launched him into a fantasy of domestic bliss.

"Kind of like having a dog," he said with a smile.

"A scruffy dog," she said, pushing loose hair from his forehead.

Her touch sent a thrill through him, but he tried to stay calm.

"How was the show?" he said.

"Oh, good," she said, stopping to think. "One of the actresses froze on a line and then skipped ahead, but the crew just jumped to the next sound cue and we went on. I'm sure the audience didn't notice."

"That's funny. It's a revelation to see how a play is put on from the stage side."

"I told you you'd like it. We'll make you a real theater guy before you know it."

"Just not *on* stage," he pleaded.

"We'll see," she said with a sly smile.

She looked around the room. "Oh, my goodness!" she said. "You didn't have to steam clean the place."

"Just being a good house guest, to thank you for saving me from another night at the Raccoon...."

He faltered as her look turned from appreciation to affection, and she stepped toward him.

In that instant, the universe folded over on itself. The room—and the whole world—swirled around him as they joined hands. It was as if he had never really looked at her before. Her eyes, which changed color with the light, now glowed a deep sea green. Her crooked smile invited him in.

It was obvious what was about to happen, but time complicitly slowed and let him savor the moment. All the drama and the danger, the moral conundrum and noble rage faded to a muted accompaniment to Genevieve's sweet face. Her look turned playfully sly, and in a husky voice she said, "What are you waiting for, big boy?"

He laughed for a moment of giddy joy, but then everything turned earnest. He pulled her in close, and they kissed.

His heart exploded in relief. Blood rushed through his veins. He hugged her so close they became one person.

The apartment filled with laughter and kissing as they comically shed their clothes and strewed them everywhere, like in the movies. Then he picked up her flawless, naked body and carried her the very few steps to her bed. She was soft as a breeze and light as a dream.

Chapter Twenty-Seven

For the second morning in a row Finn woke up late. This time he was in a bed, savoring the warmth of clean sheets and a soft blanket. Instead of cricks in his neck, he felt the fatigue of a long, blissful workout, his muscles—all his muscles, finally—tested and now at rest.

He lay still, transported by the sound of humming in the other room that told him Genevieve felt as full of life as he did.

He pulled on his boxer shorts and Derk's sweatshirt lying on the floor. He found Genevieve making coffee, dressed in fluffy slippers and pajamas patterned with snowmen and candy canes. Sunshine streamed through the living room windows, cutting the slight chill in the air.

She greeted him with a shy smile. "The heat doesn't always work so well, especially in the morning. And there's no food, but coffee's on; that'll warm us up."

"I'm feeling pretty warmed up already," he said and smiled. She turned back to the coffee pot and he stepped in close, wrapping his arms around her. The way her thin frame fit against him made him want to never let go. After so much travail in the last two weeks, he needed to hold onto this moment as long as he could.

But she slipped out of his arms. "I'm afraid we don't have any milk," she said, "and there isn't anything to eat."

"Have you checked the fridge?"

She screwed up her face at this question but reached to open the refrigerator. At the sight of all the food, she turned to him in amazement. "You went shopping...and what's this? You cooked?"

"I wanted to thank you. I can't tell you how much you've helped."

Her face lit with a kind of private smile, and then she moved the coffee pot to the table along with mugs.

"You take milk, then?" she said, and they both laughed.

They eventually cooked eggs, toast and sausages, and the morning stretched on with coffee refills and much talking. At one point she reached for his face and gently traced the old scar on his cheek.

He felt a surge of the old embarrassment, wondering how such a pretty woman could be attracted to him.

"It's romantic," she said. "What they called a 'Mensur scar,' from a duel, a serious badge of honor in Germany and Austria."

A dueling scar? Was he dreaming? This angel found beauty in a disfigurement that had mortified him through most of his life, made a trophy of his abomination? He would never again look in a mirror and feel sorry for himself.

She had only a short shift to work in the afternoon and then another performance, so they had a whole, long morning to lounge and talk.

She asked about his family. He shared the essentials of the accident, which had her close to tears. Then he moved quickly to stories about growing up with his grandfather, which added laughter to her tears.

"It's not sad," he said, gently rubbing her hand. "Without all that, how could I have ended up here?"

She beamed at this and touched a napkin to the edge of her

eye. "But your grandpa," she said, "he never got to see you happy. I wish I could have met him."

"Oh, he would have fallen for you in a heartbeat. Also, philosophers always take the long view. I think G-pa was confident the seeds he planted would take hold eventually, and despite early returns, I'd turn out all right."

"Pretty all right, I'd say."

"Ah, now you're just being nice. But my grandfather is definitely looking down on this scene from wherever he is...."

"But I'm in pajamas!" she said, crossing her arms before her chest and laughing.

He also laughed. "Yeah, I think he'd like you even in *those* pajamas, Puffy Dress Girl."

"You didn't seriously just call me that."

"It's your nickname; I couldn't help it. Maybe I'll just call you Puffy."

She smirked but could not suppress the quiet laugh that slew him every time.

To no surprise, her childhood had been much more stable than his. She grew up in another small town, outside Pittsburgh, but in a nuclear family with a younger brother and sister. Her mother had once danced ballet, which instilled in her a love of the arts. Her father had immigrated from France but, strangely, taught English at a local college, her portal to literature, in English *and* French.

"Put them together and shake and you get me," she said, "books by day, acting by night."

While she made light of her job, it was clear she took her career seriously. He had no doubt she'd make her way in the publishing business. There were dues to pay, like shelving books—though he guessed she was good at that, too—but she'd arrive where she was meant to be. And the acting, well, he figured that was for the pure joy of it. She seemed to thrive on hiding her natural shyness behind a stage role. He wished he had that kind of courage. And mostly he felt he'd been given a gift of knowing this woman. Could her vitality rub off on him?

He waited by the mailboxes at quarter to eleven, Genevieve's key in hand.

"Someone's expecting a special letter," the mail carrier said as he pushed open the door with a proprietary smile.

Finn tried to smile back but he was too apprehensive, waiting for the man to pull the familiar envelope from his shoulder bag. The manila envelope appeared, but before the mailman handed it over he looked at the address and turned a skeptical look on Finn. "You're not going to tell me *you* are Genevieve," he said, and after looking back at the envelope he added, "from the nonexistent apartment 4A."

Finn's look of relief combined with panic apparently convinced the mailman the envelope was for him, but Finn held up the key and said, "That's me, or I mean Genevieve sent me. See, here's her key."

The carrier laughed and handed Finn the envelope. "Miss Bejart and I are old friends," he said.

"Oh, right, she said you knew her. Thanks for this." He eagerly turned back to the stairs.

"Wait," the carrier said. "Don't you want the rest of Miss Bejart's mail?"

Upstairs Finn burst into the apartment and tore open his envelope, rushing to confirm it was intact and its contents complete.

Genevieve watched, seeming to relish his excitement. "I'm going to duck out to the drug store," she said, but he hardly heard her as he stood by the kitchen counter going through the contents of the envelope page by page.

He was still alone a half-hour later when he concluded, deflatingly, that he needed the documents stolen from Ted to establish the rebranding and creation of false documentation.

Genevieve returned to find him frustrated. "What's wrong?" she said.

"I've got most of what I need to go to the police except..."

"Something's missing?"

"Exactly. I'm afraid the people I work for have one missing piece of evidence, that is unless they've already destroyed it. Without those documents, I don't know if the authorities will put this all together."

"Can't they fill in the gap?"

"They could get a search warrant, but GlobalX would have time to destroy everything. No, I have to get into the office and find a folder—if it still exists."

"Can you do that?"

"Not without help. Trouble is, the kid who worked with me is in the hospital, and I'm uneasy about trusting my supposed "best friend" at the firm because I think he's the one who told them about the clubhouse."

"These people, who have the documents...?"

"Well, it's the big boss, the sleazeball-in-chief, and his right-hand man, who actually is a woman so wrapped up in her career there's no way she'd help."

Genevieve paused, looking thoughtful. "And there's no one else?"

He ran through his colleagues again but came up blank. "I really can't think...." he said and drifted in thought. "The only person I really trust is a legal assistant."

"Well, so...?"

"She's resourceful, but she's only an assistant. I don't know how she'd be able to get to those documents."

"Sounds like you have no choice."

He had hoped to keep Imani out of this mess. The jet parts fraud was not her problem. But maybe Genevieve was right: he could trust Imani, and she already knew almost everything and still wanted to help. He had no other option.

"Imani," he said when she answered her phone. "It's Finn. Can you talk?"

"Finn! The shit hit the fan here. Everyone's looking for you. Where are you? Did you hear about Ted?"

"Okay, slow down. I know about Ted."

"It's so horrible some random person would attack him."

"Maybe not so random."

"What do you mean? They said someone tried to rob him!"

"Yes, that's what they'd say, but that's not what happened. I saw it. But listen, I need your help."

"Name it."

"You already know what's involved and how we can't trust anyone at the firm...."

"Wait! You mean Ted's attack had to do with GlobalX?"

"I'm sure of it. He was on his way to meet me about the case."

"Oh, my God! It's so twisted! But there's something you should know: that greasy detective Ray brought in was here. He and this creeper guy in a suit were meeting with Victor when Ainsley barged in. Then when the cop and the other guy left, there was a big blowup. We could all hear, and Ainsley stormed out like she was going to rip someone's head off."

"Well, I don't know what that's about, but here's what's what: I copied most of the evidence and sent it off for safe keeping."

"Of course you did; you're Finnegan Alger. And so you have it all now?"

"I do but..." He paused, wondering how to put this crazy idea to her. "Thing is, Ted was carrying documents we need."

"So that was why...?"

"You got it. The man who stabbed Ted took the folder he was delivering to me, and I'm hoping Victor has it, or more likely Ainsley."

"Ainsley...?"

He sighed. "She's playing for the other team. Much as I hate to say it, or think that of anyone, even her. She had all the documents in her office, so I don't know if she still has them. Victor may have told her to destroy everything, for all I know."

"But then what was that argument in Victor's office? And when your grandfather got sick, it was Ainsley who sent flowers to the funeral."

This caught Finn by surprise. "It's funny; she never mentioned that."

"I don't think she told anyone, but her secretary told me she put in on Ainsley's personal credit card."

"Well, that was thoughtful of her, if totally out of character, but she still won't go against Victor."

"Well, I get that. But she might have the folder you're looking for?"

"If he didn't have her destroy it, yeah, more likely Ainsley than Victor. And Ainsley isn't stupid...."

"Which means..."

"Which means if she had this smoking gun, she might not let it go, not when it could prove useful."

"Then she's our best bet."

"Maybe our only bet. What we need specifically is a brown folder labelled 'Transfers.' The question is how to get our hands on it."

"I'm on it," she said with resolution. "I can check Ainsley's schedule. When she goes to lunch, I'll get into her office; it should be no problem. Of course, there's no assurance I'll find the folder."

"You're the best, Imani."

He could almost hear her huge smile through the phone line before she said, "Oh, go on. I bet you say that to all your operatives."

He laughed. "Okay, so don't let the secret agent thing cloud your judgement. Just find the brown folder; it should hold, I don't know, maybe ten or twenty pages. And don't get caught; you've got to protect yourself first and foremost."

"On it, boss."

"Okay," he said and hesitated. "I *have* to leave this to you. Take down this phone number; this is where I'm staying. If, with the grace of God, you're able to track down the folder, call me. In fact, if you find out anything about that folder or anything else to do with Global, let me know."

"And if I can't find it in Ainsley's office, do you want me to search Victor's?"

"Let's take this one step at a time."

Genevieve had to leave for work but said he should stay in the apartment until he heard from Imani. She made him promise *not* to do any more cleaning or cooking for her. He spent the next hour trying to come up with a way to make the case without the missing documents, but it didn't work. This presentation wouldn't convince anyone to take on GlobalX, especially once Victor Bolger and Hune & Buchanan ganged up on Finn.

Then the phone rang. He took a deep breath before answering.

"Finn, it's Ainsley."

His heart stopped. The plan to bring down GlobalX, his career and future, any happiness he had hoped for with Genevieve, all crashed down around him.

"Don't hang up," she said quickly. "Just listen. I don't know the details, but GlobalX was behind the attack on Ted. Vulpe was here with the head of GlobalX security, and I'm almost sure he and Ray Bagatoni were involved. I don't know what part Victor is playing, but he is at least looking the other way. And then Jimmy caught Imani going through my office, and somehow got this phone number out of her—she had written it on a notepad or something. I stepped in and said I'd handle it—because your old friend is up to his neck in this thing, too. Victor found out he used Ray to sell the stolen watches from Nashville, and has his feet to the fire.

"Anyway, I called Imani in to talk with her alone. She tried to be stoic but was clearly seething. I thought for a moment she'd take a swing at me. You've got a loyal ally there."

"But you and Victor...I heard you had a fight?"

"We did. That's partly an old story; I'm not who you think I am and neither is Victor, or maybe you know that by now. What's important is he thinks I'm under his thumb and so will keep my mouth shut, but I am as enraged as you are about what GlobalX is doing, and the attack on Ted was the last straw. Think what you will of me, we're a team, which means we take care of each other."

She paused to catch her breath. "I finally convinced Imani I knew nothing about the Ted thing and that I'm on your side. She told me what you're looking for; and just so you know, I have all the documents, including what Vulpe's guy got from Ted. Tell me how and I'll get that Transfers folder to you—and don't you need the other documents as well?"

Finn was unsure how to respond. "I," he finally said, "I made copies of the other documents and mailed them to a friend."

"Nice work, Finnegan," she said, surprised but also impressed. "But right now you've got to move! Jimmy will already have passed this number to Victor, which means Vulpe will be on you in minutes. You have to get away from wherever you are, and tell me someplace else we can meet."

Finn was still trying to wrap his head around a world where JT was the bad guy and Ainsley his savior. Was this real? Could he trust her? This was the moment where it all came together or fell apart. But the urgency in her voice stirred him to action.

"All right," he said haltingly. "I'm out of here in two minutes. Meet me at the Raccoon Lodge on Warren Street. And Ainsley..."

"What?"

"I'm all in on this. I have to trust you."

Finn collected his documents and quickly checked the room to make sure he left nothing to connect him with the apartment, all the time kicking himself for involving Genevieve. He left her extra key in a bowl by the door, grabbed his coat, threw on the backpack Genevieve had lent him and headed for the stairs.

But as the door clicked behind him, the front door closed four stories down. He stopped to listen to heavy footsteps.

He moved to the third floor, trying to make no noise. Whoever had come in surely was going to an apartment below. But the footfalls kept echoing in the stairwell.

Should he lock himself in Genevieve's apartment? No, then he'd be trapped—and he had left the key behind. He *was* trapped! There was no way off this stairwell. He'd have to walk by this person.

Maybe it was all innocent. He was just being paranoid.

He was on the second floor when a huge shadow flew up the wall at the top of the first flight of stairs. A step behind and rounding on Finn was Detective Vulpe!

Finn had almost forgotten how big this man was, not tall so much as wide, with a square head and no neck. And he looked angry.

"Finnegan Alger," Vulpe said. "We been wastin' a lot of time lookin' for you."

Chapter Twenty-Eight

"**W**hat do you want from me?" Finn demanded.

Vulpe blocked the hallway.

"I'm a little hurt," Vulpe said with a sneer. "You said you'd meet my guys at the Plaza, but here you are hidin' out in this dump like some scared little girl."

Vulpe's voice dripped with venom and arrogance. They both knew he was in control. He didn't need his gun; his massive arms and shoulders effectively cut off any way for Finn to pass.

"Sorry," Finn said. "I had things to do—and I'm on my way out."

"Well, that's not gonna happen, sonny boy, not before we have a little talk. And I'm gonna have to see what's in that bag."

"None of your business. Get out of my way."

"Oh, now that sounds really unfriendly. And you, an officer of the court. You know you gotta cooperate with a police investigation."

Vulpe squared his shoulders. He took up most of the hallway, like a heavy oak door. "Let's just start with the briefcase, right?" he said, reaching out a club-like hand.

Finn's mind shot back to his father and the wrong-hand whammy. It had been a long time since he shadowboxed, but he had practiced that move every day for years. He had never actually thrown a haymaker at a person—not a bully and certainly not a cop—but he knew the muscle memory remained.

Still, Vulpe was a brute, with a jaw the size of a toaster. Would he even feel a punch to the jaw?

Vulpe grinned malevolently, wiggling his outstretched fingers. "Don't make this harder than it's gotta be," he growled. "I just need the papers you got; I'm guessing that's what's in the backpack. You don't need to get hurt. Just hand it over."

Finn stepped toward him. Vulpe grabbed for his arm, but Finn bobbed back into a right-handed boxing stance.

"You gotta be kidding, sonny," Vulpe said, laughing derisively and clenching his fists.

Finn stepped forward again. As Vulpe swung, he ducked the blow. He moved in, throwing a jab with his left hand that met Vulpe's arm. He held back his right as if looking for an opening.

Vulpe easily fended off Finn's jab, grinning. Finn faked a punch with his right hand. Vulpe raised his arm to parry the blow and closed in. Finn hopped back, twisted his body the other way and held Vulpe off with right jabs.

Vulpe sneered, no doubt thinking Finn had no idea how to fight. He squared up and closed on Finn, watching his right fist even though Finn was now turned to his left.

Finn faked with his right. Vulpe raised his arm to block it.

Then Finn put all the power of his hips and shoulders, all the hours of practicing this one move, all the pent-up rage of years in a wrong-handed world, all his fury about Ted and Henry and Victor's betrayal, into one left-handed uppercut. The wrong-hand whammy caught Vulpe off balance and landed against his jaw. It felt to Finn like hitting a masonry wall.

Searing pain shot up Finn's arm, but Vulpe stumbled against the banister. Before he could regain his footing, Finn dashed by him, down the stairs and out the door. He saw no one on the street as he broke into a run, turned at the first corner and kept up his pace down the avenue. He couldn't fight Vulpe, but he could sure outrun him.

After another turn, he looked behind to assure himself he was clear. Then he settled into a steady jog through Tomkins Square and all the way to Avenue C, where he caught a downtown bus. He didn't know what route he was taking, but luckily the bus dropped him near City Hall. From there he walked across town, feeling out of immediate danger—although this cycle of panic and calm was taking a toll on him.

An ache grew in his left arm and hand. He had cut his knuckles and sprained his left wrist on that toaster head. But more important than aches and bruises was his upcoming meeting with Ainsley; if she duped him—like so many others had been doing—it could all be over. He wished there had been time for more than one night with Genevieve.

He made his way to the Raccoon Lodge, cradling his bruised fist and scanning the street behind him. The last thing he wanted at this point was to embroil Bridie in his problems; he had already brought chaos down on his roommates and the comedy club and Genevieve, and more seriously on Ted and Henry. Disaster seemed to repay everyone who tried to help him.

And now he would meet Ainsley Hatcher, the Ice Queen, the woman who had lorded it over him for five years while she climbed the firm hierarchy, who he was now forced to believe had morphed into his last, best hope. But if this meeting went the way of his life in general, she might just deliver Finn over to Vulpe. That would most certainly be the end.

When he got to Warren Street, the bar had not yet opened. This was bad. What if Ainsley arrived and couldn't get in? Would she wait?

He knocked, and two minutes later Patrick opened the door.

"Not open for another hour," Patrick said, broom in one hand.

"Yeah, Pat, I know, but can I talk with Bridie?"

Patrick shrugged and pushed the door open. "She's in her office."

He knocked on the office door, and the owner shouted to come in. When she saw Finn, she looked decidedly displeased.

"You again, is it?" she said. "I hope you're not thinkin' about checkin' back into the Raccoon Hotel. The maid's hardly had time to change the sheets."

"No, Bridie, I don't want to stay, but I'm still in that same mess, and I need someplace out of the way to meet someone."

"Out of the way, is it?" she said, as if offended. "This is not just a romantic tryst, now, is it?"

"Absolutely not. I'm telling you, Bridie, this is serious. I just need to meet this lawyer for two minutes and I'll be gone—and the next time you see me, I'll buy *you* a drink."

She turned her head with a pained smile. "Well, I guess in for a penny, in for a punt. Just tell Patrick I said it's okay, and hopefully you complete your assignation and get out of my hair before I have to start charging you rent."

Finn took a seat by the window so he could watch the street. But he lost himself in planning how to get the evidence to the police. He'd go to the Fifth Precinct up on Elizabeth Street; there was no way Vulpe's claws reached that far downtown. At least he hoped not.

It wasn't long before there was a knock at the door. Finn kicked himself for failing to see someone arrive. He'd have to be more careful than that. He peered out the window but could not make out who was standing close to the door. Still, he was encouraged that it looked like just one person.

Patrick paused in setting up tables and looked at Finn.

"I'll get it," Finn said. "I'm expecting someone."

Finn went to the door and opened it for Ainsley.

She strode in, looking around confidently, distinctly out of place in her expensive lawyer suit and Louboutin heels. As always, she took center stage. Patrick stopped wiping and stared.

"Interesting venue," Ainsley said.

He glanced around and looked back at her. "Yeah, I'm trying to keep out of sight."

She ignored Patrick's stare and focused on Finn. "Here's the Transfers folder and the rest of the original set of documents you gave me."

He sat at a table and sorted through the papers while Ainsley looked uninterestedly around the room. Patrick went back to work with one eye still on her.

"Yes!" Finn exclaimed. "This is it exactly."

Ainsley looked back at him. "Is that all we were missing?"

"We?"

She sighed theatrically. "Now that I've broken with Victor, there's no going back." She paused. "So, what's the plan, chief?"

He took a deep breath. She had apparently come alone and brought the evidence. He had no choice but to trust her. And with these documents and this imposing lawyer at his side, it would be much easier to convince the authorities.

He bit his lip. "We've got the case laid out. We take it to the police, to a precinct downtown so we don't run into Detective Vulpe."

"Vulpe, right," she said in disgust and then paused. "But we don't know what kind of reach that Neanderthal has within the department. And anyway, this is too complex to lay on some desk sergeant."

"What do you propose?"

"I've got a friend at FBI headquarters; it's just over by the courthouses on Duane Street."

Finn guffawed.

"What's funny?"

"Nothing. I happen to live right across the street from that building."

Ainsley looked surprised. He figured she didn't know anyone who lived this far downtown. And no one would expect people to live in *his* neighborhood, filled as it was with only commercial buildings.

"But it only matters," he continued, "if they're still parked out front."

"They're watching your building?"

"Ever since they broke in. They've been chasing me all around town. I had to fight my way out of my girlfriend's apartment this morning."

Calling Genevieve his "girlfriend" was presumptuous after just one night, but he liked the sound of it. At the same time, he felt a little sorry for Satch. More important, though, was that Vulpe and his thugs put her at risk.

"You mean you had to fight that freak, physically?"

"Well, it amounted to a bit of dodging and one left-handed slug, but yeah."

Ainsley looked at him in surprise. "Are you hurt?" she said.

He looked at his bruised knuckles, more proud of this battle scar than uncomfortable with the pain. And wasn't it one marvel after another, Ainsley showing concern for his well-being while she joined this remarkable team of women at his side? Had the whole world turned on its head?

"No, it was over in a flash," he said, trying to sound humble. "Like I said, I only landed one punch and then ran for my life."

She looked at him as if seeing him for the first time. "Well, no use waiting," she said, snapping back to the all-business shark he knew so well. "Let me just try to reach my friend."

He watched her walk to the phone booth, smiling to himself at how well she always dressed and that she wore high heels even in the snow.

When she came back from the phone, she looked hopeful. "My contact's name is Mack Rivers," she said. "He agrees it's best to avoid the police and bring the evidence to him. He'll alert his boss about what's coming and meet us at the door."

"That's great," Finn said. "It's a relief to have your help. But you look concerned."

Ainsley took a deep breath. "Mack says the jet parts angle is new, but they already have a task force looking into GlobalX for everything from influencing US elections to customs violations. And..."

"What?" he said, growing more anxious as she spoke.

"He said to get there quickly and not to trust anyone, particularly the cops."

Finn gulped. But bad as everything seemed, the end was in sight, and he was suddenly grateful for what had so often intimidated him about Ainsley. She was like that athlete you hated when she played for the other team but loved having on *your* side.

"Give me one second, and we're out of here," he said.

He knocked on the office door and opened it. "We're off for good, Bridie," he said. "Thanks a million. You saved me."

"Ah, go on," she said, rising from her chair with a joking expression that revealed more worry than she probably intended. "And don't think I'll be forgettin' about that drink you owe me."

"It'll be a round for the house," he said and pulled her into a hug. The old battle-axe gave in reluctantly but quickly pushed back, flustered but anxious. He was touched at recognizing yet another friend who turned up just when he needed her. Why had he so long felt alone in this city? G-pa's crackly voice came back to him quoting Euripides: "Friends show their love in times of trouble, not in happiness."

Finn and Ainsley decided it would be safest to taxi to the FBI building even for such a short trip. But finding a cab proved impossible. They waited on the corner of Church Street for five minutes, but the only cabs they saw were taken.

When a free taxi finally approached and slowed, two young women jogged across the street ahead of them and jumped in. Ainsley was livid. Finn wanted to wring their yuppie necks, but all he could do was make an obscene gesture as the cab passed.

"We can't stand here like this," Ainsley said.

"Then we walk. It's only, like, four blocks."

She glanced at her shoes and grimaced but then set her jaw and nodded. They set off up Church Street, the sidewalk still snow-covered in spots. Ainsley's shoes slowed them down. He couldn't help thinking how Dani could practically jog in high heels, but then she would have been no help with the FBI, or anything else for that matter.

"You know," he said, taking her arm to help her navigate Con Edison construction on Chambers Street, "I've been wrong about you."

"What do you mean?" she said, glancing up before quickly focusing back on the uneven ground.

"Well, I was convinced you were in on the coverup with Victor, for one thing...."

"And...?"

"And, well, I always thought you were driven to make partner and didn't much care about anything or anyone else."

With a sad smile, she said, "That's not far off."

"But I don't mean..."

"No, it's okay. You're mostly right. It's been all work since I started law school. Sometimes I've wondered if I'd be better off in some normal job, maybe even with a social life."

"Yeah, I don't think I've ever even seen you with a guy."

She shot him a quick look, her smile turning amused. "Well, that's a little abstruse in any event."

He tried to decipher that last statement—particularly the meaning of "abstruse"—as they turned onto Duane Street and approached Broadway. The sidewalk was more even there and cleared of snow, letting them pick up the pace.

But when they were a hundred yards from the glass tower housing the FBI offices, Finn stopped short. The black car was still parked in front of the loft, directly across from their destination.

"We have company," he said and started moving again.

Vulpe and two other men dressed in dark clothes jumped out of the car. Finn pulled Ainsley into a run.

One of the men shouted, "Police," and held out a badge.

Ainsley's heel broke. She stumbled. She'd have fallen, but he had hold of her arm.

She bent to remove both shoes, and then they ran.

Everything shifted into slow motion. A car passed along the street, forcing the cops to hold up. A siren approached down Broadway. Far off a horn blared.

"Finnegan Alger, stop!" Vulpe shouted.

One of the other cops was reaching for his holster.

"Stop!" Vulpe repeated. "This is the police ordering you to stop!"

A tinted glass door to the building swung open. A man inside in a dark suit yelled, "Ainsley! In here!"

Clutching her shoes, she rushed into the building one step ahead of Finn, and the door locked shut behind them.

Finn looked back at Detective Vulpe and the other two men outside. Vulpe pounded once on the glass, holding up his badge, frustration streaming from his face. Finn could almost hear his curses through the thick glass.

Chapter Twenty-Nine

"**Y**ou're kidding," Genevieve said when Finn called about the apartment.

"No. It's like a resort weekend, all expenses paid."

"In *Long Island City*."

"Yeah, but my man at the FBI says it's really nice."

"Oh, brother."

"I'm not supposed to tell anyone, so I hope they aren't still tapping your phone."

"Wait, they were tapping...?" she said, and stopped. "Oh, you're so funny," she went on sarcastically. "Well, if it's so hush-hush, Mr. Superspy, why are you telling me?"

"Well, I've learned to live on the edge. But after all, you're part of the special-ops team. You got me out of the clubhouse; you passed along the package; that gorilla came to your building. You really should be under government protection—at least through the weekend."

Genevieve wasn't hard to convince. Finn could not help but smile thinking how everything that was difficult with Dani was effortless with Gen.

Finn and Genevieve took backpacks on the subway, switching from the uptown local to the 7 to Queens. She tugged at his arm to see the uptown express painted with Santa on a sled and "HAPPY HOLIDAY" in big pink letters.

"Seems like it's time to take down the Christmas decorations," she said.

"Not this year," he said and hugged her shoulder.

Eight minutes on the subway and they popped up in a foreign country, with scrubby trees and low buildings. The expanse of open sky felt like a breath of fresh air and jogged another partly forgotten memory, or maybe a dream, always buried beneath Finn's former resentment against the world.

In three blocks they reached a nondescript apartment building.

"I have a feeling you oversold the resort angle," she said with an amused smile as they passed through a drab lobby to a very beige elevator.

All of a sudden, all he wanted to do was get inside the apartment and try out the bed. And, once through the safe-house door, he hardly noticed the kitchen or the balcony view of the skyline. Offered two bedrooms, he did not hesitate to choose the one on the left. He and Genevieve were horizontal before their suitcases hit the ground.

Later in the evening they were surprised to find decent food and even a bottle of wine in the kitchen.

"Do you mind opening that bottle while I put together a meal?" he asked.

"That's funny to hear from a guy," she said and paused. "Oh wait, it's that left-handed thing?"

"Corkscrews," he said and sighed. "Other than scissors, they're the worst."

"Oh, Jeez," she said, trying to repress a laugh. "I guess I'm going to have to carry you once again."

Once upon a time a comment like that from a girl had ruined many of Finn's dates. But Genevieve was different. There was no malice in her laugh; it was really more like a mating dance, teasing and beguiling.

He told himself to keep his head. If she sensed how crazy he was about her, she might scurry into the woods. It was not just how her freckles and crooked smile now filled his mind, but her strength and energy...and her sense of humor. It was no shock she won over everyone, and she would no doubt succeed in publishing, even if she might not make it to the Broadway stage. The challenge for Finn would be how to convince her to share her grounded life with him.

They settled into dinner in the dining room. The apartment felt like a hotel suite, antiseptic and impersonal but welcomely spacious and clean. All that really mattered was they were together and safe.

Admiring how slender she looked clearing the dishes in jeans and an Acme Restaurant T-shirt, he said with a grin, "Looking pretty good, Puffy."

"Go ahead and keep calling me that, Lefty Louie. And by the way, I was just reading something interesting. Do you know why the stairs in castle towers always wound clockwise?"

Finn frowned, waiting for it.

"So the defenders could freely swing their swords."

Finn took a deep breath in mock exasperation.

"Oh, that's *right*," she added. "That wouldn't work for the sinistrally challenged."

He swatted at her, but she stepped out of reach and laughed. The world felt so much kinder now that he didn't mind being kidded. And how fortunate was he to find such a smart woman? How many right-handed people could use "sinistrally" in a sentence?

"And," she added, "after tomorrow I give up tent-like costumes, except possibly to sleep in."

"I hope that doesn't mean complicated layers of nightgowns, Puffy."

She lunged for him, but he ducked. When she caught him, they tussled and then kissed.

He finally pulled away and found his wine glass. "This is nice, and we deserve it," he said, lifting his glass in toast.

"*You* deserve it."

"Hey, you saved my ass."

"It's such a nice ass."

"C'mere," he said.

He took her hand and pulled her arm up high. She twirled into his arms.

"Ouch," he said under his breath.

"The wrist still hurts?"

"No, it's fine."

"You might as well face it, Lefty, you're more a lover than a fighter."

He was okay with that depiction, especially from her. He realized he didn't mind anything she said. They kissed again for a long while. When they came up for air, they settled in on the sofa and tried to get something on the TV. But that couldn't hold their attention, and they were soon back in bed.

In the morning he woke with his heart racing, feeling it was urgent he call his grandfather. Then he opened his eyes and realized he'd been dreaming. But it wasn't the accident nightmare. Instead, he wandered through a town—maybe it was Lebanon—wanting to tell his grandfather something. What was it?

For the first time ever he woke up trying to remember a dream rather than struggling to forget it. He might have been trying to tell G-pa he had found love.

Genevieve was gone from the bed. For a mad moment he hoped he hadn't dreamed her as well, as if he could have concocted this month of tragedy and comedy. But reality took hold. He rose and threw on a sweatshirt and his boxers. He found Geneviève sitting on a stuffed chair in a shaft of sunlight, legs curled under her as she pored over a crossword puzzle.

The phone rang. He hurried to answer it.

"How's the federally funded vacation?"

He recognized Mack Rivers' voice. "You *could* have put us in the Caribbean or at least the Adirondacks," Finn replied sarcastically.

"Hey, we're on a budget here. Anyway, we need our star witness nearby for the grand jury."

"When does that happen?"

"As you know, the jury was already about to indict GlobalX; your evidence will pile on more charges with little delay at all. You already laid out the whole case—for which I personally thank you—so it's just a matter of scheduling. Plan on Tuesday. The US Attorney wants you in for prep in the morning, say ten o'clock, and you'll testify in the afternoon. Probably won't take more than two hours."

"What about Victor Bolger? Will they subpoena him?"

"He's already testified, though they'll be bringing him back."

"Did he say where he got his orders?"

"He denied any knowledge about the jet parts or the coverup."

"But I showed him the documents twice!"

"Oh, he denied meeting with you about anything other than watches."

"What a slimy bastard," Finn spit out. "You know he keeps a statue of Machiavelli on his desk?"

Mack laughed. "We probably should work that into the questioning."

"So," Finn said in frustration, "it's just my word against his?"

"Not quite. First off, we've got Ainsley coming in on Wednesday."

"But she wasn't at our meetings—which seemed strange at the time. Maybe that's how he covers his tracks."

"Well, that's likely true, but she *did* preview the evidence with him, and acted on his instructions to lock down the documents and warn off you and Ted Cummings."

And take me to one fine dinner, Finn thought with a smile. Then he shook his head in wonder. "To think: Ainsley Hatcher pulling my ass from the fire."

Mack laughed again. "It's a mistake to underestimate Ainsley. Oh, and the funny twist...."

"Yeah?"

"Turns out Bolger pulled a Richard Nixon and always taped meetings in his office."

"Well, then there's a *recording* of me telling him about the jet parts."

"Well, no. He did the *full* Tricky Dick thing; his secretary 'accidentally' erased your two meetings, his meeting with Ainsley and another with Ray Bagatoni and an unnamed man we have established was the head of security at GlobalX—and this *without* the GlobalX attorneys present."

"How does that help us?"

"By itself it doesn't do much, but the loss of the tapes of only those specific meetings supports the story of covering up the crime."

Finn was enjoying this and grateful for Mack's help. "You know," he said, "Jimmy and I used to call Ainsley the Ice Queen, although really that was just from frustration that she had no interest in us, like she was above us all."

Mack laughed. "Well, she was at the top of our law school class, too. She was a bit aloof—as you say—but there was no doubt she'd put us all to shame in the end. And, of course, she's got great legs. You didn't hear me say that."

Finn laughed, thinking how juvenile his infatuation seemed after all that had happened, and now that he had found Genevieve. Then he thought of Ted. He had suffered more than anyone to see justice done, well, more than anyone except Henry. Word was that Ted was slated to get out of the hospital in another week and would make a full recovery. And Finn felt shitty that, in all the chaos, he had missed Henry's funeral. He had called his mother, but he really needed to go visit.

"And what about Henry Ingram in New Jersey?" he asked Mack.

"We're working with local law enforcement on that. They expect arrests shortly. We should be able to connect the killing—and the attack on Ted Cummings—with the coverup."

"Okay, but listen. Henry gave his life. He deserves the credit. Is there some kind of whistle-blower award we could direct to his mother? I think she could use it."

"That's a nice thought. I'll look into it. But now let me finish. Our field office in Nashville alerted local authorities that we have information about the death of the Korean vendor who 'fell out a window.' Oh, and you'll be interested to hear Detective Vulpe and four police officers working with him have been suspended pending an investigation of break-ins and illegal surveillance. Also, Ray Bagatoni and several 'associates' are in custody on a variety of charges, including attempted murder."

"So Ray Bag-a-Donuts will be able to reunite with his old neighborhood buddies in stir. And I'll be glad not to see toaster-head Vulpe again; my wrist still hurts, and my fake right, go left trick never works a second time."

"No worries about that. It's an overall win for the good guys. We owe you an enormous debt."

"Yeah, thanks, but there's one more thing...." Finn paused, unsure if he should go on. Did good deeds wash away bad ones? Was someone keeping score?

"What's that?"

"There was this falcon statue I delivered for Bagatoni; he said it was a Christmas gift for some client named Arkadin and asked me to bring it with me to Nashville. I handed it off to a driver at the airport and thought nothing more of it."

"So?"

"Well, Victor told me it was stuffed with drugs, and the guy I delivered it to and all his cohorts were busted. There were photographs of me making the delivery and apparently some kind of incriminating tape. And they deposited money in a bank account I inherited from my grandfather."

"News to me, but I'll look into it. Do you know the driver's name?"

"He said Ed; Victor said it was Ed Wilson."

"And the other name was Arkadin?"

"Yeah, Mr. Arkadin."

"Like from the Orson Welles movie?"

"What?"

"Film noir, shot in Spain. Arkadin is a reclusive oligarch who claims he has amnesia and hires a small-time smuggler to look into his own past."

"So, what does that mean?"

"Hey, they're your co-conspirators, not mine," Mack said and laughed. "Might mean whoever put one over on you is an Orson Welles buff."

"Very funny," Finn said sarcastically.

"Relax. Given all that's gone on, I'm sure we can work through trumped-up smuggling charges as well, on the off chance your colleagues didn't make the whole thing up. Of course, you may have to return the cash. Did you stop to wonder how they happened to photograph the hand-off and why the police didn't come after you?"

"I did, but there was a lot going on. Anyway, I appreciate anything you can do."

Finn hung up and looked over at Genevieve. She was reading the paper and sipping coffee. She might be better off with a guy without Finn's persecution complex, someone like Satch. But Finn was never going to tell her that. This was his chance—once and for all—to leave behind the self-pity and get on with life. Given how things were turning out, life didn't seem so backwards anymore.

He found himself affected by the play the club was putting on, as if it were an alternate reality that replaced normal life for a few hours each evening. Finn could hear Raskolnikov say, "Finn, you have suffered a tragedy and have been targeted as an outsider. This makes you stand apart, like other exceptional men, Mohammed or Napoleon or Alexander the Great, entitled to transgress the law and cross moral boundaries." Raskolnikov reduced everything to a kind of rationalism, opinions and actions based on reason and knowledge rather than religion or emotions. If there is no God, there is no objective basis for morality, and anything is permissible for just about any reason.

Of course, Finn's transgressions hardly compared with axing a pawnbroker and her sister. And the murders in this case—of Henry Ingram and those frightened little Korean guys—had nothing to do with Finn's moral shortcomings but rather with corporate greed and corruption. Although Finn would have to come to grips with the death of a poor young guy who just wanted to see a Knicks game.

Finn did not in his wildest delusions compare himself to Napoleon. His faults fit more with the comedy club's version of a poor sap failing to return a library book—and, he recalled, *trying* to push someone down the stairs. But the fact remained, he had for most of his life felt his hardships entitled him to ignore the rules, take everything he could get from a rigged world. He wanted to believe he was over that. Like Gen's play at the clubhouse, it was time to close with singing and dancing cops, and wait for the applause.

He went to the sink to wash out his coffee cup.

"Know what I like about you?" Genevieve said, coming from behind and wrapping her arms around him.

"My good looks and indomitable personality?" he said over his shoulder.

She laughed. "I was thinking more of how well you do me... and then also do the dishes."

He turned into her embrace, filled with the pure perfume of her.

After a moment he said, "I testify Tuesday before the grand jury."

"That gives you...how long do you have this apartment?"

"Just through tomorrow night. Then I guess it will be safe to go back to the loft."

"Safe from everything but the big water bugs."

"Hey, if I knew you were squeamish, I'd have mailed the evidence to someone more steely-eyed."

"Yeah, sure. You might have tried Sylvia; she told me she likes you."

She made a face. He half-heartedly threw a pillow at her.

"Which reminds me," she went on, "I hope you know being a hero does *not* get you out of your commitment to work backstage closing night."

He laughed. "As long as we leave the police masks for the actors; that was really itchy."

Genevieve left for the matinee performance Saturday afternoon, after which she'd stay at the clubhouse for a few hours before the closing performance. There would be food there, and she could find a place to nap.

Although she had just left the apartment, he missed her already.

Being a weekend, the evening audience would dress in black tie. But as a grip working backstage, Finn could get away with black jeans and a sweater. After searching his backpack, he realized he had left his sweater at the loft, and would have to go get it.

First, though, he relished a moment to relax in the apart-ment and take a walk around the neighborhood. The waterfront was largely undeveloped, except around Hunter's Point, which seemed a great waste given the river access and wide-open views of Manhattan. In a pocket of residential development around St. Mary's Church, he found a coffee shop and sat long over *The New York Times*, the first news outside his personal trauma he had consumed in a week. Dan Rather had apparently gone after Vice President Bush in a news interview about the Iran-Contra affair, while Bush criticized Rather for walking out on an earlier broadcast. Same old same old.

Even reading about the Iran-Contra affair, he could not avoid the slight to left-handed people. The Marxist Sandinista junta came to power in Nicaragua following a revolution against an oppressive dictator. But the new government was called "leftist," so Reagan armed the opposition "right-wing" Contras. Beyond some fantasy of a monolithic, global communist threat, it was never clear why we would overthrow a country's leaders because of a label. But beyond whether the subterfuge to fund the Contras was "moral" or "legal," it rankled Finn that the bad guys were always "left," and the champions of freedom and justice consistently "right."

But nothing in the news could dampen his good mood. He had stood up for justice, the danger had passed and he had found an angel with both feet on the ground.

On his way to the theater, Finn stopped at the loft to get his sweater and see how Satch and Petra were doing. He should have remembered Satch would be at the theater, but Petra was happy to see him.

"The man of the hour," she said, turning from her work with a smudge of white paint on her nose.

"I don't know about that. Let's call it 'the survivor.' "

She smiled. "Well, the legend I intend to propagate is of the left-handed boy who reached out for justice in a world tilted against him."

Finn laughed, but he was flattered and wondered how she meant to "propagate" that image.

She pulled a canvas out of a stack and handed it to him. "For you," she said.

It was the painting of his left hand reaching to the sky, now to the "somatic complement" of scales of justice. This time the symbolism of Petra's work was clear. G-pa would have cautioned him against the perils of pride, but Finn knew he deserved this tribute and that his grandfather was smiling down on this scene.

As Finn walked around the corner onto 36th Street, a squeegee man stepped up onto the curb when the light changed and traffic started to move.

"How's business?" Finn said.

The man, dressed in only a shabby jacket against the cold, shook his head. "Ain't no love today," he said with a resigned smile.

The comment made Finn stop. It was funny how this guy mentioned love when Finn's head was swirling with the idea he might have finally found love. He handed the man a five-dollar bill.

The man looked at him, not quite trusting, but grabbed the bill and stepped back into the street to the next row of cars stopped at the light.

There was no sense waiting for a thank you. Finn continued down the block and arrived at five o'clock to a strangely quiet clubhouse. Upstairs actors were tucked away in corners, two of them stretched out on sofas.

Derk was in the kitchen nibbling at a plate of sushi. He was wearing a tuxedo shirt and bow tie, with tailored, sparkly black shorts, apparently having put aside the matching jacket for the moment. Finn thought how sensational a couple he would make with Dani, although he liked Derk too much to make that introduction.

Derk reached out his hand to shake. "The matinee was sleepy, man," he said quietly. "You could hear crickets."

"Were the actors off?"

"Not that. It was a small crowd who were mostly older, like *really* older. They enjoyed the show, but *sotto voce*. That killed the energy all around. I almost fell asleep backstage."

"And now they've all crashed?"

"Oh, that's normal for the last day, with a matinee and later the closing show and the cast party. Everything changes tonight. You'll see."

"And now for something completely different," Finn said and grinned.

"Right," Derk said, apparently appreciating Finn's reference to Monty Python. "The last night is typically a full house. Active members will be in the audience, and they're always raucous. You can feel it in the air; tonight will be radical."

Derk was right. From the moment the stage manager announced time to curtain, everything buzzed. The actors woke up and assumed their roles, and Finn tried not to interrupt as they wandered the clubhouse rehearsing lines. The women in the kitchen went into high gear preparing food. The crew set about their tasks, more than ready for the end of the run and the start of the party.

Finn didn't need closing night to be buoyant. He was flying high and savoring every moment since his universe came into alignment. He caught Satch coming back from the kitchen and took the opportunity to tie up one nagging detail in his contentment.

"Satch, man," he said, "you've been so great this last week, and a needed friend." He paused and then dove in. "I guess you know about Gen and me?"

"Yeah, well, it's kind of hard to miss the way you look at each other, and to be honest, I could see that from when I first made the mistake of introducing you."

That took Finn by surprise. He had not really been attracted to Genevieve until that night at SOBs, and even then he was reeling from Dani's rejection and not willing to step between Genevieve and Satch. But he shook off that thought; it was really important to get this straight. "I feel lousy about stepping in between you two," he said.

"No," Satch said, finality in his voice, "you didn't step in. We were going nowhere, but you guys are made; you're right for each other. Anyone can see that." He paused thoughtfully. "I don't know where I'll find another woman like Gen, but I'll be okay."

Finn was touched. His relationship with Genevieve couldn't be built on Satch's resentment, so this was like getting her father's consent. He reached for Satch's shoulder. "We'll name the first kid after you."

Satch laughed. "I'm not sure I'd saddle my godchild with Satchmo. "

The show began. The special effects went off seamlessly. The masked police characters with their puppets sang their closing number in unison with no wardrobe crisis. Finn dropped the confetti-snow, blew off Roskolnikov's hat and closed the final curtain—on the show and the GlobalX scandal.

After that everyone was hugging and most headed upstairs. Finn finished up his tasks and went to join them. His casual black clothing—in contrast to the crew and the audience all extravagantly dressed—showed he had worked backstage and thus got him handshakes and congratulations, including from an older member who insisted on mixing him a stiff Manhattan from his own stash. Finn was more than willing and found the drink came with stories of when the man had worked on club shows thirty years before.

"It all comes back to how old this place is," Finn said.

"You've got that right, young man. And we need to hang onto that."

Genevieve had invited the rest of the GlobalX special ops to the show. Petra showed up in a dress and platform heels.

"Wow," Finn said up in the Green Room, "you look so tall."

"I *guess* that's a compliment," she said and grinned.

Coming up the stairs a minute later was Ainsley. Her off-the-shoulder gown got everyone's attention. Petra, for one, seemed enchanted as the crowd parted like the Red Sea.

"Congratulations, Mr. Alger," Ainsley said. "The show was terrific."

"Well, you know," he said sarcastically, "they couldn't have done it without me. Oh, and this is one of my loftmates, Petra." He turned to Petra. "Ainsley and I work together."

The two women smiled at each other and shook hands, Ainsley almost a head taller than Petra.

"You two were both essential to the GlobalX operation," he said, causing them to lock eyes in a way that made Finn suddenly feel like the odd man out. He turned away, sensing they hardly noticed he was there, and left them talking together like conspirators.

Finn had invited Bridie, but she wouldn't leave the bar on a Saturday night. He also asked Imani, who showed up with her husband, both looking like they just stepped off a magazine cover. She wore a sleek red dress, and her hair was done up on top of her head. Her husband's tuxedo fit like a second skin.

Imani looked at Finn with a radiant smile. "I was afraid I might not see you again," she said.

"You don't get rid of me that easily."

"No, really," she said, pulling him by the elbow to a quiet corner. "I'm so sorry," she said." You gave me a job, and I let you down. Ainsley was just all over me and..."

Finn stopped her mid-sentence. "Much more experienced counsel than you have been browbeaten by the Ice Queen," he said. "Don't fret. It all worked out."

"Can you believe her?" she said, in a flash back to her natural buoyancy.

"No, actually. Not Ainsley coming to the rescue or, for that matter, JT turning out to be a rat bastard."

"Well, he always was kind of crude."

"True, and I guess that's much more annoying for women, though he ribbed me for my British ancestry, if you can believe it. But Ainsley…"

"Who is not only a force of nature—which we all knew—but who got the firm to pay my tuition in the fall."

"So Ainsley turns out to be Mother Teresa, as well," Finn said and laughed. "But are you sure you want to be a lawyer, after all you've seen?"

"I almost feel like I have to go for it. Someone has to reform your screwed-up profession."

Genevieve came out of the dressing room in a beautiful, sequined dress. As when each of the other actors appeared, people in the room applauded and crowded around her. Finn watched proudly.

She was quietly radiant, accepting congratulations. But when she looked up at Finn, her face lit up. She made her way through the crowd, reached for his arm and leaned in to kiss his cheek, whispering, "You were great tonight."

He laughed. "Yeah, you should have heard the applause when *I* came upstairs."

He wanted the world to stand still, to make this moment last. This was a happiness he had never known. Maybe he had moments before the crash, but that was another life.

Satch joined them, greeting Genevieve with a hug, and hugging Finn as well.

Finn introduced Genevieve to Ainsley and Petra. Petra gave him an approving nod when Genevieve stepped away to join Satch and the other actors for a photograph.

A bell summoned those who were invited to the cast party downstairs—and a man in a tuxedo politely invited everyone else to have a pleasant rest of their evening *somewhere else.*

It was traditional that every major production was followed by a parody during the cast party that poked fun at the play, the actors and the crew.

"A parody of a parody," one old member laughed as he stepped gingerly down the stairs, a cigar dangling from his mouth and a cocktail in his hand.

The actors now sat in the audience, and roared as the curtain opened on their set, but with a large poster of Gorbachev center stage and new actors holding scripts they had been handed thirty minutes before.

As the parody proceeded, Satch got his share of ribbing for a Russian accent that resembled melodramatic Italian. Finn had thought all along his stage voice sounded like a cartoon character, but it hadn't been his place to say since he knew nothing about acting and wasn't even a member of the club. Genevieve's role was played by a woman wearing an actual tent in place of Genevieve's voluminous costume. Down the line, the parodists poked fun at the whole cast and the director. It was impressive how these people, who had worked so hard all these weeks, were able to sit back and laugh at themselves.

Then an actor dressed like a stagehand—all in black, including gloves and a stocking hat—moved the wrong furniture onto the stage and threw handfuls of "snow" in all directions, to the frustration of the on-stage director, and then pulled on a police officer mask, jumped from the stage and ran around the audience and back on stage chased by two men waving clubs.

The audience—mostly cast and crew who had witnessed Finn's escape—stamped their feet and howled. Finn burst into laughter that cut through, not only the travails of recent weeks, but the trials of a lifetime. It was the only time Finn could remember laughing so hard he fell off his chair.

The parody concluded, and everyone wandered back upstairs. Soon, a bell rang.

"What's that for?" Finn asked Derk.

"Dinner," Derk replied as if it were obvious a meal would be served at one in the morning. Finn should have remembered nothing happened at the comedy club without eating and drinking.

Ainsley came from across the room with a relaxed smile.

"The new Ainsley," he said. "I like it."

Her smile broadened. "I'm just trying it on, but I think I like it, too."

"What will happen with the firm?"

"I'm guessing Jerry Plotkin has already taken Victor's name off the door. A few of his partners will be overjoyed to get rid of him. The old Machiavellian will probably trade his compound in Greenwich for a cell with Ray Bagatoni."

"Will you stay at the firm?"

"For now. I've spoken to Jerry, and he's behind me becoming a partner this year and taking over the litigation practice. I don't know; I need to figure out if the rest of the partners are as ethically bankrupt as Victor. But what about you? Will you stay?"

"When the dust settles, yeah, I might."

"Jimmy's office is available. In fact, when I move into the corner office, you should take mine."

He saw himself sitting behind Ainsley's big desk, with a view and plants and a sofa, making junior associates come to *his* office to meet. "Good idea. I wonder where JT will land."

"God knows, but certainly not with us. Anyway, he's got more problems than just finding another job. He sold those watches to pay off a gambling debt, so he'll be looking for defense counsel."

Finn paused, wondering how he could have been friends with JT. But he put that aside and drifted among the people spreading throughout the two main rooms until he found a seat next to Genevieve.

"So, Puffy, you and Petra seem to be getting along," he said, pleased his two favorite women liked each other.

Genevieve smiled. "Did you know she's going to paint Ainsley?"

"You're kidding."

"She just told me. Well, not a portrait, just her legs."

"She *does* have great legs."

Genevieve playfully punched his arm, and then went on, looking confused. "And she said the 'correlative' will be a Celtic triskeles, which is some kind of interlocking leg design representing birth, death and rebirth. What in the world does that mean?"

"She's an artist. Who knows?"

Finn gestured toward Satch, who was chatting up a young actress. He and Genevieve shared a smile. She hugged his arm, and said, "All's well...."

He laughed again. This late night, maybe because of the setting and the cocktails he had lost count of, felt like the last scene of a play. The demise of GlobalX and the end of Finn's life on the run closed the show.

Satch sat down across from them with a roguish look, discreetly showing them a phone number scribbled on a matchbook.

"You really have to join the club," he said to Finn.

Finn sighed contentedly. "I might just do that, assuming you're willing to sponsor me."

"You know I will, and we'll soon have you acting on stage."

"Just as long as my big scenes are all stage left."

THE END

About the Author

William Michael Ried was born on Long Island, graduated from the University of Michigan and Georgetown University Law Center, and practices law in New York City. His first novel, *Five Ferries,* was a finalist in the 2019 American Fiction Awards for Best New Fiction. In 2021 his second novel, *Backstory,* won the New York City Big Book Award for Mystery and a Silver Medal from the Wishing Shelf Book Awards for Adult Fiction, was a semi-finalist for the Kindle Book Award for Literary Fiction and was named a 2022 Eric Hoffer Award Finalist. His third novel, *Pandion,* was named a 2022 Distinguished Favorite Mystery by the NYC Big Book Awards and a Red Ribbon Winner of the 2022 Wishing Shelf Awards, made the 2023 Eric Hoffer Award Grand Prize Short List, was a semifinalist in the 2023 Kindle Book Awards for Mystery/Thriller and was awarded Honorable Mention for Mystery/Crime in the 2023 Eric Hoffer Awards. His fourth novel, *Two Degrees: A Climate Change Novel,* was awarded a B.R.A.G. Medallion, named a Finalist for Mystery/Crime in the 2024 Eric Hoffer Awards, a Finalist for Political Thrillers in the American Fiction Awards and Distinguished Favorite in the 2024 NYC Big Book Awards. He lives with his wife in Manhattan.

~

If you enjoyed this book, please post a review wherever you bought the book. For book club suggestions, the cover story, reviews and more information, see wmrauthor.com.

Acknowledgments

In publishing *Wrong Hand Right*, I have relied upon help from old friends, including Drew Dawson and Richard Maki, who offered early encouragement and incisive comments, and Bart Lazar, who reminded me what's funny about trademark enforcement. I received sinistral guidance from Ted Lowen, who, along with my fellow members Eamon Wood and Stan Goldberg, also filled me in on the history of the Amateur Comedy Club. Fellow author Mary Behan handled the next beta read, in particular honing Bridie's "Oirish," and my wife Megan helped through yet another rewrite. I also should acknowledge Gordon Greenberg and Steve Rosen, co-authors of *Crime and Punishment, a Comedy*, which was performed in the summer of 2023 at the Old Globe Theater in San Diego, for inspiration in creating my own play-within-a-novel and, of course, Fyodor Dostoevsky, the author of *Crime and Punishment*, which my imaginary play quotes several times. Christine Keleny, of CKBooks Publishing, guided the editing and publication, David Lewellen proofread the text and Lorenzo Contessa brought to the page the Left Hand Justice design. LemonLime Designs created the cover. I sincerely thank these friends and colleagues. And as to why I continue to live in and write about New York City, I quote former mayor Ed Koch: "At age 88, I wake up every morning and say to myself, 'Well, I'm still in New York. Thank you, God.' "

New York City
August 17, 2025